W9-AUD-732

Love Finds You

in

Poetry

TEXAS

Love Finds You

in
Poetry
TEXAS

BY JANICE HANNA

summerside
PRESS

Love Finds You in Poetry, Texas
© 2009 by Janice Hanna

ISBN 978-1-61129-304-3

All rights reserved. No part of this publication may be reproduced in any form, except for brief quotations in printed reviews, without written permission of the publisher.

All scripture is taken from the King James Version of the Bible.

The town depicted in this book is a real place, but all characters are fictional. Any resemblances to actual people or events are purely coincidental.

Cover and interior design by Müllerhaus Publishing Group.

Published by Summerside Press, Inc., 11024 Quebec Circle, Bloomington, Minnesota 55438.

Fall in love with Summerside.

Printed in the USA.

POETRY
1904
TEY

"Rise up, my love, my fair one, and come away."

SONG OF SOLOMON 2:10 KJV

Dedication

....

To my friend Kathy Nelson. We met on a bus in Jamaica
(of all places!) but our hearts are forever linked to your hometown
of Poetry, Texas. Thank you so much for your help!

And to the real Adeline Rose—prettier than a picture
and sweeter than a poem.

Acknowledgments

. . . .

To my editor, Rachel Meisel. I can never thank you enough for taking
an interest in this quirky, fun-loving story. May this be the first of
many awesome projects together!

To my copyeditor, Connie Troyer. Thanks for the Texas spit-shine!
The story sparkles because of you!

To my agent, Chip MacGregor. Thanks for always finding value
in my work and for placing my stories with just the right houses.
I can't tell you how much I've enjoyed working with Summerside!

To my critique partners, Kathleen Y'Barbo, Martha Rogers,
and Linda Kozar. Ladies, I'm overwhelmed by your goodness.
You are a constant source of encouragement, and I depend on your
critiques and your wisdom. Bless you all.

ON HIGHWAY 175 EAST, ABOUT AN HOUR'S DRIVE FROM THE Dallas–Ft. Worth Metroplex, you will stumble across a bend in the road that was once the town of Poetry, Texas. In this part of the country, you are far more likely to see cows and horses than skyscrapers and bumper-to-bumper traffic. Poetry was established in 1837 by Elisha Turner and initially went by the name of Turner's Point. The name was later changed to Poetry. Some say the town got its moniker because it was as beautiful as a poem in the springtime, but no one knows that for sure. By 1904 the population of Poetry was about 234, and in its heyday it boasted a hotel, a hall, a grocery store, a post office, multiple churches, a cemetery, and several saloons. Today, one can find mostly green, rolling fields covered in tiny purple flowers known as vetch and dotted with oak, elm, and pecan trees. When I visited Poetry, I felt as if I'd stepped back in time— and that's exactly how I hope you feel as you read this whimsical tale.

Janice Hanna

Chapter One
....

Poetry, Texas, 1904

"Belinda, I don't want to hurt your feelings. Truly. But what in the world has possessed you? A marriage broker? Do you really think you're...you're..."

Belinda Bauer felt heat rising to her cheeks as she waited for her cousin to finish the question.

"...q–qualified?" Greta said at last, looking more than a bit dubious.

After drawing in a deep breath, Belinda dove into her rehearsed speech. "One does not have to be married in order to *arrange* marriages," she explained. "These days, a good match is simply a matter of business. And science."

"Science?" Greta did not look convinced. "What is so scientific about falling in love and getting married?"

Belinda gave a brusque nod and continued on undeterred. "In a town such as this, filled with railroad men and farmers, women are in short supply. Elsewhere, women bow their knees at night, clutch their hands together..."—here Belinda dramatically clasped her hands as if in prayer—"and plead with the Almighty for husbands."

Greta paled. "Yes, but what does that have to do with *you*?"

"I will make it my job to reconcile the one with the other. With the Lord's help, of course." Belinda released her hands, triumphant. Surely Greta would see the good in this. And, in time, so would the others in the little town. After all, her goal to civilize the quaint town of Poetry, Texas, was a fine one. Once the women started arriving, the place would begin to blossom, possibly rivaling nearby Terrell. Or maybe—Belinda's excitement grew as she thought about it—maybe even Dallas. Yes, once proper ladies started arriving, the area would become quite citified.

"You make it sound so...simple." Her cousin paused to tie an apron around her broad waist, just as she did every morning before Poetic Notions, the town's mercantile, opened. "But if finding a mate is really as easy as you say, then why, with men surrounding us on every side, do you and I remain unattached?"

Belinda swallowed hard and then chose her words with great care as she reached to straighten several jars on a nearby shelf. "I cannot speak for you, of course." She turned to grasp her cousin's hand and gave it a sympathetic squeeze. "To be quite honest, I do not understand why some handsome fellow hasn't marched in here and swept you away to a life of marital bliss. You, of all people, would make the perfect wife and mother."

"Thank you." Greta let out a little laugh, and her cheeks turned pink.

Belinda released a sigh as she contemplated her own situation. "But I do believe, after much prayer on the matter, that I can answer the question about myself." She stood straight and tall, taking full advantage of her height. "I have come to the conclusion that I was born for a greater purpose."

"Oh?" Greta's brow wrinkled, and the color seemed to fade from her cheeks.

"Yes. And, most likely, I will never marry. To do so would only interfere with my work, my calling." Belinda let out an exaggerated sigh for effect.

"N–never marry?" Greta looked stunned. "How can you say such a thing?" A dreamy-eyed expression took over as she continued. "Why, I can hardly wait to be a bride. I've been dreaming of my wedding day since childhood. All girls do." She ran her fingertips along a bolt of delicate lace, eyeing it with a sigh, then looked up at Belinda. "Surely you have longings to marry, to have a family."

Belinda swallowed hard and hoped her glistening eyes wouldn't give her away. "I am a strong, independent woman," she said, reaching for a broom and sweeping the area near the front door of the shop. "Like most in Texas. My hard work has stiffened my backbone."

"Yes, but..."

"You've watched me, Greta. From my youth, I have labored in the cotton gin alongside Papa and my brothers. I am no stranger to work. I have managed to help Mama with the sewing, cooking, and cleaning, all the while assisting you and Aunt Hilde here at the store."

"Of course. You work harder than any other girl I know," Greta agreed, reaching to wipe off the glass case housing the cash register. "No one would argue the point." Still, she looked doubtful.

"Then don't you see?" Belinda gave her an imploring look. "I would do well with a business of my own. I would only need a small space to set up shop." She glanced around the crowded store, filled with its many shelves.

"But do you really think the local men will actually *pay* for such a thing?" Greta's cheeks flushed. "Purchasing brides from all over the country, like picking out pieces of farm equipment from a catalog? Is that...godly?"

Belinda smiled. "Greta, there's one thing I have discovered in my twenty-seven years. The good Lord most *often* moves in unique ways.

I do not claim to know the vastness of His plans, but I do promise to pray over every client He entrusts to me. I know our heavenly Father will lead me to the perfect match for each one. Besides"—she tucked a loose blond curl behind her ear—"I've created a formula of sorts. As I said, it all comes down to science."

"Coupled with faith."

"Of course."

"And how do your parents feel about this?" Greta's brow wrinkled again, this time in concern. "I can't imagine that your father is happy with the idea."

Belinda took a long strand of hair and wound it around her finger as she contemplated her response. She pictured her father—tall and broad-shouldered, his thick mustache bobbing up and down as he scolded her in his rich German accent. How would he respond to this new plan? "He will come around in time," she said at last.

"Belinda..."

"I will tell him. I promise. And Mama will be very supportive. I know her." *Once I work up the courage to tell her, that is.*

"Hmm." Greta shook her head, as if she didn't believe such a thing possible. "And your brothers? What do my cousins think of this bold venture of yours?"

Belinda squared her shoulders as she responded. "James is of marrying age—and the twins will be in a few years—so no doubt they will find the idea ingenious. As soon as the women begin to arrive, that is."

"And just where are you going to find these women?" Greta asked, still not looking convinced.

Belinda glanced out the window, distracted by a passing wagon. "Oh, everywhere. They place advertisements in all the big papers, you know. New York, Boston, Philadelphia, Kansas City, you name it. Why, our town will be filled with women from all over the country!" She turned back to Greta and offered up a confident smile. "Living this close to the railroad will be a great asset. And women are coming to Texas in droves these days. Surely you've read about it."

"Yes, to places like Dallas...or Houston. But Poetry? What would draw them here—besides the promise of marriage, I mean. What do we have to offer besides chaw-chewin' backwoodsmen and a handful of railroad ruffians over Terrell-way?"

"Greta! How dare you speak so unkindly of our little town!" Belinda's heart swelled with pride. "Why, Poetry is growing exponentially. Just look around you! We've a lovely hotel. And our restaurant boasts the finest food in the state. New shops are going in every day. Why, there's even talk of a theater. Can you imagine going to see a play or an opera, right here in our hometown?" She clasped her hands together with dramatic flair, as if she were standing before an audience of hundreds. Belinda smiled. "There's no finer cotton farming to be had in all of Texas—no debating that point. And have you seen Samuel Bromstead's wheat fields? They're prettier than a painting."

Greta stared out the window and shrugged. "I suppose."

Belinda opted to change the subject, turning her attentions to a spot near the front of the mercantile that would be perfect for her new office. She clapped her hands in glee and then pointed. "Come and help me move those shelves. I would eventually like to bring in a small desk from the back office to put in their place."

"And then what?"

"Then I will make a sign." She closed her eyes and tried to picture it: BELINDA BAUER, MARRIAGE BROKER. "Likely every single male in town will pay me a visit, and before you know it the train station will be filled with women. Think of all the new sisters we will soon have!"

Greta shrugged—and the look on her face wasn't convincing—but she did agree to help Belinda move the shelf before the store opened for morning business. Together they removed cans of homemade jams and jellies then pushed the empty shelf to a spot against the far wall. Greta looked at it with a sigh before heading to the back room for a dust cloth. When she returned, they dusted the shelves and completely reloaded them. All the way, Belinda chattered about her new plan. She could hardly wait to begin.

Greta continued to shake her head, looking at the now-empty corner of the store. "Mama's going to have a fit when she sees this."

"No. Aunt Hilde will love the idea." Belinda felt sure of it. After all, her aunt had run Poetic Notions for nearly a dozen years, since Uncle Max's death. She certainly knew what it meant to be a strong, independent woman.

Greta headed off to the back of the store to organize some lanterns, and Belinda continued on with her work. Some time later, she noticed a passel of customers through the front window and realized that eight o'clock must have passed right by. So much for keeping her head on straight. *Lord, if I'm going to handle two businesses at once, I'm going to need Your help!* With a skip in her step, Belinda made her way to the front of the store to unlock the door. Once there, she pronounced the mercantile open for business.

Customers swarmed inside, as always, greeting her as they passed by. Belinda couldn't help but smile as her gaze landed on Georg Kaufman, the town barber, as he sprinted from his barbershop across the street. His attentions appeared to be quite focused.

So were hers.

Belinda began to size him up as a potential client. Tall. Dark, wavy hair. Rich brown eyes. Well-groomed. Late twenties. Churchgoer. Businessman. Single.

Perfect.

"Mornin', Belinda." He gave her a polite nod then shifted his gaze to the razor straps under the glass at the front counter.

"Morning, Georg." She drew close and watched as he made his selections. "May I help you?"

"Yes, I'm in need of some supplies before I can open my shop this morning. Should've come by yesterday afternoon, but business was heavy. Not that I'm complaining." He flashed a smile so bright that it warmed her heart. Yes, he would surely make a fine client.

"A happy problem, indeed." She moved to her position behind the counter to offer assistance. "Glad to hear the barbershop is doing well."

"Thank the Lord for a town filled with men," he said with a nod.

"Amen to that." She fought to hide the giggle that attempted to rise.

As the store filled with customers, a steady hum of voices hovered in the air. Greta remained busy in the back of the shop, helping a couple of the local men, but Belinda's preoccupation with Georg continued. She observed him from head to toe, paying careful attention to his interactions with others.

Sure, he was a little on the shy side, but a bit of nudging would change that. When he smiled, his dimples lit the room and his brown eyes sparkled with merriment. She just had to work on getting him to smile more often. Would a little girlish chitchat be inappropriate?

Hmm. Another glance uncovered a different problem. Georg's small-town wardrobe could certainly use some updating, particularly if his wife-to-be hailed from the big city. Perhaps he would take Belinda's fashion suggestions to heart, if she dared to make them.

"Belinda? Everything all right?"

His words took her by surprise. She looked up from her inspection of his shirt, embarrassed. "Um, yes."

"Here in body only?" He ran a hand through his thick dark waves and gave her a quizzical look.

"No, sorry." Belinda's heart quickened. Was this the right time to tell Georg about her new business? Had the Lord opened a door? If so, would she step through it?

Georg paid for his supplies, and she reached over to give him his change. Her hand lingered in his a bit longer than necessary, and he looked up, confused.

"Something wrong?"

"No." After garnering up the courage, she leaned in close and whispered, "If I were to tell you that the Lord has laid it on my heart to find you a bride, what would you say?"

"I—I..." His cheeks turned redder than the paint on Samuel Bromstead's barn. "I would ask you to seek Him again for further explanation. I am quite happy in my current state."

She gave him a woeful pat on the arm, her lower lip curling down in sympathy. "You poor, dear man. You are blinded by loneliness."

"I am?" His face filled with confusion.

"Indeed. And I am just the one to bring an end to your days of solitude."

"Days of solitude?" His roaring laughter rang out, causing other customers to turn in curiosity. "Belinda, are you daft?" he bellowed. "I'm a barber in a town filled with men. My shop is crowded from sunup till sundown with talkative cotton farmers. And I can't keep enough shaving mugs for the railroad men who venture over from Terrell. Not to mention the fellas from the saloon. Why, I can't get a minute to myself. Would you have me add insult to injury by factoring a wife into the mix?

Belinda let go of Georg's hand right away, her pride instantly wounded. She stared into his accusing brown eyes, unable to believe his reaction to her gesture of kindness. Could he not see the goodness of her heart? And had he really rejected her help...so quickly?

With a lump rising to her throat, she wrapped the razor straps in plain brown paper and wound a string around the outside. Then, with a huff, she turned to wait on another customer, ready to put Georg Kaufman and his quick-fired comments out of her mind altogether.

* * *

Georg regretted the words the moment he spoke them. As he stared into Belinda's wide eyes, now filled with pain, he wished he could withdraw his statement.

On the other hand...

What could have prompted her to say such a thing? Sure, Belinda Bauer was outspoken. Everyone in town knew it. Her temperament matched her strong, solid build. And when those blue eyes got to blazing... But to spout such ridiculous nonsense? What had he done to deserve such candor? Did he really come across as lonely?

Was he lonely?

These and a thousand other things Georg contemplated as he made his way back across the busy street. He entered the barber shop, the package of razor straps in hand, and set his mind on one thing—his work.

A wife would just have to wait.

Chapter Two
....

Belinda stretched out across her bed, skirts all askew, and thumbed through a faded copy of the *New York Times*. Encouraged by a particular page of advertisements, she paused and then sat straight up.

Fortunately, mail-order brides still appeared to be in fashion these days—women looking for husbands or searching for new lives in new places. And what interesting advertisements they posted. Why, she had any number to choose from. And the women were as varied as the posts themselves.

"Marvelous!" She pressed a loose hair behind her ear, ready to do business.

Now all she had to do was find the perfect match for Georg, the one girl who would sweep into town and take his breath away. A small retainer fee upon betrothal was all that Belinda would require for her services as the liaison. Surely Georg would see his way fit to handle that.

Once he met and fell in love with the girl.

Of course, Belinda would handle the bride-to-be's train fare from New York to Texas, the business being so new and all, but she didn't mind. In fact, she had been saving up for this very thing.

"It's just a small investment in a business that will soon be known across the county," she said to herself. Her heart lit with joy at the prospect.

Likely, as soon as others in town saw the sheer perfection of her work—her keen sense of pairing up the right fella with the right gal—

men would stand in line to pay both her retainer fee and the necessary railroad fares for their incoming brides.

Right now she would focus on one thing at a time, whether Georg knew about it or not. He would come around. Eventually.

She scoured the paper, intent on finding his perfect match. Finally, she paused at one particular advertisement:

SCHOOLMARM FROM UPPER NEW YORK SEEKS HUSBAND AND NEW LIFE IN THE PLAINS. OF HEALTHY STOCK, TWENTY-EIGHT, SHORT AND STOCKY, KEEN SENSE OF HUMOR. GREAT WITH CHILDREN.

"Hmm." Belinda thought about that for a moment. Georg was a tall, stalwart fellow. Would he mind the short and stocky part? Surely not. He didn't seem to be the type to care about such things.

Then again, Georg certainly had no children. Yet. And she had to wonder if Poetry's fields would be considered plains.

Belinda drew in a deep breath, trying to imagine Georg as a father. With his quirky sense of humor and striking good looks, his offspring were sure to be both handsome and charming.

Not that it mattered—at least not yet.

For whatever reason, Belinda's mind began to wander. She began to imagine how she might describe herself in an ad such as this.

Texas spinster seeks...

No, *spinster* wasn't the right word, regardless of her age. Spinsters were women who couldn't find a husband. Belinda had *chosen* not to marry...for the greater good. That was a different thing altogether.

Again her thoughts shifted to the words she would use to describe herself. *Blond.* That part was easy enough. *Strong. Tall. Hardworking. Energetic. Talkative. Can keep up with the men. Best arm wrestler in Kaufman County.*

"Hmm." Might not be the most appealing description. Maybe she should soften her approach. *Great cook, known for hearty German fare.*

That would get 'em.

If she *wanted* to get them. Right now, she just wanted to find a wife for Georg.

Belinda scanned the rest of the page, keeping her formula in mind. The perfect match would, of course, mean that the potential husband and wife would complement in every conceivable way. Similar interests. Similar occupations. Similar points of view. Such a pairing would result in a harmonious life together as a couple. Time would bear this out.

She continued to read, searching for Georg's perfect match, his scientific equal, but nothing seemed to fit until her gaze landed on one advertisement at the bottom.

> CORABELLE WATKINS, TWENTY-THREE-YEAR-OLD
> NATIVE NEW YORKER, SEEKS HUSBAND IN SMALL
> TOWN. SHOPKEEPER BY TRADE. TALL, SLENDER, WITH
> OUTGOING DISPOSITION, CHURCHGOER. READY TO
> SETTLE DOWN WITH ADVENTUROUS, GODLY MAN.
> NO CHILDREN, PLEASE.

"Perfect!" Belinda squealed. "One plus one equals...the two of *you!*"

She sprang from her bed and rushed to the rolltop desk before locating a piece of her very nicest floral stationery paper. She reached for a pen, carefully thinking through her words before composing the letter. Belinda spoke them aloud in melodic staccato as she inscribed them on the paper.

"Dear Corabelle..." Belinda paused to smile as she placed the pen to paper once again. "My name is Belinda Bauer. I live in the quaint town of Poetry, Texas, known for its cotton gin, nearby railroad depot, mercantile, restaurant—and its conspicuous absence of women. I am currently employed at the mercantile but have established a new business as a paid matchmaker, as well. I believe you would be the perfect match for one of my clients."

Belinda stumbled a bit over the word *clients* but remained determined to continue.

"Georg Kaufman is the town barber and a handsome man in his late twenties in need of a wife."

She paused as she looked over what she'd just written. Georg *was* in need of a wife, whether he knew it or not. Time would convince him of that. *Corabelle* would convince him of that.

"After reading your advertisement, I believe that you and Georg are equal in all respects. Indeed, you are his ideal match. If you are interested in coming to Texas on a trial basis, your train fare will be covered."

Belinda drew in a deep breath at that point, wondering how much a ticket from New York to Poetry would cost. A pretty penny, no doubt. And what if Corabelle decided not to stay? Should Belinda purchase a round-trip ticket, just in case?

Perhaps a bit more persuasion was in order.

"You will love our beautiful town, especially in the springtime. And—speaking as one who has known Georg for many years—you will love him, as well. He is tall and well-groomed, with dark, wavy hair and a handsomely trimmed mustache. He is a hard worker, has all of his teeth, and has never been married, so there are no children involved in this match whatsoever." *At least not yet.*

She forged ahead. "I have always known Georg to be a God-fearing man; he never misses a Sunday service and is good and kind to all in our little community."

Belinda smiled as she thought about what she'd just written. How wonderful, that she did not have to exaggerate Georg's assets. He was every bit the man she'd made him out to be and then some. And who knew him better than Belinda, anyway? Why, they'd gone to school together. He had rescued her from several girlish mishaps through the years, including the time she'd twisted her ankle when falling down the front steps of the school.

"I look forward to your reply," she concluded. "Please feel free to write to me in care of Poetic Notions, in Poetry, Texas. Yours most sincerely, Belinda Bauer."

Lifting the letter, Belinda blew on it to dry the ink. Afterward, she skimmed over the words once more, just to make sure she hadn't left anything out. Then, just for fun, she penned a quick little poem to add to the letter:

> *There once was a town with no women*
> *With men they were a'swimmin'*
> *But a gal from the east*
> *Came to tame the wild beast*
> *And before long, the menfolk were grinnin'.*

She grinned as she read over her little limerick. "There you go! Now she will see that we are poetic in all respects."

Belinda read again the parts of her letter where she described Georg's physical attributes, confident she had done him justice. Corabelle would not be disappointed.

Hopefully Georg wouldn't be, either.

Content with her work, Belinda folded the stationery page in half. She reached inside the drawer and pulled out a matching envelope, which she quickly addressed, based on the information she found in the newspaper.

If she rushed, she could make it to town before the post office closed. Then the letter would stand a chance of leaving today. Once it was sent, there would be no turning back. Not that she minded. No, "onward and upward" remained her new motto. No hesitation. No fear.

She stood and checked her appearance in the mirror above the desk.

"Not much I can do about this mop of hair," she said. Still, she brushed the blond mess behind her ears, slipped on some shoes, and headed downstairs. She'd almost made it to the front door when her mother met her, head-on.

"Oh, you startled me, Belinda! Where are you headed to in such a hurry?"

"To town, Mother." She offered up a faint smile, hoping no more questions would come her way.

"I didn't think you were working with Hilde and Greta today." Her mother gave her an inquisitive look. "And your hair looks a bit, well..."

"No, I'm not working today," Belinda interjected. "I, um..." She slipped her hands behind her back, clutching the letter in her fingertips.

"Belinda."

"I won't be long, Mother, I promise." She rushed around her, sprinting down the front steps of the house.

"Walk, Belinda, don't run. Act like a lady!" Her mother's words echoed in her ears as she sprinted beyond the flower beds in the front yard and into the lane just beyond.

All the way to town, Belinda thought about the joy this match would bring. Georg and Corabelle Kaufman. How wonderful that sounded. How completely perfect! And what a lovely couple they would make. She could just imagine the wedding ceremony now—right down to the flowers. Daisies, of course, trimmed out with vetch, the county's fairest and most abundant wildflower.

Oh, how fun, to plan all of this without Georg's knowledge. Surely he would thank her later. But for now, keeping all of this a secret was, by far, the better plan.

With a spring in her step and a poem in her heart, Belinda continued on toward town.

* * *

Georg stepped outside the barbershop, rag in hand, to clean the front window. He basked in the glow of the early afternoon sunshine, happy for a break from his customers. Not often did he get a chance to rest from his labors—not during the summertime, anyway. No, his days were most often filled with rough, talkative men, most of them in need of a shave or a haircut.

He went to work, cleaning. It seemed no matter how hard he tried, Georg couldn't keep the large plate-glass window free from those pesky bugs. And the never-ending bits of dirt kicked up from passing wagons posed an ongoing problem, as well. He gave the window a final polish then stood back to give it a thorough once-over. Content, he turned back toward the door.

Just then, Georg felt a rush of air from behind him. The impact—hard and swift—knocked the wind out of him and threw him off-balance. He found himself belly-down on the ground, with his face in the dirt. Georg let out a groan as pain radiated through his shoulder. He looked up to discover Belinda Bauer, cheeks flushed, leaning over him.

"Oh, Georg! I'm so sorry!" She extended her hand, but he refused it and managed to get up on his own. He wouldn't be seen with a woman helping him to his feet—not in this town, anyway.

"Oh, I've ruined you!" she said, trying to brush off his shirt. "I am so sorry. Truly."

"No permanent damage done." He took over the task of brushing off his shirt. And his pants. And his face. The pain in his right shoulder continued. He did his best to shake it off, like the dirt.

All the while, Belinda stared at him, mouth agape. "My papa is right," she whispered finally. "I should've been born a boy."

Georg couldn't help but laugh at that. Though tall and solid, Belinda Bauer held every girlish charm, especially at moments such as these when tears threatened to cover her lashes. In fact, many a time she'd taken his breath away, though he had never voiced such a thing. No, she was certainly not meant to be a boy.

"Where were you going in such a hurry, anyway?" he asked. "You could've killed someone running at that speed."

"Oh? Was I running?" Again her cheeks flushed, and her blue eyes twinkled mischievously. He knew that look all too well.

"Yes, you were running." He gave her a pensive stare. "What are you up to, Miss Bauer?"

"Oh, nothing." She fidgeted with something behind her back... something tucked into her shirtwaist, perhaps? "I'm just headed to the post office before they close up for the day. That's all."

"Ah. Well, what could be so important that you'd run me down in the process?" he asked. "Something going on at home?"

"No."

"The mercantile?"

Belinda brushed the toe of her shoe back and forth in the dirt. "No, nothing happening at Poetic Notions." She looked up with a playful smile. "Don't fret, Georg. All is well. One day you will thank me for running you down in the street, just wait and see."

The oddest feeling washed over Georg as he watched Belinda sprint across the street in the direction of the post office. For whatever reason, he couldn't shake the nagging feeling that her visit to town had something to do with him.

Chapter Three
....

Less than a month after mailing the letter, Belinda steered the
family wagon through the center of Poetry, past the mercantile, the
barbershop, and the hotel, and then south toward the nearby town of
Terrell. She could scarcely keep her jittery nerves in check. A trickle
of moisture made its way down her back and she squirmed, wishing
the glaring sun overhead would tuck itself behind a cloud. Perhaps
then she could stop perspiring.

Turning to Greta on the seat beside her, she garnered the courage
to begin a well-rehearsed speech. "I, um...well, thank you for coming
with me today."

Greta fussed with her bonnet and then turned back to her with
a perplexed look on her face. "Can you tell me why we're doing this
now?" she asked, tugging at the neckline of her dress. "This is one
secret that has gone on too long. What's so important that we have to
leave the store in the middle of the day and go to Terrell? And in this
heat no less!"

Drawing in a deep breath, Belinda tried to gain her composure.
Her cousin would likely think she'd lost her mind, once she heard the
reason. Perhaps she had. These last few weeks, Belinda had begun to
wonder about that very thing herself. Many times, in fact. Oh, how
she prayed this would all work out, that she hadn't somehow gotten
ahead of the Lord. She cleared her throat. "I, um, I've been keeping
something from you, Greta."

"I've guessed as much and am glad to finally hear you confess it." Greta suddenly looked interested. Now beaming with anticipation, she leaned over and whispered, "What is it?"

Belinda carefully plotted out her next words. "Well, you know about my matchmaking services, of course."

"Who doesn't?" Greta snorted in an unladylike fashion. "People all over town are talking about you!"

"Very funny."

"*Funny* scarcely begins to describe it." Greta looped her bonnet strings in place and then gave Belinda a pensive look. "But which part of your matchmaking are you referring to? The part where you asked Samuel Bromstead to shave his beard so that he would look more appealing to Old Widow Hanson, or the part where you told Reverend Billingsley to polish up his wedding sermon because we're about to have an influx of marriages in Poetry?"

Belinda groaned. "This has nothing to do with Samuel Bromstead or Ella Hanson. I've been withholding important information because I wasn't sure how you would respond to my news. We're headed to the train station to fetch a potential bride for one of our town's most eligible bachelors."

"A b–bride?" Greta grabbed her arm and gestured for her to slow the wagon. "A real, honest-to-goodness bride? For *whom*?"

Belinda felt her cheeks heat up. *Gracious.* If Greta reacted this way, what would the others do? Her mother, father...Georg?

"Belinda?" Greta continued to stare at her as the seconds ticked by. "Who is the bride *for*?"

She took a deep breath and spit out the name as quickly as she could. "Georg."

"G–georg? Georg Kaufman?" Greta clamped a hand over her mouth and then laughed uproariously. "I don't believe it! He actually went along with you? Oh, this is priceless! He's more desperate than he appears, to be sure. I would never have guessed this of him."

"Well, I..."

"I can't believe he paid you money to do this." Greta chortled. "Wait till the others hear that he's gone and fetched himself a bride from out of state! He'll be the talk of the town. I can only imagine the chatter now."

"He, um..." Belinda exhaled sharply. "He didn't exactly fetch a bride for himself, Greta."

Confusion registered in her cousin's eyes. "What do you mean?"

"I mean..." Belinda swallowed hard and shifted her gaze. "He doesn't know I've done this. *I* fetched her. For him."

At this, Greta's eyes grew so wide that Belinda feared they might pop out. "Oh, Belinda, what have you done?"

"Do you think I'm awful?"

"Impulsive, to be sure. Awful, no. Your heart is in the right place, but I wonder about your method. Have you given this careful thought?"

Both girls turned their attention back to the road, neither speaking for a moment. The horses' hooves clopped along, creating a steady rhythm. Unfortunately, Belinda's heartbeat moved much faster—so fast that she had trouble breathing. Or was it just the heat?

Greta finally broke the silence. "Truly, Belinda, what sort of nonsense is this? Who is this woman? Does Georg even know she's coming?"

"N–no." Belinda shook her head but quickly explained. "Her name is Corabelle Watkins. She's from New York. I...well, I paid for her train ticket. I'm sure Georg will reimburse me later, when he realizes that she's the perfect woman for him."

"He will?" Greta did not look convinced. "But how do you know she's the one for Georg? How would you even begin to guess his taste in females? He's so reserved and closemouthed about such things. Always has been. Remember when we would tease him about girls in school? He would never play along. In fact, the only girl he ever spent time with was you, and even you couldn't crack that hard shell."

"I know. But don't you see? That's what makes this so perfect. He would never do for himself what I can do for him. So I *must* do it. I have no choice, really."

"Hmm. Well, I do think you're right in saying that he would never pursue a woman on his own. He's far too shy. But what you're doing for him isn't exactly yours to do, at least from my vantage point."

Belinda groaned. "So you think I've overstepped my bounds? I prayed about this, Greta. I really did. And I felt like Corabelle was supposed to come to Poetry. She's just what we need—a woman from the big city to share a sense of refinement and culture with those of us who, well, with those of us who need it."

"A refined city woman?" Greta shook her head. "Marrying a small-town barber? This, I must see to believe. And what about your scientific notion that a husband and wife must share common interests?"

"I feel sure they are as much alike as they are different," Belinda said. "Corabelle is a shopkeeper. Georg works in a shop as well. She is a godly woman. He is a godly man. I daresay they will get along splendidly."

"We shall see. But I have a feeling this refined city woman is going to take one look at our little town and board the next train back to New York."

Belinda bit her tongue to keep from adding fuel to the ever-growing fire. Instead, she lifted up a silent prayer, asking the Almighty to move mightily on her behalf.

They arrived at the train station in short order, and Belinda waited alongside Greta for the two-fifteen from Dallas. After a cursory glance at her reflection in the station window, she turned back to her cousin. "How is my hair? Do I look a fright?"

"You look fine, but why does it matter?"

"Well, Corabelle is from New York, as I said, and I want her to think that we Texans are civilized. I don't want her to bolt simply because she's put off by the external."

Greta snorted again.

Minutes later, a long blow of the whistle from the approaching train pierced the air. Belinda took a few steps closer to the track, her nerves more jumbled than ever. The grinding of the brakes tightened them even further. Plumes of dark gray smoke now filled the air, along with the familiar taste of ash and soot. Belinda put her handkerchief over her mouth to keep from coughing as the train came to a halt just yards from where they stood. Off in the distance another train unloaded cattle cars. A light afternoon breeze picked up the heady scent of the animals and blew it their way. Belinda coughed, all the while thinking what a poor first impression this might make on their guest.

She watched as passengers stepped down from the cars. One by one they came, but none looked like the Corabelle Watkins she'd pictured in her head. Surely this woman would rival the debutantes from Dallas or Houston.

Finally, just about the time Belinda was ready to give up, she heard a female voice rise above the noise of the other passengers. "This unbearable heat will be the death of me yet!"

Belinda looked up, taking in the young woman exiting the train. Her honey-colored hair was twisted up in the latest fashion and fastened with silver combs. The hairstyle showed off a slender face with delicate features, right down to the perfectly placed cheekbones and flashing green eyes. And that dress! Belinda had never seen such finery. Well, not since her last trip to Dallas, anyway.

The porter, a weary-looking fellow, followed along on the woman's heels, muttering several "Yes, ma'ams" and "No, ma'ams" as she ordered him about.

"Do you suppose that's her?" Greta asked, her eyes narrowing.

"I'm not sure," Belinda whispered in response. "Only one way to know for sure." She took a few steps in the woman's direction, doing her best to appear both professional and courteous. "Corabelle Watkins?"

"Indeed." The wrinkles in the woman's brow faded, and those green eyes suddenly sparkled with anticipation. "Are you Belinda Bauer, then?"

"I am." She extended her hand but the woman seemed not to notice. Instead, she began to fan herself.

"Is it *always* this hot in Texas?"

"Only in midsummer," Belinda explained. "Our winters are quite cool, and the in-between seasons are lovely. Not too hot, not too cold. The springtime, as I told you in my letter, is absolutely beautiful."

"Folks come from all over the country to see the wildflowers," Greta said.

"Oh yes, the vetch is quite exquisite," Belinda explained. "The grounds around this part are covered with tiny purple blossoms in the springtime. And, rest assured, the other seasons—barring summer—are mild in comparison to the North."

"I see." Corabelle seemed to relax a bit. "So, no snow, then?"

"Rarely."

The lovely young woman laughed. "Perfect! Perhaps I have moved to the right place after all."

Belinda quickly made introductions. "Miss Watkins, I'm happy to introduce my cousin, Greta Klein."

"Happy to make your acquaintanace." The woman extended a gloved hand, and Greta took it with a welcoming smile.

Minutes later, Corabelle's many possessions filled the back of the wagon, and the women were on their way. As they made the ride to Poetry, the newcomer complained without pausing for breath—about the train ride, the food she'd eaten, and, of course, the heat. She finally turned her attention to their surroundings. "My, Texas is rather... flat. You do have some lovely plains, but nothing in the way of mountains."

"Not in this part of the state," Belinda explained. "But out West—"

"I always love a nice trip to the mountains," Corabelle said. She followed this statement with another sigh. "But I suppose I will get used to the terrain, over time. The cotton fields are nice. And you do have some pretty trees. We don't have many of those in the city."

"Oh, but the things you *do* have!" Greta said, the tone of her voice escalating to one of sheer delight. "Tall buildings. And opera houses. And museums. I've heard so many wonderful things about New York City!" On and on she went, singing the praises of city life. Belinda wanted to pinch her. How could she ever persuade Corabelle to stay if Greta continued to carry on so?

"So, tell me about this wonderful man I'm to wed." Corabelle's eyes now sparkled with excitement. "I've come so far to meet him, and yet all I know is that he's a godly man who shaves other men's faces."

Greta giggled.

"Georg is really nice," Belinda said, trying to redeem the conversation. "Quite handsome."

Greta wrinkled her nose and shook her head.

"What?" Corabelle looked at her with a worried expression on her face. "You don't find him handsome?"

After a shrug, Greta said, "To be quite honest, I never thought about it before. He's all right, I suppose. But he's like a brother to me, so I never paid much attention."

Again, Belinda wanted to pinch her. She would have to remember to give her cousin a speech on matchmaking etiquette.

Corabelle pursed her lips and her eyes narrowed. "So I'm to marry a plain man." After a pause, she said, "Well, no bother. Looks aren't everything. At least he owns his own business. A barbershop. That's nice."

"Owns his own business?" Greta slapped her knee. "That's a good one. His pa owns the barbershop. Always has. Georg just works there. And I don't think he particularly likes it."

"Oh, I see." Corabelle sighed again, this time more dramatically. "So, I'm to marry a plain, *discontented* man who works for his family but isn't terribly happy about it. Anything else I should know?"

"Yes." Belinda was determined to get in a few words before Greta ruined this whole thing. "You will find that Georg Kaufman is one of the kindest, noblest men you will ever meet. He is friendly to everyone and actively participates in community and church events.

1904

Unlike my friend here, I do not find him one bit plain. Why, he's the handsomest man in all of Poetry." How could anyone doubt it?

"And he does have all of his teeth," Corabelle added with a smile. "That's a plus." She turned to Belinda, the creases between her eyes deepening. "You weren't exaggerating about that part, were you?"

"No, I assure you, he has a mouthful of teeth."

At this, Greta almost fell off the wagon laughing. After coming up for air, she turned to Belinda and whispered, "Since when do you find Georg handsome?"

Belinda shushed her and continued to look at the road ahead. Greta glanced at her with a hint of suspicion in her eyes.

Corabelle seemed oblivious to their quiet conversation. She continued to comment about the weather, the surroundings, and the fact that she hadn't had a good night's sleep in days. Eventually, she got around to talking about Georg once again. "So when do I meet him?" she asked. "And why didn't he come to fetch me at the station? If I'm to be his bride..."

"We need to talk about that, to be sure," Belinda said. "There is one other little detail I've left out." She paused for a moment then rushed her next words. "Georg doesn't exactly know I've sent for you."

"W–what?" Corabelle paled.

"He doesn't even know you exist." Greta doubled over with laughter. "Isn't this fun!"

Corabelle began to fan herself once more, her eyes narrowing into slits. "How am I supposed to wed someone who does not know I exist, pray tell?"

"Oh, don't fret." Belinda nodded, hoping to offer some assurance. "You just leave the details to me. I'll manage just fine, I assure you."

Funny, even as the words were spoken, she felt a knot in her stomach. How in the world could she manage to convince Georg to fall in love with—and marry—Corabelle Watkins? The way things were going, she'd be the laughingstock of Poetry.

Belinda guided the horses around the bend to the outskirts of town, preparing herself for the inevitable questions from their guest.

"Gracious, the town is small," Corabelle observed, looking this way and that. "Quite different from the city, no doubt about that."

"Yes, but we have a lovely mercantile," Greta explained. "We call it Poetic Notions."

"And look over there." Belinda pointed to the hotel. "That's Stanzas. The owners have a fine reputation in these parts. Folks come from all over to visit our area. The restaurant is one of the best in the state."

Corabelle pointed at a sign reading RHYME AND REASON. "What is that, pray tell?"

"A bookstore," Belinda explained. She pointed across the street. "Peter Conrad runs it. He carries the best poetry ever written and is a wonderful storyteller." She smiled as she thought of the older man with his long, flowing beard and unusual wardrobe. "If you ever need a poem, he's your man. He keeps the finest books in the state—all of the classics and more." Just then, Peter came out of his store with Mayor Edwin Mueller on his heels. The two men glanced up as they passed by. She couldn't help but notice the curiosity in their eyes when they saw Corabelle. Not that she had time to stop and explain right then. That would come later.

Belinda continued to point out the shops as they drove along. "And over here we have Limerick's Livery."

"I see." Corabelle nodded. "But these business names are so..."

"Unusual?" Greta asked with merriment.

"Yes. Quite different."

"Oh, but it's wonderful," Belinda said, her heart swelling with pride. "Everyone does such a fine job of contributing to the poetic feel of the town."

"I see." But what about the barbershop?" Corabelle nodded in the direction of the sign above Georg's shop, which simply read KAUFMAN'S BARBERSHOP. "Am I to marry a plain, discontented man with no imagination?"

Belinda released a groan.

Just then, Georg stepped out of the front door of the barbershop onto the boardwalk. He slapped one of his customers on the back, a broad smile on his face. Then he looked up as the ladies rode by, his eyes widening as he took in Corabelle Watkins. A smile wider than the Sabine river lit his face.

Belinda looked his way and grinned. Well, praise the Lord! Maybe this wouldn't be so difficult after all.

* * *

Georg looked up as a passing wagon blew dust all over him. He groaned and brushed himself off. The sound of a couple of cackling females caught his attention, and he gave the wagon another look. Belinda Bauer and Greta Klein waved, and he smiled in response. He'd just lifted his hand to wave when he caught sight of the woman seated on Belinda's left. His breath caught in his throat, and for a moment he stood frozen in place.

The blond beauty looked his way with a girlish smile. He managed a nervous wave, but, in doing so, knocked over the broom he had leaned against the side of the building moments before. Scrambling, he picked it up and clutched it in his hand.

Above the clomping of the horses' hooves, he distinctly heard the sound of the women laughing.

Well, never mind that. He could laugh at himself, all things considered. If only he could get another look at that beautiful stranger.

Chapter Four

....

After thoroughly introducing Corabelle to the town of Poetry, Belinda stopped at Poetic Notions to drop off Greta. Afterward, she made the drive to her house, with Corabelle chattering a hundred miles an hour beside her.

"If I'm not to marry the plain, discontented barber right away, then where will I stay?" she asked with a perplexed look on her face. "I will need a place. And time to woo him." Her expression shifted to one of concern. "Though I hadn't counted on having to win his heart, so I do feel a bit deceived, in that respect."

"I'm so sorry." Belinda blinked away the tears that threatened to come. She hadn't been completely honest...with anyone. How could she redeem this situation? There was only one way. Georg had to meet Corabelle and fall in love with her. Right away. Belinda would see to it, no matter how difficult the task.

"Do you think it will take long to win him over?" The lovely New Yorker's eyelashes fluttered, and Belinda managed a smile.

"No time at all, I assure you. You are quite beautiful and kind. Georg will fall head over heels in short order."

As she spoke the words, a strange twisting feeling grabbed hold of Belinda's heart. Georg had to go along with this. If he refused, the whole plan would fall apart. Who would want to hire a matchmaker incapable of making one simple match, after all?

Belinda remembered the expression she'd seen on his face in town and relaxed a bit. Surely that was a hopeful sign.

They arrived at Belinda's home minutes later. As she pulled the wagon up to the front of the house, her three brothers ran out to meet them, the expressions on their faces quite a sight to behold. In fact, she'd rarely seen them so boisterous. At once, Belinda sensed a potential problem.

"Let me help you down, miss," James said, extending his hand with gentlemanly flair.

Belinda gave her oldest brother a look of warning, though he didn't seem to notice. No, his eyes were firmly fixed on their new guest, whose cheeks were now crimson.

As Corabelle extended a gloved hand in his direction, her eyes twinkled. "Why, thank you, kind sir. You Southerners are ever-so-polite."

His eyebrows elevated mischievously and he cleared his throat. "Thank you, ma'am."

Corabelle giggled. "I don't know if I'll ever get used to all of this *ma'am* business," she proclaimed, as James slipped an arm around her slender waist and lifted her from the wagon. "But I do have to say it's quite flattering." Her feet landed solidly on the ground, but James never released his grip from her waist. Instead, the two continued to stare into each other's eyes, their faces only inches apart.

Sensing trouble ahead, Belinda took the opportunity to interrupt. "You will find that the men in Poetry are, for the most part, gentlemen." Not that she spent much time thinking of her brother as a full-grown man. He might be twenty-three, but his boyish actions put her in mind of someone much younger at times. Still, she could not deny the look of interest in his eyes as he gazed at Corabelle.

At this, her twin brothers, Elijah and Elisha, took to squabbling, one punching the other. Belinda groaned and gestured for them to fetch Corabelle's trunk. They climbed aboard the wagon and flexed their muscles to show off for their guest. She responded with a ripple of laughter.

Minutes later the boys finally settled down, and Belinda led Corabelle inside.

Her mother appeared wearing her plainest calico dress and a faded apron. Her hair, usually pulled up in tidy fashion, looked a bit limp—likely from the heat. "Belinda, I've been worried about you. I went into town, and you weren't at the store. Wherever did you run off to?"

"Oh, well, I..."

Thankfully, Mama turned her attention to Corabelle. "Well, who have we here?" she asked, giving Corabelle a brisk once-over. "A guest?"

"Yes." Belinda had been dreading this part. She knew her mother would have a hundred questions but hoped she'd put them off till after dinner. Bringing a visitor to the home unannounced had never been done before, especially not a visitor as refined as this one. "Mama... everyone...this is Corabelle Watkins, from New York City. I went to the train station to fetch her."

"Well, forevermore! You should tell a person." Belinda's mama swept the young woman into her arms. "Welcome to Texas, Corabelle. I'm Hannah. We're happy to have you, of course. To what do we owe the pleasure? Are you here visiting friends or relatives?"

"Oh, no. Neither of those. I've come in want of a husband." Corabelle puffed her shoulders back and made direct eye contact with James, whose cheeks lit up redder than a rooster's comb.

Mama laughed. "Well, I daresay you've come to the right place. We've men aplenty in Poetry. And more than a few handsome ones in this very household, if one happened to take a second glance." She gave James a look, and he winced.

"Mama, can I speak with you? Privately?" Belinda gave her a look, but her mother seemed too distracted to notice.

"You must be exhausted, Corabelle." Mama took their guest by the hand and smiled with her usual tenderness. "Why don't you let the boys take your trunk to your room and you can rest awhile before dinner. We're having pot roast and potatoes with biscuits. Folks all over Kaufman County rave about my biscuits."

"Sounds delicious." Corabelle slipped a gloved hand over her mouth as she yawned. "So sorry... I guess I am tired."

"Show her to your room, sweet pea," Mama said, turning her daughter's way. "Our guest looks tuckered out." She paused a moment, gazing at Belinda. "For that matter, you do, too. Maybe you should both catch a few winks before supper."

Belinda hated to admit it, but it wasn't exhaustion she was feeling. No, it was sheer terror. But she had to tuck those feelings away, at least for now. She led Corabelle to her room, her mind moving in a thousand different directions at once.

The young woman squealed with delight when she saw the four-poster bed. "Oh, this is lovely, Belinda. Just beautiful!"

"Thank you." Belinda couldn't help but smile as she looked at the exquisite handiwork. "Papa made it. He and the boys are wonderful with a lathe. I'll show you more of their creations later. And Mama made the quilt, of course. She tried to teach me, but I never took to it."

"I'm quite good with a needle and thread," Corabelle said. "Perhaps she could teach me."

"Perhaps. But for now, go ahead and take a nap. I'm sure you are exhausted."

"What about you?" Corabelle asked as she unbuttoned her shoes. "Aren't you sleepy?"

"No. I, um...well, I have a few errands to run. I will wake you when I get back. By then it will be suppertime. Georg will be here to share the meal with us. I'm sure you're going to adore him."

"Fine." Corabelle yawned. "Although right now wooing a man is the furthest thing from my mind. I just need a few hours to rest. Perhaps then I'll feel differently about things."

"Yes, surely a bit of rest will do the trick."

After getting Corabelle settled in, Belinda headed off to the barbershop. She managed to avoid her mother's questions by slipping out the back door and running across the lawn. The trip to town seemed shorter than ever—something to do with how fast she ran, she was sure. Urgent matters called for urgent actions. And nothing could be more urgent than making sure Georg Kaufman came to dinner.

* * *

The heady smell of mint hung in the air inside the barbershop. Georg finished up with one of his customers—a railroad fella from Terrell— and then turned his attention to cleaning out the mugs. His thoughts traveled back to the young woman he'd seen earlier with Belinda Bauer. He'd never seen such refined beauty...not in this town, anyway. Women like that were few and far between in a place like Poetry. And the ones who did come through usually didn't stay long or look twice at him.

But he planned to remedy that. Something about this new girl captivated him. Stirred up his curiosity, at the very least. As he pondered her great beauty—the fancy clothes, the twinkle in her eye—a familiar voice rang out. Georg turned to see Belinda standing in the open doorway of the barbershop.

"Belinda." He couldn't help but smile. "To what do I owe this honor?"

"Georg, I need to ask a favor." She took a step inside, wringing her hands.

"A favor?" He shrugged, trying to imagine what she might say. "Of course."

"Would you come to supper at our house tonight?"

He paused a moment, more curious about the fear in her eyes than the question itself. "Supper? Why?"

"Well..." She paused and seemed a bit flustered. "James is thinking of planting a peach orchard and needs your opinion. Your orchard is the finest in the county. Everyone agrees."

Georg shrugged. "Sure, but if your brother needs my opinion, why not just ask me himself?"

"Yes, I see. You're right. He could do that himself." She paused again then looked his way with another explanation. "The twins are old enough to start shaving soon."

"And?"

"And perhaps they could use some pointers. A razor in the hand of a sixteen-year-old boy could be dangerous. I once heard a story about an inexperienced shaver who did himself mortal harm."

"Belinda, you don't seriously expect me to believe you've come on behalf of Elijah and Elisha. They would have a fit if they heard what you just said. And besides, I have it on good authority that they've been shaving for years."

"Oh? Perhaps you are right." She squirmed a bit more. "Well, how about this one? Mother is making peach cobbler and remembered that it's your favorite. She insisted you share the meal with us. See? You can appease both my mother and my brothers and enjoy a wonderful meal to boot."

This time, he couldn't stop the smile. He could always be won over with the words *peach cobbler.* "What time?"

"Six o'clock." She turned to leave but turned back. "Oh, and Georg...?"

"Yes?"

"Wear that blue shirt you wore to church on Sunday. And your mustache could stand a bit of trimming."

"My blue shirt?" He crossed his arms at his chest and frowned, overcome with suspicion. Surely Belinda Bauer had something up her sleeve. "Why do I need to do that?" He glanced in the mirror, taking in his mustache. "And whyever do I need a trim? My mustache is perfectly fine as it is."

"We have a special guest staying at our home, so we're hoping everyone will look—and behave—their best." She gave what appeared to be a warning look, one he couldn't yet interpret. "We are hoping to make a wonderful impression on her."

"Her?" His heart began to race, thinking of the young woman he'd seen with Belinda earlier. For the honey-haired stranger, he would wear his blue shirt and dance a jig. Or, at the very least, comb his unruly hair.

Suddenly he could hardly wait for supper.

Chapter Five

As soon as Belinda arrived home, she went straight to the kitchen to help Mama with supper. She did her best to answer the questions her mother posed but found herself stumbling over words more than once. As the grandfather clock in the parlor gonged six times, Belinda pulled off her apron and rushed to check on their guest. As she rounded the corner into the parlor, the beautiful young woman sashayed down the stairs wearing the most exquisite white dress Belinda had ever seen. She gasped when she saw it. "Oh my goodness! Georg's eyes will pop. Truly."

"Do you think?" Corabelle turned in a circle. "I worked at the loveliest hat and dress shop in New York and saw the finest items, even before the customers did. This dress was perfect for me, especially the lovely trim and white fabric." She whispered, "I thought it might double as a wedding dress. I'm pleased you like it."

"It's remarkable. I don't know when I've ever seen anything so nice." *At least not around here.*

Corabelle offered a gracious smile. "Thank you. I must put my best foot forward tonight when I meet my future husband. I will win him or give my life in the attempt!" She paused to look at her reflection in the mirror on the wall and then turned back with a shrug.

"I daresay, it won't come to that." Belinda giggled. "You are a vision of loveliness, and he will see it immediately."

"So, tell me what I am to expect with Georg," Corabelle said, easing her way down onto the settee and folding her hands in her lap. "You find him agreeable?"

"In every way." Belinda paused to think about Georg as a little boy. In so many ways, he had differed from the other ruffians in her class. He'd always been more kindhearted than most, even then. And now... She smiled, thinking of his daily treks in and out of Poetic Notions. These days, he was known for his caring manner, both with the men who entered his shop and the people at church.

Belinda didn't have time to think much more about it. When the knock sounded at the door, the twins came bounding down the stairs.

"I'll get it!" Elijah hollered, nearly tripping over himself to get to the door.

"No, I'll get it!" Elisha countered, shoving his twin out of the way.

The two began their usual scuffling, one of them finally landing a punch in the other one's belly.

Belinda rose from her seat and gestured for Corabelle to do the same. The two women moved in the direction of the door. They entered the foyer just as the boys flung the door open. A very well-groomed Georg Kaufman stood on the other side, holding his hat in his hands. The twins grunted a hello then disappeared into the kitchen. Belinda could see the interest in Georg's eyes as he stepped inside at her bidding.

She did her best to sound professional as introductions were made. Belinda smiled, realizing that this was the very first couple she would officially introduce. "Georg, I'm pleased to introduce our guest, Miss Corabelle Watkins from New York City."

Corabelle extended her gloved hand, and he took it, planting a light kiss on the back side of it. "I'm so pleased to make your acquaintance, Miss Watkins," he said with a spark of excitement in his eyes. "Indeed, it isn't every day we get someone from the big city to our fair town. To what do we owe the honor?" He took a seat on the chair across from them, gazing into her eyes.

Belinda cleared her throat as she closed the door, hoping Corabelle would take the hint. It would be better not to say why she'd come to town. Not just yet, anyway.

"Well, I've dreamed of coming to Texas for simply ages," Corabelle said, her eyelashes fluttering shamelessly. "And then I received a letter from Belinda, who extended an invitation. She gave me reason to believe I might like to settle here." Corabelle's cheeks turned crimson as she gazed into Georg's eyes. "I do hope that turns out to be the case."

"Indeed." Georg looked mighty pleased at this revelation. "But, pray tell, how did you come to write to her, Belinda?" He turned to her, his brow now wrinkled. "I didn't realize you had friends in New York."

"Oh, we never met till now," Corabelle said, before clapping a hand over her mouth. "I—I mean, we only ever exchanged letters."

He looked more confused than ever. Thankfully, Belinda's mother entered the room at that very moment with Elijah and Elisha on her heels. "Dinner is ready, everyone. I hope you're hungry. We've cooked enough for half the town."

As they entered the dining room, James loped in, smelling of lye soap and looking as if he'd had a serious Texas spit-shine. Indeed, Belinda couldn't ever recall seeing her brother so done-up, even for church. Yes, there was something mighty suspicious about his cleanliness today. And that goofy grin on his face. Even his boots had been polished! *What are you thinking, brother?*

James took one look at Georg, and his smile quickly faded. With a brusque nod, he offered up one word: "Georg."

Georg reciprocated with one word: "James."

Everyone gathered around the dinner table. Georg fumbled all over himself pulling out Corabelle's chair but had to nudge James aside to accomplish the feat. The New York beauty gave him a nod then sat. After Papa's prayer, Mama engaged Corabelle in conversation.

"You must tell us all about your life in New York, darlin'. None of us have ever been out of Kaufman County."

"Well, of course we have," Belinda debated, thinking Corabelle might find them all country bumpkins. "We've been to Dallas many a time, and Papa has even been to Houston."

"I have, I have." Papa nodded and then turned to Corabelle to explain. "My brother works in the oil business in Beaumont, just outside of Houston. He offered me a job at Spindletop, but I refused it."

"Spindletop?" Corabelle's eyes grew wide. "Truly? Spindletop has made the papers in New York. Why didn't you take the family and move there?"

"Move away from heaven to an oilfield?" He laughed. "When I saw those ruffians—heard their language, saw the greed—I said to myself, 'Poetry is the place for you.' I might be a small-town man at heart, but my own hometown is truly a slice of heaven. Why go elsewhere?"

Belinda could've given her papa a kiss right then and there. Surely his words would settle the issue in Corabelle's heart. If only Georg would play along. Belinda looked across the table from him and cleared her throat. He took the hint and swallowed a bite of roast beef then turned to their guest with an anxious smile.

"Miss Corabelle, I would be honored to show you around our fair county tomorrow afternoon, if you are so inclined." His mustache bobbed up and down a bit, probably the result of nerves. "The countryside is lovely, and I happen to know of a beautiful stretch of land with some of the handsomest horses you've ever seen."

"She has already agreed to let *me* show her the county," James interjected. "Our plans are set."

Belinda turned to her brother, astounded. "And when was this decided?"

"Well..." Corabelle twittered. "I came downstairs to fetch a glass of water just before you arrived home from wherever you ran off to today. James and I were standing in the kitchen, looking through that little window onto the lovely wildflowers outside. When I commented on them, he offered to take me on a little drive in the wagon tomorrow." She sent a warm smile in James's direction and his gaze shifted downward.

"We're going midmorning, though," he said. "Afternoon's too hot."

"Indeed. Isn't he sweet, to take the weather into consideration?" Corabelle gave him a look of longing, and Belinda's heart settled into her toes. This would never do...but how could she fix it now? She peered at Georg, hoping he would say something, but he did not. Instead, he sighed and returned to his food, as if that had been the real reason for his visit.

"Corabelle is interested in opening a shop in town," James said. "We talked about it at length, so I've agreed to take her into town to look around for a piece of property."

"W–what?" Belinda looked at her new friend, flabbergasted. "You're opening a shop?"

"Perhaps," Corabelle said, dabbing the corners of her mouth delicately. "As we drove through town earlier, I had the loveliest idea for a hat shop...fitting to such a poetic place. I do hope you all like my idea."

"Oh?" Mama looked her way, curiosity etched on her face. "And what is that?"

"Sonnets and Bonnets." Corabelle beamed. "Don't you love it?" She turned to James with an admiring look. "James thought it was a simply wonderful idea."

"But, dear...are you not looking for a husband?" Mama paled. "Once you marry, you couldn't keep the shop."

"Forevermore." Corabelle let her napkin fall to the table and looked at Mama, her face turning pale. "Why not?"

Mama began to fan herself. "Working after marriage? Why, it's simply not done. Women marry to become mothers...to raise their children. Many work *before* marriage—like Belinda, here—but when the vows are shared, the workload shifts to the home."

"Perhaps where *you* come from." Corabelle retrieved her napkin and spread it in her lap. "But that's not a city notion. In New York, several of the shops are run by married women. Many are quite famous. I enjoy my work. Always have and always will. No doubt I will go on working after marriage for as long as I please."

Mama's gaze shifted down as she took a bite of her pot roast.

"I, for one, find her work ethic admirable." James grinned, his blue eyes sparkling. He paused, his gaze firmly locked onto Corabelle's. A rosy color spread across his cheeks, and he gave a boyish smile. "And I think the idea of the hat shop is perfect. Just what the town needs."

Corabelle turned her attention to Georg.

"And what about you, Georg? What do you say on the matter?"

"I say that..." He paused, tugged at his collar, and then shrugged. "I say this is a matter for prayer."

"Indeed," Belinda said with a nod. Finally, someone with a bit of logic. "I agree wholeheartedly. And in the meantime, let's all share a story about Poetry, something to make our guest feel welcome."

She turned her attention to redirecting the conversation. Surely the Lord could make sense of all of this...with a little time and a lot of prayer.

* * *

Georg looked across the table, not at Corabelle, whose attentions were given over to James, but to Belinda. While he sensed her frustration with the situation, Georg couldn't help feeling a little betrayed. Had she—or had she not—implied that Corabelle might be available for courting?

Looking at James, Georg came to the very short conclusion that James would carry this thing through till the very end. Still, Georg couldn't give up on the idea that he should try to woo Corabelle, as well. Belinda would help him. She seemed to know a lot about such things. From the time they were in school together, she'd played the role of matchmaker. And several of her matches had actually led to happy endings. Take their childhood friends, Mary Lou and Tad, for example. Belinda had done a fine job of pairing them up. Were they not happily married with a baby on the way?

Yes, this would simply take a bit more work. But with Belinda at his side and the Lord smiling on, Georg would surely accomplish the task.

POETRY
1904
TEX

Chapter Six

. . . .

On the Sunday after Corabelle's arrival, the local Presbyterian congregation held a picnic on the grounds after the morning service. Belinda settled onto a quilt with her mother and the twins, looking about for Corabelle and James. They'd been missing for ten minutes, at least. How was Belinda supposed to shift her new friend's attentions to Georg if she kept disappearing with James?

Belinda reached for her fan, overcome by the heat. These midsummer picnics were a great idea in theory, but the heat often altered the mood of those in attendance, especially on days like today when the temperature soared into the upper nineties. Belinda watched as her papa brought the picnic basket from the wagon and set it on the colorful quilt. She scooted over to help Mama pour some lemonade. Settling back, she took a long, cool drink, enjoying its tangy sweetness.

A few minutes later, Georg appeared, looking quite dapper in his Sunday suit and hat. My, but he looked especially handsome. The better to win the lady with. He eased himself down onto the blanket next to Belinda, his gaze darting across the church lawn. She knew, of course, who he was looking for.

"So..."

"I know." Belinda shook her head and whispered the rest, holding her fan up so that no one would be the wiser. "Surely they will turn up shortly. I have it on good authority that James took her to meet the pastor. I do hope that's true." Her mother opened the picnic basket and began to unpack their lunch.

Georg gave her a knowing look. "Could I have a moment of your time away from the group?"

"Certainly." She folded her fan, fussed with her skirts, and, with Georg's help, rose to her feet. "Mama, I will be back shortly."

Her mother gazed up with a curious look on her face. "Take your time, Belinda. It will take me awhile to get things unpacked. Papa will help."

Her father glanced up with a nod. "Go on, you two. But be back soon. You don't want to miss Mama's fried chicken and biscuits."

Belinda smiled as she took Georg's proffered arm. They strolled beyond the groups of people, Georg whispering all the while. "I require your help, Belinda," he said, keeping his focus straight ahead.

"Oh?" She gazed at him, confused. "What can I do?"

He prompted her to keep walking. Clearly, he did not want others to glean anything from their conversation. "I've given this a great deal of thought. In fact, I've scarcely slept all week. I need to woo Corabelle, but I don't have a clue where to begin. She's from the city and is accustomed to fine things and fine words. She needs to be romanced. I am not a man of words. And surely you can see that I am not the romantic sort."

"Well, of course you are!" Belinda stopped and gazed at him, astounded at his confession. "Why, you're the kindest, most thoughtful man I know."

"Thoughtfulness and romance are not one and the same," he debated.

"On the contrary." She took his arm, and they began to walk once again. "I find it quite romantic when a man is thoughtful."

"Still, I believe something more is required here." He paused and gazed into her eyes for a moment. "Surely the only way to win Corabelle's heart is through a poem. A...well, a love poem."

"Oh, marvelous idea!" Belinda practically squealed. "Have you written one?"

He groaned. "I tried, but it sounds ridiculous. I thought maybe you could help." He paused a moment. "In exchange for your help, I will cover the cost of Corabelle's train ticket. Greta told me that you paid for it yourself, and I want to do what I can to help, since you've obviously arranged all of this for me."

Belinda felt her cheeks turn warm. She opened her fan once again. "I do hope you will forgive me for that. It was rather presumptuous, I know. But I'm thrilled that you have taken an interest in her. That's wonderful news. Of course I will help you. Just show me what you have written and we will build on it."

Georg gestured toward the steps in front of the church, and they both took a seat. He pulled a piece of paper from his coat pocket and slid it her way. "This is it." He shrugged. "Not much."

"Let me be the judge of that." She skimmed over the page and then began to read aloud, using her most romantic voice:

Oh, lady fair
With golden hair
And winsome smile
You've crossed the miles
To meet me here
And now, my dear,
I offer you
My heart so true

Belinda paused and gazed at Georg with new admiration. "Georg! This is lovely."

He sighed. "Do you think? The ending needs some work, wouldn't you agree? Seems rather open-ended. And what am I offering her, after all?" He rose and began to pace, finally turning back to Belinda. "You see my dilemma? How can I say I'm giving my heart to a total stranger? I don't even know my own heart yet."

Belinda rose and put her hand on Georg's shoulder. "Well, of course you do." She placed her palm against his chest, feeling the beat of his heart. With a smile, she added, "Don't you see? It's been with you all along. If anyone can read its messages, you can." For a moment, she held quite still, feeling the beat of his heart against her hand. Then, realizing that a couple of youngsters were looking on, she pulled back. "So sorry."

"No." He shook his head and gave her a funny look. "No apology necessary. You're trying to help."

"Yes, well, let's get busy on this poem, shall we?" She took a seat once more and read the words of the letter. "What are you thinking for the end? If you're not offering her your heart, then what?"

Georg sighed. "That's just it. I don't know. Maybe my time? My attentions?"

"Yes, I think that will do." Belinda stared at the page once again. "Though I'm not quite sure what rhymes with attentions." She chewed on that problem for a bit. Suddenly an idea came to her. "I know what we can do. Tomorrow, when we're both on our lunch breaks, we should visit Peter Conrad at the bookstore."

"Of course." Georg looked over with a hopeful expression. "He's the best poet in town." After a moment's pause, his enthusiasm seemed to wane, however. "On the other hand, I don't know that I care to expose my feelings—if that's what they are—to Peter. What if word gets around town?"

"I think Peter can be trusted," Belinda said. "But if you are concerned, I will go to him myself and ask for his help in advance, and then we can meet with him at an appropriate time. I know he will give it. He's our town's poet laureate, after all! Corabelle will never know that he helped."

"Hmm." Georg sighed. "I don't wish to be deceptive."

"No, you won't be. Don't you see?" She gazed into his eyes, overcome with excitement. "You've laid the foundation with what you've already written. He will build on it, but it will still be yours. And I promise, Corabelle won't see it until you put your stamp of approval on it. Agreed?" She stuck out her hand.

Georg paused a moment then slowly extended his hand. "I suppose that would be all right."

"Wonderful! Just watch and see what the Lord does, Georg! I have a feeling He's up to something mighty big here!" As she spoke the words, Belinda looked up and discovered the widow Hanson and Samuel Bromstead walking side-by-side and talking. Wonder of wonders! The Lord really was up to something here. Something grand!

Overcome with joy, she folded the paper and tucked it into her waistband, far from watchful eyes. Then she linked her arm through Georg's and they made their way back across the church lawn to join her family for dinner on the grounds.

* * *

Georg couldn't help but feel that something was amiss all through the meal. It wasn't just the fact that Corabelle scarcely looked his way. It was the overwhelming sense that James might very well take his head off if he dared to engage her in conversation. Well, he would do his best, regardless. By the time they'd finished their dessert, Georg had worked up the courage to open his mouth.

"Might I have a few minutes of your time, Miss Corabelle?" he asked as he swallowed down the last of his peach cobbler and lemonade.

She turned from a giddy conversation with James to respond. "Why, certainly, Georg."

Moments later, the couple walked arm in arm beneath the overhanging trees. Finally, Georg could speak his mind. Only, when he tried to, the words stuck in his throat. Something about being next to this beauty caused him to lose his ability to think clearly. Or to string two words together in a sensible sentence. He found himself babbling...about the weather, the barbershop, and other ridiculous nonsense. He would've slapped himself if she hadn't been watching.

Corabelle, ever gracious, appeared to play along, but he could tell that her heart wasn't really in it. Only when they rounded the back side of the church and met James face-to-face did her eyes light up.

"Do you mind?" James asked, with a twinkle in his eye. "Miss Corabelle and I have some unfinished business to take care of."

Georg nodded on the outside, but inside his heart twisted. Looked like it might take something more than a poem to woo this big-city beauty.

Not that it would make much difference. No, as he observed the way she came alive in James's presence, as he caught a glimpse of the undeniable sparkle in her eye, Georg had to ask himself a question: "She is a beautiful woman...but is she the woman for me?"

Chapter Seven

. . . .

The Saturday after the picnic, Belinda sat at the edge of the creek, beneath the shade of her favorite oak tree, with her bare legs dangling over. Dipping her toes in the water was a familiar, comforting pastime. Here, she could think clearly—and pray. She held a fishing pole in her hand, as always. Something about coming to the creek for a little quiet time always put her in a better frame of mind. Besides, she had a lot to think about today. She and Georg planned to meet in town to visit Peter Conrad at his bookshop. He would advise them about the poem, and Georg's relationship with Corabelle could move forward as planned.

Pushing thoughts of the poem out of her mind, she attempted a prayer. "Lord, I know You see all things. You know what's going to happen long before we do. Father, I ask You to work a miracle here." She focused her prayers on Georg and Corabelle, of course, but threw in an extra one for Samuel Bromstead and the widow Hanson. Surely if just one couple could be happily matched, her business would begin to blossom. Men would come from out of the woodwork to find wives. And the town, of course, would thrive as a result.

After she whispered a soft "Amen," her thoughts shifted back to Georg. They had been friends for so long...all the way back to grade school. Oh, the merciless teasing he'd endured from the little girls. He wasn't like the other boys; he didn't tease or cajole. No, Georg Kaufman had always been the kindhearted one. The one who got overlooked at game-playing time. The one you knew you could count on if you were in a jam.

And now the poor fellow was subjected to torment of a different kind.

"Poor Georg." Belinda sighed as she thought about his plight. All week he'd been forced to watch James and Corabelle's growing relationship. He'd endured it like a champ. But today all of that would change. With Peter's help, Georg would craft a beautifully written poem, one guaranteed to win any woman's heart.

A squeal rang out and Belinda turned, surprised to see Corabelle running her way.

"W–what happened?" Belinda dropped the pole and scrambled to her feet, fearing the worst.

"Oh, Belinda!" Corabelle paused to catch her breath. "I—I can't believe it! He—he—asked me to marry him!" She stuck out her left hand and showed off a delicate opal ring. "Isn't it beautiful? I'm getting married! I'm really, truly getting married!"

Belinda scrambled to her feet, overcome with joy. "Really? Oh, this is marvelous!" She could hardly believe it! Even without the poem! "Georg actually proposed?"

The color drained from Corabelle's face and her lips curled down in a pout. "Not *Georg*, silly. *James.* Your brother!"

Belinda felt as if her stomach had plummeted to her toes. James... proposed? Could such a thing really be possible? She tried to force a smile but could not, for happy as she was to have Corabelle join the family, there would be one whose heart was supremely broken over this news.

Corabelle's grabbed Belinda and gave her a tight squeeze and then laughed. "We're going to be sisters! And you have to help me with the wedding. I've got the dress, of course, but I know nothing about the rest of it. Flowers. Cake. Veil. I have nothing ready!" She squeezed Belinda's hand. "Please say you'll help me."

"I suppose I could help...." Belinda's voice drifted off as she found herself distracted. In her mind's eye, she could see the look on Georg's face when he received the news. She pulled on her shoes and laced them up, trying to stay focused.

Corabelle grinned from ear to ear. "Oh, thank you, thank you! If I hadn't come to this wonderful place, I would never have met your James. And now I have! I'm so blissfully, gloriously in love! I've never felt this way before. Why, it's the happiest feeling in all the world."

"I'm sure you're right." Belinda swallowed the lump in her throat. She couldn't help but wonder how Georg would feel about all of this, however. Perhaps the word had already spread through town. Or would by day's end.

Swallowing her pride, she rose, grabbed her fishing pole, and tagged along on Corabelle's heels. Once at the house, the feisty New Yorker spent a good hour making plans for her big day. Mama was beside herself with glee at the whole thing. She chattered on and on, clearly thrilled with it all.

"We want to marry right away," Corabelle explained and then blushed. "James says there's no reason to wait."

"But you two hardly know each other," Belinda argued. "Surely you don't mean to rush things."

"Your papa and I met in May and married in June," Mama said with a girlish smile. "Honey, when you find the right one, there's no disputing the fact. All the waiting in the world won't stop the hands of time."

"Yes, but..." Belinda wanted to argue. Wanted to say, "But if you wait, perhaps you will see that you've snagged the wrong groom."

Instead, she kept her thoughts to herself, pasted on a smile, and joined the conversation about the ceremony.

"You will stand up for me, of course!" Corabelle said, turning Belinda's way. "I have you to thank for this...for all of this!" On and on she went, talking about the wedding, which would take place at the church in two weeks.

Two weeks. Two short, sweltering-hot, midsummer weeks. Two weeks to keep Georg from taking back the money he'd given her for Corabelle's train ticket. She would need that money to secure another bride—from who knew where—for Georg. Surely someone *somewhere* would want to marry the town barber.

After lunch, Corabelle and James went off for a ride in the buggy. Belinda used this opportunity to sneak into town. Speaking with Georg was critical. She had to tell him herself, though the very thought of it made her ill. She made her way onto Main Street, dragging her heels all the way. Oh, how she dreaded sharing this news.

As she arrived at the barbershop, Georg happened to walk outside to sweep the front porch. "Belinda." He turned to her with a smile. "You're early. I thought you were coming at four thirty. Peter isn't expecting us till then." He grinned. "You'll be so proud of me. I've been working on the poem. The ending is really coming along, so I think Peter will have a strong foundation."

"I see." She drew in a deep breath. "Georg, I have something to tell you. Are you busy?"

"No. In fact, there's not a whiskery man in town, apparently." He grinned. "Business has been slow today. I finished up with the mayor over an hour ago but haven't seen anyone since."

"Ah. Well, I'm here to talk about Corabelle."

His eyes lit up at once. "I'm so glad you brought her up. You're not going to believe what I've done. I went off to Terrell yesterday afternoon and fetched a ring."

"You didn't." Belinda began to fan herself as a wave of dizziness passed over her. She pushed aside her fears as best she could.

"I did!" He raced to the back of the store and came back carrying a small velvet box. "A man can't very well propose without a ring, can he?"

His hand trembled as his fingers uncurled, revealing the most beautiful ring she'd ever seen. Belinda felt her heart plummet to her toes as she stared at the lovely silver band with a shiny blue stone. She couldn't help but gasp at the ring's beauty. "What is that stone, Georg? I've never seen anything like it."

His hand continued to shake as he extended it her way. "A sapphire. The jeweler said there's nothing like it in this area, so Corabelle will be able to wear it with great pride. No other woman in the county has a ring like this."

Belinda took the ring in her hand and held it out, examining the stone's many facets. She'd never seen anything so beautiful in all her life.

"Try it on," Georg whispered. He looked around then grabbed the ring and pressed it onto her left ring finger, though he had to struggle a bit to get it past her knuckle—probably swollen from the heat.

Belinda gasped once more, this time astounded by the feelings that came over her with such a lovely ring on her finger. What would it feel like, to wear a ring like this...forever? She could only imagine.

Belinda pondered this and a great many other things as she stared at the exquisite stone. Oh, how she hated to tell Georg the news, especially now. She looked up, wishing she could mask the tears that sprang to her eyes. "Georg, listen, I have something to tell you."

"What? It's the wrong color? I should have purchased a diamond. I knew it."

"No, the color is perfect. The ring is quite unique—and beautiful, to boot." Belinda extended her hand, more than thrilled with his purchase. "It's about Corabelle." She squeezed her eyes shut and whispered a prayer. Opening them, she forced the words out. "James proposed and they're getting married in two weeks at the church."

"W–what?" Georg's face took on an ashen look. "I think you'd better repeat that."

"James and Corabelle are engaged. There's just no other way to say it. The wedding is planned. We're...well, we're all invited. The whole town."

Georg slumped down onto the bench in front of the barbershop. Belinda watched the tips of his ears turn red. For a moment, he didn't say a word. Then, finally, he extended his hand. "I guess I won't be needing the ring, then."

She reached to pull it from her finger, but her breath caught in her throat as she realized it was stuck. "Oh, Georg!"

"What?" He rose to his feet and grasped her hand. "Don't tell me it's—"

"I'm trying. Hold on a minute. Please." She wrestled with it, unable to get it to budge.

"Here, I know." Georg turned to the right and then the left, making sure no one was watching. Then he took hold of her arm and led her into the empty barbershop. "I'll lather it up. The soap will help it come loose."

"Are you sure?" She continued to fight with the stubborn ring but couldn't get it past her knuckle. "Ugh! This is so humiliating! I always told Mama I had a boy's hands. Now I have the proof."

"Don't be silly," Georg argued. "That ring is very small. I knew it would have to be sized, most likely."

"Still." Belinda shook her head, more embarrassed than anything else. She watched as Georg took some of the minty lather and worked it into her finger, the slippery stuff now encompassing the ring on every side.

"Let's try this one more time." Georg grasped the ring and pulled it. Unfortunately, it came flying off with such speed that it shot across the room and landed in one of the shaving mugs on the other side.

Belinda sprinted that way and dished it out. Holding it up with her lather-covered hand, she grinned. "Your ring!"

"Yes." He frowned. "My ring that I no longer need."

"Don't be silly, Georg." She shook her head, determined to make the best of this. "God has the perfect woman for you, and I plan to find her. Just give me a little time and I'll make good on that, I promise."

"I really don't think you need to bother," Georg said, looking more disheartened than ever.

"Oh, but I must! You paid for Corabelle's train fare, and I can use the money to bring someone else."

Georg put his hand up and she stopped talking right away. "Belinda, listen. I appreciate your help, but I think it's clear we're getting ahead of the Lord on this. You go right ahead and help the other men, those who feel called to marry. As for me...well, I do believe I was right, that day in the mercantile."

"Oh?" She shook her head, not remembering.

"You asked how I would feel if you told me the Lord had laid it on your heart to find me a bride. Do you remember how I responded?"

A rush of emotion came over Belinda, along with a wave of guilt, which niggled at her conscience. "Y–yes." She whispered the word.

"What did I say?"

"You asked me to seek Him again for further explanation because you were quite happy in your current state." She sighed as she glanced his way, ready to dispute his words. "But I told you then...and I'll tell you now...you are a lonely man, Georg Kaufman. And I will find the woman of your dreams, if you'll just give me one more chance. As I've said before, it's all a matter of science. Merged with faith, of course. Your perfect complement is out there. I know it!"

He opened his mouth as if to speak but then closed it right away. After a moment's silence, he gave his response. "I would ask that you turn your attentions to the other men. Perhaps one day I will require your services. When that time comes, I will let you know."

"Promise?" She gave him a hopeful look.

"I promise."

"Wonderful!" She reached up to give him a warm embrace then pulled back, embarrassed. "I'm so sorry. Don't know what came over me. I'm just so grateful you're not mad at me." She turned and headed for the door, pausing only for a moment to look back. "Don't give up hope, Georg! I know God has matrimonial plans for you. I can feel it right here." She put her hand on her heart, gave him a wink, and then sprinted toward home as fast as her legs could carry her.

* * *

The minute Belinda disappeared from view, Georg dropped into a chair and raked his fingers through his hair. So Corabelle and James were engaged. *Engaged.* To be married in two weeks. The news still stunned him. All week he'd dreamed of wooing her. And the ring was meant to seal the deal. Clearly the Lord had other plans.

He stood and began to pace the room, ranting all the while. "Lord, I am a sensible man. A sensible man. I do my best to behave rationally and not step out ahead of You. I need to ask for Your forgiveness, Father. Clearly, this was not Your will. But I got so caught up..." He paused, thinking of Corabelle's beautiful green eyes and her flirtatious smile. "I got so caught up in the idea of having a wife like her that I actually believed it was Your plan. I don't need a wife, Lord. I don't. I'm doing just fine here on my own. Wouldn't You agree?"

"I'm not altogether sure I do."

Georg stopped dead in his tracks and turned to discover his father standing in the open doorway of the shop. *Oh no.*

"So, we're arguing with the Almighty about the need for a wife? Or would it be...the lack thereof?" His father entered the room with a crooked grin on his face.

"No, I..."

"Listen, son. This is something I should have told you years ago. When the time is right for you to marry, you won't have to go looking for a wife. Trust me when I tell you this. The Lord will drop her in your lap. You'll turn around...and there she'll be."

Georg sighed and dropped into a chair. "I suppose. But until then, I think I'll just keep my eyes focused on the business. Can't go wrong there, can I?"

"Keeping your eyes on the business is a good thing," his father said, reaching for an apron. "But I'll tell you the truth. It's a lonely life for the man who is married to his work."

Georg never had a chance to carry through with the conversation. The moment he opened his mouth, a rush of customers streamed through the door. In that moment, he made up his mind to do exactly what he'd said he would do: focus on his work. Nothing more, nothing less.

POETRY 1904 TEY

Chapter Eight

....

The morning after Corabelle married James, the men came from all corners of the county to inquire about Belinda's services. First it was Myles Lott, the schoolmaster. Belinda couldn't help but smile at his enthusiasm as he approached her desk. Who knew the forty-something bachelor had always longed to wed? As his student, she'd never contemplated the possibility. Still, he looked particularly intrigued by the idea. Excited, even. Belinda promised to search for the perfect woman, one suited to the life of a schoolteacher's wife. And Myles agreed to locate a poem from among the many books in his classroom to use as enticement. She knew he would come up with the perfect verse to win a woman's heart.

Next came Charlie Grundy, the blacksmith. The poor fellow had lived a lonely life, with few bridal prospects. Of course, his rough exterior could be to blame. Belinda would have to find someone special to accomplish this goal. She knew better than to ask Charlie to compose a poem. Perhaps Peter could help with that one. Or maybe she could come up with something herself. It would really have to be something, to counterbalance the man's physical appearance.

Bucky Williams, who ran the local gristmill, showed up next. With his hat in his hands, he explained that life would be much sweeter with a wife in the picture. Bucky was a handsome enough fellow, though exceptionally tall and thin. Still, he was quite amiable and always treated others with respect. Surely Belinda could find his perfect match. She promised to speak with Peter about something poetic to include with any letter she might write.

Ironically, Reverend Billingsley showed up next, looking more than a little nervous. He pulled off his hat then peered at her with embarrassment in his expression. "Belinda, I, um—well, I know you must find this rather shocking...a man of the cloth looking for a bride in such a way."

"Heavens, no, Reverend!" She smiled, hoping to offer him a bit of reassurance. "The Lord moves in mysterious ways, after all."

"Indeed." The pastor sighed. "And to be quite honest, ever since Evelyn passed on, I've been quite lonely. I love preaching to my congregation, but I miss the joy of having a wife to come home to. And I need someone to aid me in my endeavors to win the lost. So if you're able to put that into the letter, I would be grateful to pay for your services."

"Indeed." Belinda leaned forward and whispered, "How are you at writing poetry, Reverend?"

"P–poetry?" He paled. "Not good. Why?"

"I am a firm believer in wooing women with beautiful words. Perhaps you could write a little verse to include with my letter."

He paused and appeared to be in thought about it. Finally, he snapped his finger. "Indeed! I know just what to do. I will include a verse from the Song of Solomon. It's quite poetic." After a moment's reflection, his cheeks turned a ruddy color. "Of course, I will have to choose my passage carefully. The Song of Solomon is quite, well, romantic."

"Yes." Belinda stifled a laugh. "Please err on the side of caution."

After the reverend left, several other men showed up, each anxious for a wife. She refused to take money from any of them, even as a retainer. No, until she located the women, she could not.

Once left her to her own devices, Belinda fetched copies of two
newspapers—one from Kansas City, the other from Philadelphia. The
one from Philadelphia was outdated, but she located the bridal letters
inside just the same. One of the letters caught her eye at once. The
woman, Marta Schuller, appeared to be highly educated.

Belinda settled into the chair at her desk to read:

FORTY-FIVE-YEAR-OLD PHILADELPHIA NATIVE.
EDUCATED AT THE UNIVERSITY OF PENNSYLVANIA, ONE
OF ONLY FOUR WOMEN IN MY CLASS. WORK AS A PRIVATE
TUTOR. SEEK NEW LIFE IN SOUTHERN TOWN WHERE I
CAN USE MY COLLEGE EDUCATION AS WELL AS MY SKILLS
WITH CHILDREN.

Belinda could hardly believe her good fortune! Why, Marta
Schuller was perfect for Mr. Lott, the schoolmaster. His scientific
equal. No doubt about it. They could combine their efforts and teach
the children while enjoying a life of marital bliss. Belinda wrote to her
right away. Surely Myles would find the perfect poem from one of his
books to sweeten the pot.

Next, she set her sights on finding someone for Bucky Williams.
Someone who might make a good gristmill-owner's wife. She had to
smile as she stumbled across the perfect advertisement:

SOUTHERN GAL SEARCHING FOR A TRUE-BLUE
SOUTHERN GENTLEMAN. READY TO SETTLE DOWN AND
RAISE A FAMILY. SMALL-TOWN LIFE WOULD BE IDEAL.

As she read the rest of the piece, Belinda had to admit, this woman—Katie Sue Caldwell—sounded just right for Bucky. Belinda reached for another piece of stationery and filled it with an apt description of Bucky's attributes. Once done, she tried to come up with something poetic to add, but nothing came to her.

Ironically, just as she gave up on the idea of composing a poem, Belinda heard a familiar voice. She looked up to see Peter Conrad, the town's most famous poet. The timing could not have been more perfect. She ushered up a silent, "Thank You, Lord!" and then turned her attention to her guest.

"Making matches, Belinda?" the elderly man asked with a twinkle in his eye.

"Indeed." She smiled as she took in his rugged appearance. Not many men could wear a beard that long, and his mustache hadn't been trimmed in ages. She often wondered what he looked like, underneath all that hair. "Are you looking for a match, Peter?"

"Certainly not." His eyes twinkled as he shook his head. "I can assure you, I will never require your services. Life is complicated enough, I daresay. And you know me. I'm a confirmed bachelor. Fifty-nine years without a woman, and I've done just fine. I'm of the firm opinion that you shouldn't try to fix something unless it's broken."

"No arguments, then!" She laughed. "Well, if you're not looking for my help, could I ask for yours?"

"My help?" As his brow wrinkled, the bushy salt-and-pepper eyebrows came closer together. "With what?"

"I am in need of love poems. Perhaps I could pay a set fee for love poems to include with the letters I send out to potential brides."

Peter stared at her, clearly troubled by this suggestion. "You know what the great Leo Tolstoy once wrote, do you not?"

"No, I'm afraid I don't, sorry."

Peter sighed, as if finding her to be completely devoid of sense. "He said, and I quote, 'One ought only to write when one leaves a piece of one's own flesh in the inkpot, each time one dips one's pen?'"

"Beg your pardon?"

"People do not have any business composing poems unless they've dipped their lives into the inkwell. That's what he was trying to say, and I agree completely."

"O–oh. I see." Suddenly Belinda felt ashamed for asking.

"No, I'm afraid you don't understand." Peter shook his head. "For if you did, you would know that asking a true poet to write love poems for others is virtually impossible. Only when a man or woman's own heart is involved is the deed possible. I can only write a poem from the depths of my soul if I have actually visited the depths of my soul. And if you are asking me to compose such a piece for another human being, it is simply not possible."

Belinda nodded, finally understanding. "So you're saying you cannot help me?"

"No, I'm saying that the poems won't be as genuine as they should be, for my heart won't be involved."

"Ah." So there was hope. "Peter, you know poetic form. Structure. And surely you can piece together the right words to sound good."

Peter slapped himself in the head. "This is why writers write and others do not. There is a vast ocean between the two that none can cross, lest they pour out their blood like ink in the attempt."

"Hmm. Well, that sounds messy," Greta said, passing by. "And

I think you're making too much of this. Just a couple of simple poems, Peter. Nothing more."

He rubbed his chin, his brow now wrinkled. "How soon would you need them?"

Belinda gave him a sheepish look. "Well, to be quite honest, I would like to get these letters out today. The pastor is coming up with a verse from Song of Solomon, so we won't need one for his letter."

"Song of Solomon, eh?" Peter waggled his brows. "We can only pray he will choose carefully."

"He will." She giggled. "And Mr. Lott has agreed to find something from among his books. But that still leaves two letters."

"Who are the gentlemen?" Peter asked. "Knowing will help me personalize anything I write."

"Charlie Grundy and Bucky Williams."

"Ah. I see." He began to pace. "I have my work cut out for me, then."

"Yes." She sighed. "But I know you can do it, Peter. You're a born poet."

"Mm-hmm." He paced a bit longer, finally turning her way. "Tell you what. Let me go ahead and make my purchases and then I'll head back to my shop to think on this. I'll have something to you within the hour. Would that work?"

"Beautifully!"

He nodded. "Fine. In the meantime, I've come into the store to buy flour and sugar. Could you help me? Greta has gone missing."

Belinda looked around, finding the store completely empty. Her cousin must be in the back room organizing goods. She flew into action, helping Peter with his purchases, then headed off to find her.

"There you are!" Belinda gasped as she spotted Greta perched atop a chair, trying to reach something from a top shelf in the storeroom. "Let me hold that chair. You could fall."

"Thanks." Greta filled her arms with empty canning jars then scrambled down, her skirts all askew. "I didn't mean to leave you with the customers. But I'm woefully behind on things."

"Now that I'm so distracted with my work, you mean?" Belinda sighed.

"Oh, I think what you're doing is a noble thing, so I don't mind. Not really." Greta gave her a reassuring smile. "I'll manage fine." She chuckled. "Besides, I'm anxious to see how everything turns out. Matchmaking is a lot of fun!"

"You really think so?"

"Really." Greta nodded. "But what was all that silliness Peter was spouting? Sometimes the man perplexes me."

"He is of the opinion that the poems won't sound genuine unless they're written out of real emotion. And perhaps he's right, but I don't know what to do about that."

"What can you do?" Greta echoed. "The other fellows aren't poets."

"Right. Neither do they possess Peter's wit." Belinda sighed. "I really need him right now. So, concerned or not, I hope he can come up with a couple of poems for me. Otherwise, I will never find matches for these gentlemen!"

"I daresay you will, if you will look in those newspapers" Greta pointed at a stack of them sitting nearby. "There's one from Philadelphia, one from New York, one from Kansas City, and another from Biloxi. All filled with advertisements. So get to work, Belinda! Make some matches."

Belinda grinned then snatched the papers and headed back to her desk at the front of the store. Finding someone to suit the reverend's needs would definitely be a good place to start. Belinda reached for the newspaper on top—the one from Kansas City—distracted by an ad from a young woman who seemed better suited to Georg. Suddenly, a familiar voice rang out. She looked up to discover none other than Georg himself, coming through the front door. Pressing the newspaper under her chair, she stilled the shaking in her hands and rose to greet him.

* * *

Georg took a few pensive steps in Belinda's direction. His mind was still reeling from yesterday's wedding. Watching Corabelle take James's hand in marriage had been difficult, but in the end, Georg had to conclude that it hadn't exactly broken his heart. No, as the ceremony passed, Georg came to the obvious conclusion, the one he wished he'd come to before making a fool of himself over Corabelle. A bachelor's life suited him just fine, thank you very much.

Still, there was that matter of the money he'd given Belinda the day of the church picnic. Surely she would return it now. He approached her desk and offered a firm smile. She looked up and batted her eyelashes.

"Georg."

"Time for a lunch break," he announced.

"Oh, I don't dare." She looked up at him, stunned. "I have so much to do."

He extended his hand, gesturing for her to stand. "We have some things to discuss."

Belinda sighed and then rose to her feet. They made their way to the back room, and he leaned against one of the empty barrels and gestured for her to do the same. She settled onto one and looked his way.

"What can I do for you, Georg?"

"Yes. Well. About this whole wife thing—" He never had a chance to say anything else, because she interrupted him.

"I'm so glad you brought that up! I was just looking in the Kansas City paper and stumbled across a woman who will be perfect for you." She scrambled off the barrel, ran to her desk, and grabbed a newspaper, which she brought back and thrust into his hand.

"But that's just it," he argued. "I'm not looking for a perfect woman."

"Well, good!" Belinda laughed. "Because you will be sorely disappointed if you are! There are no perfect women in the world, I assure you! I was just saying I'd found someone suited to you. A good match, as it were." She opened the paper and pointed to a section he'd sooner avoid.

"I see. But, Belinda, about this whole arranged-marriages thing..."

"You know me better than almost anyone, Georg," she interrupted. "I've always been the sort to arrange things."

"Yes, but...lives?"

"Only the Lord arranges lives. I, well, I just offer any assistance I can to move things along." She gave him a winsome smile. "Just consider me a marriage broker. Now let's get to work, shall we?"

He sighed, unsure of what to say next. It looked like Belinda would persist with this matchmaking nonsense regardless. It might be easier to play along and then convince her in the end that he was a happy bachelor when no suitable woman could be found. Yes, that would surely work.

He glanced through the newspaper, reading blurbs about the various women. In the meantime, Belinda fetched a couple of apples and tossed one his way.

"What about this one?" She pointed at an advertisement in the paper as she took a bite.

Georg shook his head. "Look again, Belinda. She's in her sixties."

"Ah. No wonder she sounds so settled."

He sighed. "Yes, very." *And so am I. So why am I even looking?* "Belinda, I do not need a wife. That's what I've been trying to say. I enjoy my life. I have friends, church, family.... My father and I run a good business. I'm doing well for myself." He put the paper down and took a bite of the sweet, juicy apple.

The corners of her lips curled down in a pout. "Really? Truly?"

"I'm not lonely. I enjoy spending my days as I do. And if I got married, well, nothing would be the same."

"Yes, you're right about that." She swatted him with the newspaper, and he grinned. Now this was the Belinda Bauer he remembered from school—playful, fun, often in trouble with Mr. Lott. Thinking of the schoolmaster, perhaps this would be the perfect time to change the direction of the conversation. He could talk to her about reimbursing his money later.

"I hear our old schoolmaster was in here looking for a wife." Georg waggled his brows. "He came over to the barbershop just after, telling us all about it. What sort of woman do you have in mind for him?"

"Oh, I've found his match!" Belinda grinned and sprinted back into the store, coming back with yet another newspaper. She read about a woman in her forties from Philadelphia, and Georg's interest was piqued at once. In fact, it almost sounded too good to be true.

"She sounds wonderful," he admitted. Maybe there was more to this marriage brokering that he'd considered. Perhaps it really was, as Belinda said, a matter of science. Matching the right man with the right woman. Like-minded people with like-minded interests.

"Well, you can't have her. She's for Mr. Lott." Belinda picked up another paper. "Now I have to find someone for the reverend."

"The reverend? He's looking for a wife?"

"Yes. You can help me." She put down the Philadelphia paper and looked through the one from Kansas City once more. Georg drew near, more curious than anything else. "What sort of woman is he looking for, do you think?"

"Oh, sensible. Practical. Someone in her late fifties. Likely a widow. A woman who enjoys Sunday services, of course."

"What about this one?" Georg read aloud an advertisement about a lady named Sarah Jo: "'Petite widow seeks new life in quiet rural town. Searching for a man who loves the Lord, enjoys reading, and relishes Sunday afternoon strolls in the countryside.'"

"Georg!" Belinda looked at him, clearly dumbfounded. She turned her attention to the newspaper to read the rest of the advertisement. "You've done it! You've found the perfect wife for Reverend Billingsley. And look! She bakes pies. The reverend *loves* pies. And she plays the piano. Our church has a piano and is in dire need of a decent pianist. Oh, this is a match made in heaven! No doubt about it! Do you see now what I mean about a scientific match? These two have much in common!"

Georg laughed. Maybe it was a match made in heaven. Maybe this woman would come and sweep the pastor off of his feet. And maybe—with Belinda's matchmaking skills at work—all the menfolk in Poetry would be happily married.

Well, all but one.

1904

Chapter Nine

On the first Tuesday in August, Belinda met with several of the townsmen at the church. The pastor attended, of course, as did the mayor, who looked more than a little concerned. Georg came along as well. How she had grown to depend on him these past few weeks. She looked around the room, trying to figure out how to settle them down. They were quite excited. And spiffed up, to be sure. She'd never seen the menfolk this polished-looking outside a Sunday service.

Belinda clapped her hands to quiet the crowd in the church. "Gentlemen." She raised her voice. "Gentlemen!" The roomful of excited clients looked her way, the noise level in the room dropping dramatically. "I need your attention, please."

She drew in a breath, realizing the time. Any minute now, Papa would arrive from the station with potential brides for several of the fellows. In the weeks since she'd set out to find wives for the pastor, the schoolmaster, and two others, several other men had inquired about her services, as well. Most of those men had shown up today out of curiosity, no doubt. And perhaps a few thought they might steal one of the incoming brides for themselves. She would work diligently to make sure that did not happen. Still, with so many people to accommodate, Belinda wondered if she could keep everything straight in her head!

Reverend Billingsley looked at her with a twinkle in his eyes, no doubt excited about his incoming bride. Mr. Lott paced the room, occasionally pulling out his pocket watch and staring at it. Bucky Williams, who stood a good head taller than everyone in the room, was easy to keep track of. He stood off in the corner, talking to Charlie Grundy. Unfortunately, Mr. Grundy hadn't gone to any special effort with his appearance today. Belinda prayed that it would not turn out to be a problem.

With the room now quiet, she made her announcement. "Gentlemen, we don't want to frighten these women away. With that in mind, I believe we should have some sort of protocol. There must be a way to greet them without coming across as anxious. Agreed?"

A few of the men grumbled, especially Charlie. "I've waited thirty-eight years for a wife, Belinda. What would it hurt to act excited now that I've actually got one?"

"If you want her to stick around, you'd better give thought to a gentle welcome," Belinda explained. "Your wife-to-be"—*should she agree to marrying you after seeing you in person*—"is accustomed to working in a library. A library is a quiet environment. We don't want to frighten her away."

He grunted but eventually took a seat.

She reached for her fan and began to work it in front of her face, overwhelmed by the mid-August heat. Hopefully the women wouldn't be frightened away by it.

Belinda never had time to give it a second thought. She heard the wagon pull up outside and watched in horror as the men turned and stampeded out of the church and onto the grounds below, whooping and hollering as they went. Whispering a prayer, she turned to Georg. "Oh, help."

He shook his head. "I daresay it's out of our hands now. Only the Lord can manage this mob."

"I know." She swallowed hard. "That's what scares me. They're out of control."

"Don't let them see your fear, Belinda," Georg instructed. "Just hold your head high, march out there, and take control. They are paying for your services. You have to be authoritative. Trust me on this. I don't know much about many things, but I know a lot about how men act."

"Okay." She drew in a deep breath and then looked into his eyes for reassurance. "And, Georg, in case I haven't said it before, I'm awfully sorry I didn't find someone for you this time around."

"Don't fret over that." He shook his head. "I've already told you, I'm blissfully happy single."

"Well, I know, but..."

He put a finger over her lips, offering up a boyish grin. "No arguments. We can talk about me later. You have a passel of menfolk to quiet down. Better get to it."

"Yes." She offered up another silent prayer for help as she headed outside to take charge. She finally reached the wagon, where Papa sat with four unfamiliar women clustered around him. The two youngest ones looked terrified. One—the older woman—grinned from ear to ear. And one—probably the schoolteacher—well, she simply looked bewildered. Who could blame her?

The men continued their howling until Papa rose from the wagon, put his fingers in his mouth, and let out a loud whistle. "That'll be enough of that!" he hollered. "Stop it now, or I'll turn this wagon around and take these ladies back to the station!"

Belinda breathed a sigh of relief as the crowd fell silent at once.

The men took a giant step backward as the women began to descend from the wagon. The first—a woman in her late fifties with a mixture of red and silver hair—took Papa's hand and stepped onto the ground below. She wore a colorful frock pinched in at the middle, but it wasn't enough to hide the plump physique. Still, with such a whimsical smile and bright blue eyes, who would care about a few extra pounds?

The woman glanced around as she introduced herself in a loud voice: "Sarah Jo Cummings, at your service!" When no one said anything, she hollered, "Well, what's everyone so quiet about? C'mon, now. Fess up. Which one of you fine fellas is my man? Don't tell me I've come all the way to Texas to be stood up, now!"

She put her hands on her hips and stared out over the crowd. Belinda gasped as she saw the look of shock on the reverend's face. He gingerly took a couple of steps in the woman's direction and extended his hand. "I am Reverend Billingsley. Pleased to make your acquaintance, Sarah Jo."

"And yours." The woman's whimsical smile faded as she looked at his collar. Slapping herself in the head, she said, "So it's true. You're a preacher."

"Why, yes."

"Well, if that doesn't beat all! I was afraid of that." She groaned. "Thought maybe you'd elaborated a bit in your letter like I did in mine. That verse from Song of Solomon sent shivers right down my spine!" She gave him a wink and then slapped him on his backside. The men apparently found this incredibly funny, and a roar of laughter went up.

The good reverend's face turned all shades of red, and Belinda was pretty sure she felt her heart hit her toes.

Determined to stay focused, she turned her attentions to the women still climbing out of the wagon, summing them up as she went. The one in front must be Marta Schuller, the schoolteacher from Philadelphia. Behind her came Prissy Finkelstein, meant for Charlie Grundy, the blacksmith. So then, the short, rotund one in the very back had to be Katie Sue Caldwell, from Biloxi...Bucky Williams's intended.

Instead of following her earlier instructions, the men drew near the ladies, much like a group of hunters coming in for the kill.

"Gentlemen! Gentlemen, please!" She tried in vain to quiet them, but they would not be quieted. A lump rose in her throat, and she tried to force it down. How could she regain control, now that it had been lost? Without divine intervention, this whole plan was suddenly destined to fail.

* * *

Georg looked on, half amused and half terrified as the scene unfolded in front of him. While he hated to see Belinda's pride injured in any way, he had to admit that she'd brought most of this chaos on herself. Had she not promised wives for some of these men? And wives they now had...whether they wanted them or not. Not that anyone had exchanged vows just yet. Georg had to wonder if any of these fine folk might run for the hills, now that they were seeing each other face-to-face. A few would likely be tempted.

He gave the four women a once-over, starting with Sarah Jo. The plucky gal was slightly rounded in the middle, not that the reverend would mind that. Still, she was not at all the demure churchgoing lady he had pictured, based on her advertisement. Quite the opposite, in fact. There was nothing demure about this boisterous woman.

Sarah Jo's outgoing personality made him smile, though, as did her whimsical expression. He had to wonder what Reverend Billingsley thought of her. Probably wouldn't take long to find out.

Marta Schuller, the schoolteacher, seemed nice enough. She wore her dark hair pulled up tight, and her wire-rimmed spectacles sat perched atop a thin nose. Her plain, practical dress would be fitting to a classroom. He watched as Belinda introduced her to Mr. Lott, who gave her a boyish grin. She smiled back. Sort of. He couldn't quite tell. Her thin lips curled up a bit, he supposed.

At this point, Georg watched Bucky Williams—tall and slender— look down upon his intended, Katie Sue. The top of her head barely met his shoulders. That might prove to be problematic, should they ever decide to kiss. And to say that Katie Sue was plump would be putting it mildly. She matched Bucky's height with her width, to be sure. Oh, but the smile on the young woman's face would win anyone over. That and her twinkling blue eyes. They almost matched the merriment in Bucky's.

And then there was Prissy Finkelstein. Georg wasn't sure when he'd ever seen a more, well, *pristine* woman. Her traveling clothes were fresh and clean, her hair beautifully tended to, and her white-gloved hands impeccable. He watched in rapt awe as she took in the not-so-tidy Charlie Grundy. The look on the poor woman's face was priceless. Georg chuckled, in spite of his intentions to the contrary. Oh, the adventures that lay ahead for those two!

The townsfolk gathered round, everyone talking a mile a minute. Then Belinda ushered the four women toward Stanzas, the town's hotel. He followed along in case she needed him for anything but stayed to the side of the group where he could watch the interactions between the potential brides and grooms.

More than anything, he felt the need to protect the four women from any unnecessary heckling. Not that he needed to bother with that. Mr. Grundy guarded over Prissy with great care. And the pastor, heaven help him, seemed to be fully overwhelmed with Sarah Jo, who talked a mile a minute—not just to the reverend, but to any man who would listen. Katie Sue peered up at Bucky Williams, batting her eyelashes. And Marta Schuller—the schoolteacher? Well, she marched three feet ahead of the whole crowd, clearly a born leader. Poor Myles followed along in her dust, his hat in his hands and a disappointed expression on his face.

Georg couldn't help but laugh. The town of Poetry was filled with a passel of brides, that was for certain. But how would their budding romances fare? Only time would tell!

Chapter Ten
....

The week following the arrival of the brides was truly the most chaotic of Belinda's life. She did her best to help Greta and Aunt Hilde at the store, but every time she turned around, someone interrupted her. The menfolk, mostly. Many of them were now itching to be hitched. They arrived by the bushel-full. Still, she decided to slow things down until the four couples were happily wed. Or until she heard a heavenly angel choir telling her to continue this reckless pursuit.

On a Thursday afternoon, with the early August heat wrapping the town in its embrace, Belinda received a visit from Corabelle and James. Her sister-in-law's face lit into a smile the moment she sashayed into the store. "I'm so thrilled to see you!" she said, her green eyes shining with mischief. "Can you slip away for a moment? We have something to show you!"

"Greta, do you mind?" Belinda untied her apron in anticipation.

"No, not at all," Greta responded. She turned to Corabelle. "But if you've got a secret, I want to know it, too!"

"You will, you will. In time." Corabelle winked and then took James by the arm.

Belinda made her way outside and followed the enthusiastic couple down the boardwalk to the old, abandoned feed store, where they stopped and turned to her with curious grins on their faces.

"You'll never guess." Corabelle flashed a smile. "Go on. Try."

"Mmm." Belinda shook her head. "You're going to build a house in town?"

"No, silly." Corabelle giggled. "You are looking at the future home of Sonnets and Bonnets, my new hat shop! We just purchased the building today and will begin renovations next week!"

"You're going to do it?" Belinda grinned then reached to embrace Corabelle. "Oh, what a fabulous idea. This old building was just sitting here doing nothing. What a happy solution for us all." She paused a moment. "But where will you get the hats?"

"I will design them myself," Corabelle explained. "I've done ever-so-many drawings. Just wait till you see!"

"She has quite a gift," James said, planting a kiss on Corabelle's cheek. "My bride is a woman of many talents."

"Well, let's just say the Lord was preparing me for this all along," Corabelle responded. "I feel like my years in the city were a prerequisite to coming here. Isn't it amazing how God arranged all of this?" She paused, putting a gloved hand to her lips as she smiled at Belinda. "With your help, of course, my dear."

Belinda laughed. "I daresay, the Almighty doesn't need my help. If He formed the world and all upon it in a week's time, He can bring about a match between two parties without my intervention."

"Still, you played a role, and we will be forever grateful." Corabelle reached over and gave her hand a squeeze. "That's why you had to be the first to hear the news about the shop."

"Thank you for telling me." Belinda chuckled. "Though Greta is going to have a fit if I don't share the news. Do you mind?"

"Of course not!" Corabelle said. "We want everyone to know. The sooner, the better. It will be good advertisement." She grinned.

"You've not seen me in action yet, Belinda. I'm quite the shopkeeper. Just wait and see."

"Oh, I'm sure! How long till the store opens?" Belinda asked.

"Soon, I hope. Now that so many women have converged upon our fair town..."

At that very moment, Prissy Finkelstein, Sarah Jo Cummings, and Marta Schuller came out of Peter's bookstore. The women stopped to chat.

"We're headed to the restaurant to have our lunch," Prissy announced. "I do believe Charlie Grundy is meeting us there." She batted her eyelashes and Sarah Jo jabbed her in the ribs.

"He could use a little polish and shine, but we'll get him cleaned up," Sarah Jo said.

"And the reverend?" Belinda asked.

"Well, he doesn't need any cleaning up, that's sure and certain," Sarah Jo said with a wink. "He's so clean that he squeaks when he walks." She clapped her hands together as laughter pealed forth. "Don't rightly know if he's coming to the restaurant today, but there are plenty of other menfolk to catch a woman's eye, if not. Why, this town is swimming in men!" Her gaze shifted to Peter, who had closed up the bookstore and was heading across the street to the restaurant. Sarah Jo leaned in to whisper, "And I do mean *swimming* in men!"

"Where is Katie Sue?" Belinda asked, determined to change the direction of the conversation.

"Where she always is," Prissy said, giggling. "With Bucky Williams. With those two, it was love at first sight. I've never seen anything so sweet in all my born days."

"I'm so glad." Belinda smiled. Well, at least one of the couples seemed fitted to each other. Perhaps two, if Charlie Grundy managed to bathe or don a fresh shirt.

"Why are you standing out here, anyway?" Sarah Jo asked. "Business slow at the mercantile, Belinda?"

"Oh, not at all. Corabelle was just…" She clamped a hand over her mouth, not wanting to give away too much without her sister-in-law's permission.

"You might as well hear our news." Corabelle turned to the women with a smile.

"Oh, honey!" Sarah Jo practically hollered. "Are you having a little one? When is the baby due?"

Several townspeople stopped and turned their way at this loud proclamation.

"No, no." James paled as he lowered his voice. "That's not it."

Corabelle giggled. "Not at all. I'm opening a shop. A hat shop." She went on to describe Sonnets and Bonnets in detail, even giving details about some of the hats. At once, the three women began to chime in, each giving her opinion of this venture.

"I want to order seven hats, then," Sarah Jo announced. "One for every day of the week. I'll take one in blue, one in green, another in yellow…" She went off on a tangent, talking about the various colors and designs.

When she came up for air, Marta got in a few words. "I could use a sensible hat for walking outdoors. The heat is quite unbearable here."

"Oh, who cares if it's practical?" Prissy said, fussing with her bonnet sash. "Just give me a fashionable hat any day. I miss the millineries from home so much. This is a sweet little town, but it's lacking in so many ways."

Belinda sighed. "I'm sorry. Are you disappointed?"

"Not disappointed, so much," Prissy said, tying her sash into a perfectly looped bow. "It will be interesting to see how things change, with so many ladies about."

James coughed and then shifted his gaze to the barbershop.

"I see, well, I..." Belinda wasn't sure how to finish her sentence, for while she longed for Poetry to grow in both respectability and numbers, she didn't want to see it flipped up on its ear. At least not by these three.

"I, myself, have always wanted to open an opera house," Sarah Jo said. "Where wonderful theatricals could take place. I'm a piano player, you know."

"Fabulous idea!" Corabelle clapped her hands together. "An opera house! Why, think of the shows we could put on. Of course, we would have to hold auditions, but what fun!" Her cheeks pinked. "I, um... well, I do a little singing, myself. And I daresay my acting skills are something to behold. At least that's what I've been told by my friends in New York."

"Indeed?" Prissy turned to her, clearly stunned. "Why, I know you won't believe this, but I was a sponsor at the Grand Opera Society in Kansas City. I can think of nothing finer than to have an opera house. I'm quite skilled at drawing in a crowd."

"Still, we've no building," Sarah Jo said, looking about. "That could be a problem."

"A new opera house has gone in over in Terrell," Belinda shared. "That's only six miles away. Perhaps you could get involved in their program. Building an opera house here in Poetry will be a hard sell to Mayor Mueller. He will say we don't have the budget for it."

"Posh! If the folks in Terrell can have one, we can, too," Sarah Jo announced. "I will head up the venture myself—and I'll get the menfolk behind it, even the mayor." She winked. "If I know anything, it's how to rally the men."

Belinda sighed. This would likely drive the nail in the coffin between the reverend and Sarah Jo. Not that he minded opera houses. No, it wasn't that. But it was clear that Sarah Jo intended to woo any man who would look her way. Clearly, the pastor would take issue with this.

As Sarah Jo, Corabelle, and Prissy took to jabbering about the opera house idea, James excused himself to head over to the barbershop. Marta, who had remained painfully quiet until now, looked Belinda's way. "Might I have a moment of your time, please?" she asked in a hushed voice.

"Yes, of course."

They took a few steps away from the crowd. Marta looked up with tears in her eyes. "Belinda, let me start by saying that I really like this little town. Truly, I do. Even with the heat. It's as pretty as a picture from a book, especially with so many wildflowers about. And the trees are so very green. Why, the whole place is simply alive with color."

"I'm thrilled you like it here," Belinda said. "That makes me very happy."

"Yes, I love the town, but..." Marta sighed. "I do not, nor do I think I ever could, love Myles Lott."

"Oh dear." Belinda gestured to the bench in front of Poetic Notions, and the two took a seat. "Are you quite sure?"

"Quite. I've tried. You have no idea how I've tried. But I cannot fathom loving him. And that's not all. I am completely and totally opposed to the way he teaches the children."

"O–oh?"

"Yes. Are you aware that his teaching methods are outdated?"

"Really? I guess I never thought about it. I was one of his students. He was a bit dull at times, I suppose, but…" Belinda didn't say any more for fear of tarnishing the man's good reputation.

Marta leaned in close. "Well, if *I* had the privilege of teaching at that school, I would rectify the situation at once. You would see. I have a modern way of thinking. He's quite old-fashioned. And very…male."

"Well, yes, of course. But I rather thought that would be a good thing," Belinda teased.

"I haven't yet made up my mind about a great many things," Marta said, brushing her hands against her skirt. "Particularly, whether I will stay or go. But I cannot marry Mr. Lott. And I'm counting on you to tell him that. I cannot be persuaded to do it myself."

Belinda sighed. *If I must, I must.* She had, after all, stirred up this hornet's nest. She would have to be the one to deal with any resulting stings. Still, there would be the issue of the money for Marta's train ticket. Myles had paid for it, in good faith. How would they rectify this situation?

Marta fussed with her collar then turned Belinda's way. "Don't fret about the way this turned out. Honestly, I'm trusting the Lord to bring the right man into my life, if indeed that is His plan. I have to wonder if I put the cart ahead of the horse by placing that advertisement in the first place. A good friend talked me into it, but I must admit, I was hesitant. Even more so now that I see how it turned out." Her lips curled down as she sighed. "Perhaps I can find work as a tutor while here in Poetry."

"Oh, that's a wonderful idea," Belinda said. "My twin brothers are in need of tutoring with their higher mathematics. And the two

Donaldson girls have had a terrible time with spelling. Yes, I think this will work nicely." She wanted to add, "And perhaps, in doing so, you will learn to like Myles Lott," but refrained. Still, she would continue to pray in that direction.

Marta offered a smile then joined the others. Minutes later, the women crossed the street to have lunch at Stanzas. Belinda went back to work inside the store and helped Greta and Aunt Hilde move one of the heavier shelves. They were barely halfway into their work when the reverend arrived, looking pale and a bit unnerved. "Belinda, might I have a moment of your time?"

She looked up from the shelf with an apologetic look and he quickly slid into place, moving it for her.

"Thank you so much," she said. "Now, what can I do for you?"

He gestured to the side of the room and she walked alongside him, away from her aunt and cousin.

"First, let me say that Bucky and Katie Sue have decided to get married at once," Reverend Billingsley explained with a smile. "This Sunday, in fact."

"Marvelous!" A rush of joy filled her heart as she thought about their pending wedding. One out of four matches. Not great odds, but at least they weren't *all* dismal failures.

"Externally, they are as different as night and day," the reverend continued, clearly oblivious to her thoughts. "He's so tall and slender, and she's so...anyway, they are quite the opposite, one from the other. And yet they are happily matched." The reverend's smile quickly faded. "I wish I could say the same about my relationship with Sarah Jo. She is rather..."

"Rough around the edges?"

"To say the least." He grinned. "Not that I'm opposed to rough around the edges. I rather think I might enjoy the challenge, so long as the woman was the one God had chosen for me. It's just that she's quite the opposite of what I envision Him sending my way. I need a woman who is steady. Reliable. Not given to..." He shook his head then gave her a sheepish look.

"It's all right, Reverend. I understand completely. And if you want me to refund your money..."

"No no no." He put up a hand to stop her from continuing with that train of thought. "I am not saying that. I have never been one to give up. I will give this my best shot. I just wanted you to know what I'm up against so you can add your prayers to mine."

"I think it's fairly clear to all of us what you're up against." Belinda gave him a wink. "So I will be praying. I promise."

"Indeed. So shall I." He took a few steps toward the door then turned back. "Did you hear that she wants to open an opera house? An opera house!"

"Yes." Belinda nodded. "Are you opposed to the idea?"

"Well..." He paused then shrugged. "I suppose not, in theory. I would imagine folks might come from Wills Point, Royce City, and Terrell. Not sure they'll venture all the way from Dallas. But it should bring in some revenue, to be sure." He shook his head. "I somehow imagined that Sarah Jo would put her piano-playing skills to work in the church, not in a theatrical environment." He shrugged. "Of course, if I marry her, the church will be *become* a theatrical environment, will it not?" With a sigh, he turned back toward the door.

Belinda tried to return to her work at the register while Greta went to work arranging shelves. However, she found herself distracted, both by Marta's unhappiness and the reverend's uncertainty. For the first time, she paused to consider the fact that she had actually caused this dilemma. "It's my doing."

"What's your doing, honey?" Aunt Hilde asked, approaching the register.

"Oh, I, uh..." Belinda sighed. "I think maybe I've jumped the gun, to use one of Papa's expressions."

"Gotten ahead of the Lord, you mean?"

"Maybe." She shook her head. "Oh, I don't know. I prayed before sending out those letters. And I know Peter prayed as he wrote the poems. He told me as much. But I never once thought about what might happen if the people weren't happy with my choices."

"You are a girl who arranges things," Aunt Hilde said with a nod. "That's sure and certain. But arranging lives is a bit more difficult than placing jars on the shelves in the store."

"Georg said as much, though not in those exact words." Belinda paused to think about all this. "I do like to arrange things, but I'm only human. I'm going to make mistakes."

"Those letters you sent out to the potential brides..." Aunt Hilde's brow wrinkled. "Do you tell the women that you will cover the cost of their train tickets home if things don't work out?"

"Yes."

"Then leave it in the Lord's hands, child." Her aunt patted her hand. "These women made the decision to come of their own accord. They were not manipulated, merely presented with an opportunity. I daresay most were wise enough to figure out ahead of time that things might not work to their best advantage, but they were willing to take that risk. And I can't help but think the Lord has had a hand in all of it. Bringing them here, I mean. It's not up to you to shoot Cupid's arrow into anyone's heart. You simply act as a mediator."

"True." Belinda threw her arms around her aunt's neck. "Oh, thank you, Aunt Hilde. You always have such a way of making me feel better."

"I think we're more alike than we admit," Aunt Hilde whispered. "I've often been accused of being an arranger, myself." She gave Belinda a wink. "Oh, and by the way...Samuel Bromstead was in the store earlier today. Want to guess who was with him?"

"Really?" Belinda grinned. "The widow Hanson?"

"Yes, and he and Ella looked quite happy to be together. So you see, my dear, many of your instincts are right. Just be careful how you apply them. Otherwise it will be two steps forward, one step back."

"Yes, ma'am. I understand. I will move cautiously."

Over the next couple of hours, Belinda did her best to focus on the customers. Still, she couldn't help but think about how all of this might end. In many ways, this whole thing felt like a train barreling down the track. Where it landed was anyone's guess.

* * *

Georg spent all afternoon getting the menfolk spiffed up. His shop had never been so full. Turned out every single fellow in town had his eye on one or more of the women who'd arrived last week. And not necessarily the men who were supposed to be interested in them.

He couldn't help but laugh as he thought about the woeful mismatches. Poor Myles Lott. Everyone in town had already figured out that Marta Schuller didn't exactly have eyes for him. But what a sad dilemma, to face rejection from your bride-to-be in such a public fashion. Myles had shuffled into the barbershop for a few moments early this morning. After taking a look at the crowd of men, he'd left immediately. Surely he knew that a good many of these rowdy fellas now had their eye on his intended.

The situation with Reverend Billingsley and Sarah Jo Cummings was as humorous as Myles's story was sad. All morning long the menfolk had speculated about that one, and the chatter continued as Georg worked through the afternoon.

"I think the reverend will feel compelled to marry Sarah Jo, even if he doesn't want to," Charlie Grundy said, as he settled down into a chair for a haircut.

"But how could a man marry a woman he didn't love?" Old Man Miller asked. "It's not fair—to either party."

"Indeed." The word slipped out of Georg's mouth, but he realized just how close he'd come to doing that very thing. He didn't love Corabelle, and yet he'd nearly offered her a ring. Oh, how he thanked the Lord that he hadn't made that mistake. In so many ways, he felt liberated by his decision not to look for a wife.

Still, there was some fun to looking, as evidenced by these men and the enthusiastic expressions on their faces.

"I think the reverend's caught between a rock and a hard place," Peter said, walking in the door.

Georg turned to smile at his good friend. He'd never quite figured out why Peter Conrad spent so much time at the barbershop. The man's beard hung to his chest, and his hair—what was left of it—he wore long behind his back. Quite different from the other men in town, for sure, but no one dared question it. No, everyone loved Peter far too much to quibble about his looks. Or lack thereof.

Peter took a seat and then pulled out a scrap of paper and began to scribble something on it. Another of his many poems, no doubt. He seemed to come up with at least one a day, if not more. With so many incoming brides, his verses were mostly romantic in nature these days.

"That Sarah Jo's a mighty strong woman," Peter continued, looking up from his work. "Probably too strong to be the reverend's wife. She'd be calling all the shots."

"Wearing the pants in the family, that's for sure," Charlie added.

"I don't think we need to be speculating about who is or isn't suited for someone else," Georg said, trying to focus on his work. "That is the Lord's doing. We are merely...observers."

"Might be," Charlie said with a shrug. "But you can't tell me you haven't played a role in this, too."

"Me? Well, I—" Georg looked at the roomful of men, stunned. "What are you getting at, Charlie? Speak your mind and make it plain."

"Belinda told me weeks ago that you were the one to match up Sarah Jo and the reverend. That you found the advertisement and made the suggestion."

His heart suddenly felt like a lead weight. "Oh, I—I suppose I did. But I was just..." Just what? Playing along with Belinda in something that had felt like a game at the time. Sure, on paper Sarah Jo Cummings had seemed perfect for Reverend Billingsley. But things weren't always as they appeared on paper, now were they?

Unfortunately not. And—also unfortunately—this was no game. It was very real. And now a very real Sarah Jo Cummings resided at the hotel, courting every man in town...except the reverend.

"What do you think of Bucky and Katie Sue's upcoming wedding?" Charlie asked.

Georg stopped trimming Charlie's hair to think about that. Seemed like a lot of folks were making impulsive decisions without taking the time to think—and pray—things through. Still, how could he fault a man like Bucky Williams for wanting to marry a girl with a smile like Katie Sue's? The young woman had won the hearts of nearly everyone she'd met. Why, the joy of the Lord shone through in everything she did. Who wouldn't fall in love with that?

"Cat got your tongue, Georg?" Peter asked with a laugh.

"Sorry." He startled back to attention. "Just preoccupied today."

"So am I," Charlie responded. "Gotta head over to Terrell to pick up a ring for a certain young women named Prissy."

"Really?" Georg asked, as he began to trim Charlie's unruly locks. "You're going to ask her to marry you? Don't you think you should wait awhile?"

"I'll give it another few days," Charlie said. "Got to clean up a few things first. She seems like the kind of woman who likes things tidy. And my house, well...let's just say it needs a woman's touch."

"Everything about you needs a woman's touch, Charlie." Peter erupted in laughter. "But I daresay this will shake out the cobwebs."

"Speak for yourself," Charlie said as he turned to examine himself in the mirror. "I am a man transformed. Just watch and see."

"Mm-hmm." Peter reached for a newspaper, slapped it open, and grew silent.

Georg paused, trying to think of a way to join the conversation. Prissy was definitely the sort to like things tidy. Looked like she had a lot of work on her hands, whipping both Charlie Grundy and his house into shape.

Still, as Georg stared at the man with shorter hair and a clean-shaven face, he had to admit...the possibilities were there. And stranger things had happened, after all.

At once, he thought of Belinda. How she planned to change the town by bringing in these women. With all the trouble brewing between Sarah Jo and the reverend...and with the obvious ill feelings between Marta and Myles...there was sure to be a mess to clean up.

Might take a lot of elbow grease on Belinda's part to clean things up. He couldn't help but think she was up to the task.

Chapter Eleven
....

Bucky and Katie Sue were married the following Sunday in a
simple but delightful ceremony on the church grounds. Reverend
Billingsley led the festivities, of course, though Belinda took note
of the pained look in his eyes every time he looked Sarah Jo's way.
Sarah Jo was hard to miss, since she played the role of maid of honor.
Her bright green dress stood out against the purple wildflowers, but
she didn't seem to mind. Neither did Katie Sue, who only had eyes
for Bucky.

Belinda's favorite part of the ceremony came when Bucky
read a poem he'd crafted just for Katie Sue. Belinda had it on good
authority—from Peter, of course—that Bucky had had very little to
do with the actual creation of the poem. Still, it was perfect for the
occasion. Bucky's voice trembled as he read the words:

> *One waits for years with hopeful heart*
> *Believing always from the start*
> *That somewhere, somehow, another waits*
> *To take his hand, to be his mate*
> *Then she arrives and time stands still*
> *Heaven whispers God's perfect will*
> *And two are one, mysterious plan*
> *The love between a woman and man*

There were several oohs and aahs from the crowd as he finished reading, and more still as he took his new wife in his arms and leaned down to kiss her for the first time as her husband. The oddest feeling came over Belinda as she watched it transpire. Certainly she felt some sense of relief, even satisfaction, for playing a role in bringing them together. Still, seeing the two of them made her want to search out Georg, to see the expression on his face. Would he—with her assistance—end up happily matched, as well?

She caught his eye and he gave her a wink, which sent her heart into a tailspin. *Lord, Georg is so special. He deserves the perfect woman. Perfect for him, I mean.* Yes, surely he would one day stand before the congregation and speak such words of love over his bride-to-be. Once Belinda located her, of course.

After the morning service, everyone picnicked on the grounds, as was the custom after summer weddings. Belinda watched with a sense of pride as Bucky and Katie Sue made their way through the crowd, greeting their wedding guests with smiles and conversation. Both beamed ear-to-ear, clearly happy to have found each other. Belinda whispered a prayer of thanks that the Lord had given her the foresight to bring them together, though all of the credit truly belonged to Him.

Belinda smiled as Georg approached. "What do you think, Georg?" she asked. "Isn't it all so wonderful?"

"All?" He gestured to Reverend Billingsley, who now chatted quietly with Myles Lott. Neither looked terribly happy.

"Well, maybe not *all*," Belinda said. "But I have a feeling the Lord will take *all* of it and use it for His glory, even the parts I've made a disaster of."

Georg laughed. "He has a habit of doing that, doesn't He? The Lord takes our blunders and uses them for His glory. I can't tell you how many times I've been grateful for that."

"Amen." Belinda nodded, her enthusiasm mounting. There was some consolation in the fact that the Lord would fix whatever she happened to break. Still, she didn't want to go overboard to test that theory.

"Did you hear about Prissy Finkelstein and Charlie Grundy?" Greta asked, drawing near.

"No, what?" Belinda swallowed hard, preparing herself for more bad news. Had Prissy left on the early morning train out of Terrell, convinced that Charlie would never change his messy ways?

"They're courting. But that's not all..." Greta pointed off in the distance, and Belinda gasped as she laid eyes on Charlie. "I don't believe it! He's as clean as a whistle."

"No doubt about it," Georg said. "I trimmed his hair myself."

"And I sold him a comb just yesterday," Greta whispered. "Can you believe it?"

"No!" Belinda gave him another look, stunned at his fresh appearance. Who would have guessed? "The man is even wearing a new suit!"

"I sold him that, too," Greta said. "And who knew he was so handsome underneath all of that dirt? Or maybe he's just glowing because he's been transformed by love. That's what he's telling everyone, anyway."

"Transformed by love." Belinda shook her head. "Amazing." She had to smile as she thought about Charlie Grundy in love. Surely if she could find a match for Charlie, there was a suitable woman to be found for Georg. She gazed at her friend with a smile as he spoke.

"I wouldn't have believed it if I hadn't witnessed it myself," Georg said with a brusque nod. "He's been into the shop nearly every day for a clean shave. And trust me when I say he's cleaned up more than his appearance. Even his language, which was somewhat questionable, has been put through the wringer. I haven't heard a foul word from him in days."

"It's a miracle," Greta whispered. "Next thing you know, the Lord will be parting the Sabine river and asking Charlie to walk across."

"He does clean up nice, I must admit," Belinda said, smiling as she took it all in. "See what the hope of new love does to a man?"

"Yes, but look at the opposite," Greta said. She pointed to Marta Schuller, who sat alone on a quilt at the side of the church property. "Poor thing. I have to wonder if she's giving thought to going back home now."

"I hope not." Belinda bit her lip, deep in thought.

"Perhaps we should go over there and spend some time with her," Greta suggested. "Offer a little gentle persuasion that Poetry is the place for her even if she and Myles aren't suited."

They took a couple of steps in the woman's direction but stopped suddenly when something happened to change everything.

"Would you look at that!" Belinda's enthusiasm grew as she watched the reverend approach Marta and offer her a glass a lemonade.

"Thank goodness for Reverend Billingsley," Greta said, fanning herself in an attempt to dispel the stifling heat. "Such a kind man. He must sense her pain."

"Well, think about it, Greta," Belinda whispered. "He's unhappy with his match, too." She sighed. "Though I don't know what to do about that. I feel just awful for getting his hopes up."

"Who says you have to do anything?" Georg asked.

"Well, I feel compelled to fix the things I've broken."

"I think it would be wiser to let the Lord fix them," Georg said. "I daresay His plan is the best."

"You're right." Belinda looked at him with a smile. "Why is it that you're always right, Georg Kauffman?"

"Me? I'm not. On the other hand..." He gestured with his eyes to Marta and the reverend, who had taken a seat on the quilt next to her. Within seconds, the two were talking nonstop.

Greta looked at Belinda, a stunned expression on her face. "Do you suppose it's possible...?"

"Who knows?" Belinda laughed. "Stranger things have happened."

"Indeed. And are continuing to happen before our very eyes." Greta nudged her and gestured off in the distance, where Peter Conrad stood on the porch steps at the front of the church with Sarah Jo beside him. "If I didn't know better, I would say Sarah Jo has her eye on Peter."

Georg snorted. "If I didn't know better, I'd say Sarah Jo has her eye on every man in town."

"Still..." Greta whispered. "If you pay close attention, you will see that she focuses her real attentions on one. The others are simply a diversion. This I have already taken note of." Greta grinned as she looked over at Belinda. "Maybe I should try my hand at matchmaking. I daresay I would do a good job."

"Indeed. Though I would spend my hours focusing on finding a match for myself, if I were you. You will make a lovely bride someday, Greta." Belinda nodded. Then something caught her eye. She focused once again on Peter, who had taken off running across the church lawn. Folks turned from every direction, and a roar of laughter went up.

"Come on back here, honey!" Sarah Jo called out, her voice rising and falling above the crowd of parishioners. "I ain't finished with you yet!"

"I'll bet she's not," Georg whispered. He forced the smile away and then cleared his throat. "Maybe I'd better go after him and make sure he's all right. I will meet you for lunch in a few minutes."

"Do that," Belinda said. "I will check on Sarah Jo, in the meantime."

She took Greta by the arm as she headed off to check on the older woman, who remained on the church steps with her hands on her ample hips.

"I know you're hiding behind that building, Peter Conrad!" Sarah Jo hollered, waving her finger in the air. "C'mon out and face me like a man."

" 'Like a man' being the key words," Greta whispered with a giggle. "She might as well be wearing pants herself! Have you ever seen such an almighty-powerful woman?"

"Never," Belinda added. "But I think that's half of her charm. Trust me, Sarah Jo Cummings might be wearing a skirt on the outside, but she's definitely wearing men's pants on the inside. It's going to take a doozy of a fella to calm her down. Still..." Belinda's eyes scoped the crowd. "I've got to believe there's at least one man in Poetry, Texas, who's man enough for the likes of her."

* * *

Georg walked around the back of the church building, where he found Peter bent over and gasping for breath.

"She wearing you out?" he asked, drawing near.

"Mm-hmm." Peter looked up and shook his head. "What am I going to do about her, Georg? She's got her claws into me."

"And you're opposed to the idea?"

"On every conceivable level."

"Then you have but one choice," Georg said. "You've got to speak it plain."

Peter shook his head. "You know me, Georg. Have you ever met a plainer-speaking man? I don't mince words. Even my poems are brutally honest." He paused to wipe his brow with his handkerchief. "But I have never in all my born days come up against a handful of a woman like that Sarah Jo Cummings. She—she—" He shook his head again. "Well, anyway, I'm wound up tighter than a clock when she's around, and I don't know that my heart can take it." He put his hand on his chest. "On top of it all, she wants to involve me in this nonsense about an opera house. Because I'm artistic, she says. I love literature, true, but artistic? Do I look the sort to be hopping around on stage in a theatrical getup?"

Georg shook his head and laughed. "No. And I can see that she has you worked up. Perhaps it will do you good to write down your thoughts on paper. That is your natural inclination, after all. Share with her what you are really thinking, really feeling."

"There is no poem on planet Earth to do that woman justice, and I don't mean that in a good way." Peter sighed. "Still, I will give some thought to what you've said. Perhaps I could come up with something to put me out of this current misery."

"Yes." Georg nodded. "And in the meantime, come and have lunch with us. I'm eating with Belinda and her family. We'll have a great time."

"Perfect." Peter nodded, and a look of relief swept over his face. "If I'm with all of you, Sarah Jo will leave me alone. She wouldn't dare interrupt our lunch for any of her flirtatious wrangling."

They rounded the building, and Georg looked around until he saw Belinda in the distance. She looked up with a girlish smile and waved. A sense of wonderment came over him as he took in her beautiful blue dress and whimsical smile. Strange, he'd never noticed how the sunlight played with the lighter strands of her hair. And how the sun kissed the tip of her nose.

Snap out of it, Georg. What in the world is wrong with you?

He pushed the feelings of awkwardness away and chided himself silently as they made their way to the Bauer family. He and Belinda were only friends. They'd always teased one another. More often than not, he'd been on the receiving end. But he had never felt anything more. What had brought this on? Probably just the idea that everyone else in town was now happily matched.

Well, almost everyone. As they approached Belinda's family, Peter groaned. "Tell me it isn't so."

"What?"

Peter pointed to the quilt, where Sarah Jo now sat beside Belinda and her mother. The red-haired woman looked up with a flirtatious smile. "Well, Peter Conrad, as I live and breathe. Have you come back to have lunch with me after all, you silly man? Ready to repent for your wicked behavior?"

"*My* wicked behavior?" Peter let out a groan, pulled off his hat, and whacked the nearest tree branch with it. "Dad-blame it, woman! How many times do I have to tell you that I'm not interested in courting you?"

"Oh, I don't need courting," she said with a wink. "Courting's for kids. I'm a full-grown woman. You could just up and marry me and I'd be happy as a lark. 'Course, I could stand to hear a love poem every now and again. Like that one you wrote for Bucky to read to Katie Sue, I mean."

Peter slapped himself in the head. "How in the world did you—"

"Oh, never mind that," she said. "I have my ways of finding out what's what around here. But I'm also interested in finding out who's who. And my *who* of the day is *you*!" She roared with laughter. "What do you think of that, Peter Conrad? I just wrote a poem, did I not?"

"Your metric pattern was off a bit," he said. "But I cannot deny its rhyming scheme."

Georg could see that was not the only scheme at work. Sarah Jo clearly had designs on Peter Conrad. But what could be done about it?

"You're my perfect match!" Sarah Jo said said with a coy smile. "And I promise you, honey, I'll give you a hundred reasons to write love poems, if you'll just give me a chance. And I'll promise you the starring role in our first theatrical, too. Why, with a face like yours, you were born for the theater. No doubt about it!"

Peter closed his eyes and shook his head. After a few moments, he shoved his hat back on his head, then took a seat—not next to Sarah Jo, but on the end of the quilt nearest Belinda's father. Georg joined him and found himself seated next to Belinda.

"Is everything okay with Peter?" she whispered.

"Mm-hmm." He wanted to say more, but the scent of lemon verbena caught him off guard. And something about the sound of Belinda's voice, like the breeze moving across fields of wildflowers... It captivated him.

Have I lost control of my senses? What's happening to me?

"Georg, you don't look well." She placed her hand on his arm and gave him a pensive look. "Do I need to fetch Doc Klein?"

"No." He tugged at his collar, pushing away all strange thoughts of Belinda. "I'm sure I'm just overheated. After I have something to eat, I'll be fine."

"Let me make you a sandwich, then." She began to sing one of the hymns they'd sung in church that morning. Her voice rang out across the grounds, almost sounding angelic. Her smile. That beautiful blond hair. The blue dress.

Georg found himself humming the song. For a moment anyway. He shook it off as Peter asked him a question. He wanted to answer. He really did. But something about all this had him in a state of complete and utter confusion.

And he was loving every minute of it.

Chapter Twelve

....

Three days after Katie Sue and Bucky's wedding, a new shipment of newspapers arrived at Poetic Notions. Belinda sat at her desk, devouring them, on a quest to find brides for several new clients. She had almost given up on the idea of locating someone for Georg, when she came across the perfect advertisement. A match conceived in the heavenlies, no less.

"Greta, look!" Belinda ran with newspaper in hand to the register, looking for Greta. "You're not going to believe it, but I think I've found a wife for Georg. Finally! He's going to be thrilled."

Her cousin, who was working diligently to clean the glass case at the front of the store, looked over at her with interest. "I'm not so sure about that last part, but I'm intrigued. Who is she? What makes her perfect for him?"

"Oh, she sounds delightful. Her name is Adeline. Very lyrical, don't you think?"

"Very."

"Listen to this." Belinda cleared her throat and then began to read in her most romantic voice: "'Woman of refinement from the East Coast. Late twenties. Pleasant appearance and disposition. Happy to settle down in small town with amiable man. Must be of good Christian character and ready for a family.'"

"Ready for a family?" Greta looked at her. "Is Georg wanting children?"

"I'm sure he wants them eventually," Belinda said. She paused to think about that. It would be a crime, really, for Georg not to have children. Why, he would be wonderful with them. She could almost see him now, tossing a ball with his sons or rolling a hoop with a daughter. Yes, surely Georg would want children.

"Something about that sounds odd," Greta said. "Do you suppose she already has a child?"

"Ooh, I never thought of that." Belinda read the advertisement again. "You know, she might. It sounds as if she has a ready-made family. Still, I think I will write to her and let her know about Georg. But I promise to pray about it first, as always."

"You're saying you pray before each transaction?" Greta looked doubtful.

Belinda sighed. "I try to remember to do so, but sometimes I forget, especially when the match seems so obvious. I think, when it came to Sarah Jo, I might have forgotten." She smiled. "Still, that one is Georg's fault. He's the one who actually located her, you know. Not me. He stumbled across her advertisement in the newspaper quite accidentally."

"So I've heard." Greta stopped working and gave Belinda a pensive look. "But Belinda, I don't think it was an accident. I love Sarah Jo. She's an asset to this town, whether she weds or not. She brings life and joy to us all. In a unique way, but life and joy nonetheless."

"She brings more to some than others," Belinda said, fighting back the laughter. "But one thing is for sure—she is never boring!"

Her words were interrupted by Peter Conrad, who came racing into the store, breathless. He took one look at her and paled. "Belinda, you've got to help me."

"H–help you?" She stared at him, stunned, and then quickly folded the newspaper. "Help you with what?"

"Sarah Jo Cummings."

"What about her?" Belinda placed the newspaper on the glass case and focused on Peter.

"She's after me. Again." His wide-eyed look let Belinda know this was no joking matter. Still, she couldn't help but laugh.

"Peter, do you mean to tell me that Sarah Jo Cummings—" She never had a chance to finish the sentence, for at that very moment, the fast-footed woman came sprinting into the store. She wore a red plaid dress and a matching bonnet.

Sarah Jo stopped for a moment, her breathing labored, and then grabbed Peter by the arm. "Why, Peter Conrad," she crooned. "I felt sure that was you. Did you not hear me calling your name out there?"

"Oh? You were calling my name?" He turned to look at her, his eyes narrowing. "I will have to get my hearing aid checked."

Greta perked up at that one. "Hearing aid? Since when do you wear a hearing aid, Peter?"

Belinda jabbed her in the arm.

"Oh. Oh, I see." Greta giggled. "So sorry."

Sarah Jo continued on, oblivious to their playful attitudes. "Peter," she said, her voice dripping like honey, "you simply must help me. I've been looking for a book to read and can't find a thing at that old hotel. But it seems like every time I come to your bookshop, you're just closing up for the day. My, but you do keep odd hours."

"Ah. Well, see, I..."

"I'm looking for something romantic in nature," she said. "Though action stories and adventures are good, too. Do you have dime novels?"

He groaned. "I believe we have a few in stock, though, of course, I prefer the classics."

"Oh, the *classics*. Of course. I prefer them myself. My favorite is that *Romeo and Juliet* story by Frederick Shakespeare."

"That's *William* Shakespeare."

"William, of course." She continued to grip his arm and now gazed up into his eyes with admiration. "I just love a man who knows so much. I'm intrigued by your brilliance. Oh, if only I could study and learn as you do. Wouldn't that be a wonderful thing?"

Peter muttered something about there not being enough schooling available in the state of Texas to accommodate her, but she appeared not to listen. Instead, she chattered on and on about how his shop needed a woman's touch. When she got to the part where she said she wanted to reorganize his shelves, his face turned such a deep shade of red that Belinda feared he might have a heart attack right there on the spot.

"I have arranged a meeting with several of the townsfolk for next Saturday," Sarah Jo said. "We're going to talk about the new opera house. I believe I've located the perfect spot on the south end of town, not far from Grange Hall. The mayor has agreed to lend his support. Isn't that wonderful?" She laughed. "I knew I could win the man over."

"Mayor Mueller has agreed to build an opera house without the vote of the people?" Peter looked stunned.

"That's what the meeting is about," Sarah Jo said. "To garner their vote. Oh, but I know it's a shoo-in. Everyone wants an opera house. Right, Belinda?" She turned to face Belinda, her eyes wide with excitement.

"It would bring in revenue," Belinda agreed. "So I can see the good in it."

"And talk about fun," Greta added. "It would certainly draw a new, sophisticated crowd to our town."

"And I know just who will star in the first performance." Sarah Jo gripped Peter's arm, and he groaned.

Belinda felt for the poor man. "Sarah Jo," she said, taking the woman by the arm. "I wonder if you would do me a favor. I'm searching for a wife for Mr. Ogilvie, the butcher, and I've had trouble finding an appropriate match. Perhaps you could help me choose someone for him."

"Really?" Sarah Jo released her hold on Peter, who looked like he'd been given a reprieve, and clasped her hands together. "Oh, why didn't we think of this before? I've made plenty of wonderful matches in my day. Why, I'm the perfect person to help you. Just watch and see."

She babbled on about the various women she'd matched up back in her hometown, but Belinda didn't hear half of it. She caught Peter's eye and gestured for him to slip out the front door. He did, in record time.

Now for the hard part. She'd promised Sarah Jo she could help find a bride for Mr. Ogilvie. They headed off to the back room to thumb through the newspapers. Sarah Jo squealed with delight at every single advertisement.

"Look at this one!" She pointed to a paper from Boston. "This gal says she's pretty as a picture!" Sarah Jo snorted. "I'll tell you right now, Belinda, half of these women exaggerate."

"Do they, now?"

"Indeed." She chortled. "I did, myself. All that stuff about being petite and loving Sunday strolls. Not that I'm opposed to a nice stroll, as long as my arm is linked with the right fella's." She gave a flirtatious wink then went back to looking at the newspaper.

"Can I ask you a question, Sarah Jo?" Belinda took a seat on one of the barrels and gave her a pensive look.

"Well, sure, honey. Sarah Jo Cummings is an open book. No doubt about that."

There was no disputing that fact. Still, Belinda had some unanswered questions. "Have you ever been married before?"

Sarah Jo's expression shifted immediately. Gone were the laugh lines and the upturned lips. Gone was the twinkle in her eye. She paused for a moment and then folded the newspaper and took a seat on the barrel next to Belinda. She whispered, "Yes. I was married for thirty years."

"I see." Belinda wanted to ask more but now felt hesitant about the matter.

Sarah Jo seemed reticent to say more. At first. Finally, she burst like a dam, talking a mile a minute. "I met my husband, Joe—a railroad man, by the way—when I was working at a shop in town. A general store, much like Poetic Notions. He swept me off my feet. That fella was always such a looker, and kindhearted, too."

Belinda didn't interrupt but let her continue.

"We married the year I turned twenty-two. Had a baby girl that next year." Now the smile returned.

"Oh, you have a daughter?"

Sarah Jo rose and began to pace the room. "*Had* a daughter. Kelly Jo was only three when she passed. Scarlet fever stole her from me."

"Oh, I'm so sorry." Belinda hardly knew what to say.

"Joe and I wanted other children, of course, but the good Lord never blessed us with any." She shook her head. "Trust me, I had plenty of words with Him about that—the Lord, not Joe."

"I understand, and I'm sure He did, too."

"Well, we lived our lives the best we could. I took over the running of the shop, and he worked his way up with the railroad. We lived in a fine house and had every good thing at our disposal." She gestured to her dress and bonnet. "I never went without, Belinda. The man made sure I had the things that pleased me."

"He sounds wonderful," Belinda agreed.

"He was." Sarah Jo sighed as she took a seat once more. "I lost my Joe four years ago. Doc said it was from working around the coal for so long. Damaged his lungs. Terrible way to go." Her eyes filled with tears, and she reached for a hankie to dab them away.

Belinda's heart wrenched as she saw Sarah Jo's pain. "Oh, I'm so sorry. I had no idea."

"Did you think I was just an old spinster?"

"No. Well, I don't know what I thought. When I wrote to you, I only saw those few words in the paper, and they certainly didn't tell the whole story."

"Indeed, they did not. And I can assure you, the other women each have a story, as well. We can't very well sum up our lives in a few lines, any more than the men can sum up theirs in a love poem. Our stories are longer, more complex. They have their ups and downs and probably a few tears along the way."

Belinda rose and moved to Sarah Jo's side. "Thank you for telling me all of that."

"Well, there's one more thing, if you don't mind my saying it."

"What's that?"

"I know my Kelly Jo would have been a little older than you are now, but I'd like to think she would have turned out as lovely as you. When I see you, I think of her. I can't seem to help myself."

Belinda's breath caught in her throat. "That's the nicest thing anyone's ever said to me."

"Well, honey, you're long overdue, then, for you are truly one of the sweetest girls I've ever met." Sarah Jo winked. "And if a certain fella hasn't figured that out yet, then I daresay he's deaf, dumb, *and* blind."

She gave a little wink and Belinda's heart tumbled to her toes. Surely she didn't mean...certainly she wasn't talking about...Georg?

They ended their conversation and Belinda returned to her work. All afternoon, she thought about Sarah Jo's story. She was right, of course. Every one of those women had her own tale. And each carried secret joys and pains. Marta, for instance. Surely she had a story. The worry lines on her forehead said as much. Perhaps, with a little nudging, Belinda could get her to open up. Maybe then she could ease the guilt of mismatching her with Myles Lott.

As the evening shadows fell, Belinda rushed to finish her work. She wanted to head home for supper. Mama was making chicken and dumplings tonight, one of her favorites. As she left the store and made her way down the boardwalk, Belinda couldn't help but gasp. There, on the other side of the glass in the town's restaurant, she laid eyes on Reverend Billingsley...and a woman. And not just any woman. Oh, no. The good reverend appeared to be having dinner with Marta Schuller! Right there in plain sight!

Hmm. Perhaps the dear woman needed his counsel. She was, after all, quite disappointed with how the situation had ended with Myles.

Only, she didn't look disappointed. No, Belinda had to admit while looking through the window, Marta did not look disappointed at all. In fact, she appeared just the opposite. Her eyes sparkled and her cheeks flushed as the pastor spoke. Marta took a bite of her steak then dabbed at her lips with her napkin, but she never took her eyes off Reverend Billingsley.

Wonder of wonders. Could it be? Belinda stopped to contemplate the possibilities as she turned toward home. At once, she began to pray. "Lord, You are, indeed, a miracle worker! Your hand was at work in this, after all. You did have a bride for the pastor. Just not the woman I thought." She paused a moment and then added, "Now, Lord, about Sarah Jo..."

She never had a chance to finish. At that moment, Peter came running out of his shop with the fiery redhead on his tail. Belinda stopped in her tracks, laughter emanating from the deepest places within her without restraint. Oh, how she laughed. One of these days Sarah Jo might actually catch Peter Conrad. In the meantime, it was surely fun to watch her try!

* * *

Georg looked out of the barbershop window, smiling as he caught a glimpse of Belinda laughing at Sarah Jo and Peter. He stood, captivated, watching her. Her cheeks were a nice rosy color as she laughed, and as she leaned forward, her pinned-up hair tumbled around her shoulders in golden waves. His breath caught in his throat. Georg wanted to take a step outside to ask what was so funny, but he got the answer to his question when Peter Conrad came bolting into his shop.

"She—wouldn't—dare—come—in—here!" Peter dove into one of the barber's chairs and opened a newspaper, covering his face.

"Actually, Peter, I was just closing up shop for the day." Georg didn't have a chance to finish his explanation before Sarah Jo Cummings appeared at the door.

"Oh, Georg!" she called out. "I do wonder if you would be so kind as to ask that handsome man in the chair to come out and speak with me."

"I'm busy, woman," Peter said. He gestured for Georg to grab a razor, and Georg flew into action at once.

"Shave or haircut, Peter?"

"Both."

"Both?" Georg leaned down and whispered, "I can't tell if you're pretending or if you're serious. You really want a shave and a haircut?"

Peter spoke through clenched teeth. "If it will keep that woman from chasing me all over town, yes. A shave and a haircut."

"Oh, but Peter!" Sarah Jo's voice rang out. "You can't cut your hair! Why, it could turn out like that tragic story in the Bible. You know the one?"

"Samson?" Georg interjected.

"Yes. He cut off his hair, and you know what happened next. He lost all of his strength."

"I've already lost it, woman!" Peter hollered back. "You've drained every ounce out of me. Now, if you don't mind, I really need some time to myself."

"But I need to speak with you." Sarah Jo rambled on—something about *Romeo and Juliet*. Something about Frederick Shakespeare. But Georg never really heard the particulars. He was too overcome by Peter's impulsive decision to shave and cut his hair. And intrigued, as well. No one had seen Peter clean-shaven for thirty years. What sort of transformation were they talking about here?

He went to work, starting first with the hair. Before he took the first cut, Georg whispered, "You're sure about this?"

"Sure as I've ever been about anything in my life."

Sarah Jo watched in rapt awe from the doorway, finally disappearing from view when the pastor and Marta happened by in conversation with the mayor. Georg could still hear her voice ringing as she moved away from the store.

Peter whispered the words "Good riddance" and then focused on the mirror.

Georg drew in a deep breath and then clipped away the first long piece of hair. Then the second. Then the third. Within minutes, he worked skillfully to bring shape to what was left of the man's hair. Turned out, the salt-and-pepper strands looked mighty nice short. Mighty nice.

Now to deal with that scraggly beard. He'd imagined cutting it dozens of times before but never thought he'd have the honor. Now that the opportunity had presented itself, he could hardly think where to begin.

"Take it off, Georg." Peter stared at his reflection in the mirror, lips pursed. "All of it. No arguments, now."

"Even the mustache?"

"No." Peter fingered his bushy mustache and appeared to be deep in thought. "Leave it. Just trim 'er back a bit."

Georg did as he was told, though it took awhile to accomplish the task. When he finished, both he and Peter stared in awe at the mirror. The transformation was unbelievable. Underneath that rough, hairy exterior, a handsome, clean-cut man resided. It made Georg wonder what Peter had been hiding from all these years. He also couldn't help but wonder about Sarah Jo's Samson comment. Would the strong, confident Peter Conrad crumble like a wilted flower without his hair to protect him?

Georg never had the chance to voice his thoughts. The second the haircut and shave ended, Peter sprang from his seat, tossed a few coins Georg's way, then headed for the door. Georg grabbed a rag, following behind him, pretending to wipe down the store's windows. In truth, he wanted to see how this might end.

Peter didn't make it three paces into the street before Sarah Jo's squealing voice rang out. "As I live and breathe! Why, forget everything I said back there about Samson! You are the handsomest man I've ever clamped eyes on!" She turned away from Marta, the reverend, and the mayor and focused all of her attention on Peter, who headed up the road toward his house.

Mayor Mueller headed Georg's way. "I'm not sure I would have believed it if I hadn't seen it with my own eyes. Whatever possessed him to do it?"

"I haven't got a clue." Georg shook his head. "Maybe he thought it would act as a deterrent, but that doesn't appear to be the case. Looks like Delilah got to him."

"Delilah?" The mayor looked puzzled.

"Ah, never mind." Georg chuckled. Maybe he could explain later.

"Any logical man would've known that a woman prefers the clean-cut look," Mayor Mueller said, shaking his head. "If you ask me, he was asking for it."

"Asking for it?" Georg shrugged, not quite understanding. "Asking for what?"

The mayor gestured to Sarah Jo. "Asking for it, that's all." He turned and walked away, chuckling all the while.

Georg pondered the mayor's statement for a moment. Was it possible Peter was secretly enamored with Sarah Jo? Had he cleaned himself up to seal the deal? Though it seemed preposterous at first glance, stranger things had happened, especially lately.

And speaking of stranger things... Georg shifted his attention to Reverend Billingsley, who stood on the boardwalk, deeply engaged in conversation with Marta Schuller. The look of pure joy on the reverend's face spoke volumes. In fact, Georg couldn't ever remember seeing the man so content.

For whatever reason, seeing the two of them together made Georg feel a little wistful. Not sad, really. But every day, with each new match, he secretly longed for the one thing he insisted he did not need. A wife. Yes, he could argue the point all day with Belinda, but in the end he had to admit the truth, if to no one but himself.

He needed—and wanted—a wife. Someone to greet him at the end of each tiring day. Someone to laugh with, to share stories with. Someone he could bring flowers to and perhaps even write a poem for. Someone who would understand his dry sense of humor and not laugh at his wardrobe choices. In short, someone who would love him just the way he was. Day in and day out. Year after year.

The more Georg thought about this possibility, the more real it became. Perhaps Belinda had been right all along. Maybe he shouldn't have given up on the idea of bringing in a bride from out of state. Yes, perhaps he'd jumped the gun in saying she should stop looking. Look how well it had worked for the others. Prissy and Charlie were happy as larks. And Georg didn't know when he'd ever seen Bucky Williams more at peace. Samuel Bromstead and the widow Hanson had been seen taking a stroll through town earlier in the day...hand in hand. Why, even the reverend and Marta appeared to be matched. And Corabelle and James? Much as Georg hated to admit it, they were perfect for each other.

He dropped down onto the bench, watching as Reverend Billingsley and Marta rounded the corner together, with the reverend's hand on Marta's back. What would it be like to have a woman reach for your hand? To slide your arm around a woman's waist and escort her through town? What would it feel like to have someone greet you at the door every evening and kiss you good-bye in the morning?

For some reason, every time he thought about any of those things, the only hand he could envision in his own...was Belinda's. The thought of this so startled him that he couldn't think straight for a moment. Was it possible he'd really fallen for her and not known it?

Georg quickly reached for his broom then headed inside, trying to act as if everything was normal. On the inside, however, he wondered if he would ever feel normal again.

Chapter Thirteen

....

In the weeks following Peter's physical transformation, Georg wrestled with his aching heart. Oh, how he longed to deny the obvious, but he could not. By the end of the second week, after several restless nights, he came to a conclusion that should have been clear from the beginning. He didn't need a mail-order bride. Never had. Never would. He needed—and wanted—Belinda Bauer. Wanted her kiss first thing in the morning. Wanted her smile to greet him after a long day's work. Wanted to hear her laugh at his jokes and reach for his hand as they walked down Main Street. He suddenly wanted the one thing he'd never even known he wanted...until now.

This revelation both terrified and thrilled him. Now if only he could manage to convey his thoughts in a way that would not terrify her, then all would be well.

Bright and early on a Thursday morning, Georg worked up the courage to visit Belinda at Poetic Notions. All night long he'd wrestled with the sheets. Every time he thought about sharing his feelings with Belinda, he felt ill. Nerves, most likely. As a result of his wrestling, Georg had awakened feeling stiff and sore...but still very much enamored with Belinda Bauer. And now that this fact was clear in his mind, he had to know if she felt the same.

Georg took a few steps inside Poetic Notions and found it full of customers. So much for a private conversation.

Belinda looked up from the register and waved. "G'morning, Georg!"

"Good morning to you, too." He forced a smile then headed her way.

"What can I do for you on this fine day?" she asked. "Need razor straps?"

"No, I, um..."

"Shaving mugs? A new batch just arrived." She reached into the glass case under the register and pulled out one in a style he'd never seen.

"Sure. I'll take four of those."

The corners of her lips curled into a smile. "I thought you might like them. I was thinking of you when I ordered them from the catalog."

Somehow knowing she'd been thinking of him made his heart want to sing. "So, how do you feel about the new opera house?" he asked, making small talk. "Seems a lot of townsfolk like the idea."

"And why not?" she queried. "Poetry is becoming quite the place to be! Why not an opera house?"

"I only hope Sarah Jo doesn't try to dress me in tights and put me up on the stage."

Belinda giggled. "Surely she won't humiliate you with the costume, but you do have a nice singing voice." She paused and gazed directly into his eyes. "I remember that from our school days. So don't be surprised if she calls on you to participate. I do hope you'll join in the festivities."

He shook his head. "I don't think I'm quite ready for that, thanks all the same. But from the sound of things, they're going to start building right away. That's progress for you."

"I daresay."

He paused, trying to think of something else to say. Anything to spend a little more time with her would suffice. "So who are you matching up today?" Georg asked, hoping to ease his way into the conversation.

Her face lit into a smile as she leaned in to whisper, "Doc Klein was in a while back, looking for a bride. I believe I've found the perfect person for him. Listen to this." Belinda read an advertisement from a woman named Rebecca Morgan, a nurse from Virginia.

"Interesting," Georg said.

"Yes, I sent off the letter in today's mail. Hopefully she will be agreeable."

"Sounds too good to be true," Georg said. "A nurse? For Doc Klein?"

"Yes, I've explained my scientific formula to you, remember? I try to find women with similar likes and dislikes. That way, the happy couple will be suited to each other. Doc Klein and Rebecca Morgan will make a lovely match."

"Perhaps too lovely," Georg said. "Have you not already figured out that pairing up folks who have too much in common may not be a good thing? Haven't you learned from Myles and Marta?"

"Hmm." She thought about that for a moment. "I don't know. As you know, I've always believed that matching people was simply a matter of practicality. The doctor gets his nurse. The preacher gets his piano player."

"Oh, but he didn't."

"True. But that was a fluke." She paused and then groaned. "Oh, all right. I'll admit, my plans are riddled with flaws, but I have the strongest sense that Rebecca is supposed to come to Poetry. Call me crazy, but—"

He flashed a smile as he interrupted. "Belinda, I would never call you crazy. Impulsive, maybe, but not crazy. Your ideas are a bit far-fetched, but they appear to be working to everyone's advantage. Our fair town is filled with happy-go-lucky couples, and we have you to thank for that."

"Thank you." She leaned in to whisper, "Have you heard about Prissy and Charlie?"

"That they eloped?" Georg nodded. "Heard all about it at the barbershop. They ran off to Dallas and found a justice of the peace. Who would have thought such an unlikely thing possible?"

"Me!" Belinda grinned. "Deep in my heart, I knew." She paused a moment and then added, "Of course, I would have preferred to stand up with her in a church wedding, but that's all right."

He paused a moment, contemplating her words. Perhaps this would be the perfect opportunity to shift the conversation. "So, who else are you matching up these days?"

"Mr. Ogilvie."

"The butcher?" He could hardly believe it! "Why, I didn't know John Ogilvie was looking for a wife. He's always been sort of a loner, hasn't he?"

"I think his mother convinced him to do this. He still lives with her, you know. I get the feeling he's a bit of a mama's boy." Belinda quirked a brow, letting him know her opinion on that matter.

"Ah yes." Georg cleared his throat, realizing for the first time how it sounded for a man in his late twenties to still live at home with his parents. He wondered if Belinda thought of him as a mama's boy. "Who have you paired John Ogilvie with?" Georg asked, more than a little curious.

"A woman named Cassie from Charleston. She's a seamstress. I thought it would be nice because they both have a trade. Do you see now what I mean about having common interests?"

"Yes, though I'm not completely sure I agree with the theory, in general. If a man and a woman have too much in common, they might be bored with each other. A little variety is nice." *Take the two of us, for example. We are different in nearly every respect.*

Belinda squinted her eyes and appeared to be deep in thought. "Perhaps you're right. Still, I feel they will be a good match. Cassie made it clear in her advertisement that she hopes to go on working after her wedding, and John told me he would be happy with a wife who works."

"I suppose that's all that matters," Georg said with a nod. "Making sure both the men and the women end up happily paired." He drew in a deep breath, trying to work up the courage to change the subject.

"Oh, they will be happy, I can assure you. And it looks as if I've located a match for just about everyone," Belinda said, clearly oblivious to his thoughts. "Oh, speaking of matches, I want to talk with you about something personal." She gave him a wink, which sent his heart in a hundred different directions at once. Then she leaned in and whispered, "Something I think you're *really* going to like."

"Oh? That's ironic." He reached out and took her hand, and she looked at him, confusion registering in her eyes. "I want to talk to *you* about something personal, too. Something I'm hoping *you're* going to like."

"Truly?" She gave his hand a squeeze, and her eyes took to sparkling even more than usual. "Oh, Georg! I can guess, and I'm so pleased! You want to talk about finding someone for you? Because, actually—"

"No, no. I want to tell you that—"

"Oh, but Georg, I've done it!" She clasped her hands together, clearly pleased with herself. "I've done it...again!"

"You've done what?" He looked at her, perplexed.

"Found her. Found your perfect match!"

"You—you what?" Everything he'd wanted to say slithered away like a snake in the grass. He released his hold on her hand and stepped back, horrified at this revelation.

Belinda clamped a hand over her mouth but then quickly pulled it away to speak. "Please, oh please, don't be angry, but I've written to someone on your behalf. A young woman named Adeline Jewett from Boston. I have every reason to believe she's the one for you."

"But..." What could he say in response to such a preposterous notion?

"She sounds ideal, Georg. Absolutely ideal. She's pretty and young and genuinely loves the Lord."

"You can sense all of that from an advertisement in a newspaper?"

"Yes. When I read her words, I just knew she was supposed to be here. And you will know it, too. Once you meet her, that is. She's set to arrive next week. On Monday."

He stared at Belinda, unable to think of a sensible thing to say. Could she not see that he didn't want her to bring any women to Poetry on his behalf? That he was finally trying to say the one thing he probably should have said weeks or even months ago? That he was interested in courting Belinda and Belinda alone? That he'd stayed up half the night trying to figure out how to tell her?

Obviously not.

Georg shook his head, but she never seemed to notice. Instead, she gazed at him with the same excitement he always saw on her face these days. When she was up to something, anyway. He finally managed to squeeze out five words: "So you've done it again."

"I have." Her hands trembled as she reached to brush a loose hair from her face. "Sent for her two weeks ago, in fact. Oh, but don't be mad. I couldn't sleep at night if I knew you were mad. You are absolutely the last person I would ever want to hurt, and I mean that with my whole heart."

"Why?" He asked the question hoping she would speak her thoughts clearly.

"Why what?"

"Why am I the last person you would want to hurt?" *Go on. Say it.*

"Well, I..." She fussed with her collar, finally offering up a shrug. "You're my friend. I would never want to hurt a friend."

"I'm your *friend*?" He stressed the last word, just for emphasis.

"Of course you are!" Her eyes filled with tears. "Oh, you *are* mad at me, aren't you? You don't want my friendship?"

"Of course I do." He reached to take her hand once more and gave it a gentle squeeze. *It's just that I want more than that, don't you see?* His heart thumped madly, but no words would come.

"Georg, I know I have let you down on more than one occasion. I'll be the first to admit that. But please don't stop being my friend just because I've done some foolish things. It would kill me. I would die a thousand deaths. I wouldn't be able to look at my own face in the mirror ever again. I would give up all of this in a heartbeat if I thought it was somehow hurting you. That's the last thing I want to do, trust me. How could I hurt you?" She shook her head. "Next to Greta, you are the dearest person in the world to me."

He drew in a deep breath and shook his head, trying to figure out what to say next. Though he took some comfort in her words, he still couldn't come up with a sensible response. No, she would surely misunderstand anything he might say at this point. Perhaps it would be easier to play along with this ridiculous scheme of hers until he could figure out what to do. Besides, it already looked as if she'd fetched him a bride from halfway across the country, whether he wanted the woman or not.

Not that it really mattered. No, this one would probably end up married to the butcher. Or the baker. Or the candlestick maker. Anyone and everyone but him. He did not—he would not—he could not—fathom going through any more heartbreak. Other than the obvious one facing him right now.

Georg gazed into Belinda's misty eyes and sighed. "I need to get back to work, Belinda." He fished in his pocket and came up with the money for the shaving mugs. "I hope you have a nice day. See you at church on Sunday."

* * *

Belinda's eyes filled with tears, and she tried to swallow the lump in her throat as she rang up Georg's purchase. She could tell from the look on his face that she'd hurt him. But how? Sure, she had acted impulsively, but surely he knew to expect that from her by now. Her news shouldn't have startled him. After all, she still owed him a bride. He'd given her money to fetch a bride, for heaven's sake. How could she not deliver, especially when so perfect a match came along?

As she watched him walk out of the door, she tried to console herself. "He will be fine once Adeline arrives on Monday's train," she whispered.

"Who will be fine?" Aunt Hilde said, approaching.

"Oh, I..." Belinda turned away, dabbing at her eyes. "No one."

"Mm-hmm." Hilde's one-word response spoke volumes.

"What?" Belinda turned back, suddenly not caring if her aunt saw the tears.

"You're smitten with Georg Kaufman, that's what. I've known it for months now but never spoke my mind about it."

"W–what?" Belinda's eyes widened. She stood in shocked silence. "Of course I'm not!"

"Of course you *are*," Hilde said. "It's as plain as the nose on your face. To everyone but you, apparently. It's about time you admitted it to yourself, Belinda. Otherwise you're sure to bring more pain to Georg and to you."

"But, Aunt Hilde, I've never even contemplated such a thing."

Perhaps that wasn't altogether true. There was that one moment, when the blue sapphire ring had gotten stuck on her finger. She'd thought perhaps she might end up married to him simply because she couldn't get the ring off. But that was just foolishness. She'd never given a serious thought to Georg Kaufman in all the years she'd known him. Right?

"Sometimes we can't see the forest for the trees," Aunt Hilde said, placing a hand on Belinda's shoulder. "At least that's why my mama used to tell me. I think you've got so many brides coming and going from Poetry that you don't see yourself as one."

"Well, I don't. That's true." Belinda nodded. "I've already told Greta that I don't believe I will ever marry. I'm to stay single...for the greater good."

"*Whose* greater good?" Hilde gave her a pensive look.

"W–what?"

"Whose greater good? Yours? God's? Whose?"

"Well, I don't rightly know." Belinda sighed. "For the community, I suppose. I have to give my life in service to others."

"We all give our lives in service to others. That's what the body of Christ is called to do. But that doesn't mean you should deny your own happiness, child. The Lord has a husband for you out there. I know it in my knower." Hilde put her hand on her heart. "And one day you will know it, too. So don't be so quick to discount your own happy match, all right?"

"A–all right." Belinda stumbled over the words, but not as much as she stumbled over the idea. Did the Lord have someone out there for her? Was she, as Hilde said, missing the forest because of the trees? Had God already sent her the perfect man and she'd assigned him to another?

These and a thousand other thoughts tumbled through her head as she continued her work throughout the rest of the day. For now, she had to admit the truth, if to no one but herself. She had been so intent on finding Georg a mate that she'd never considered the possibility that she might have overlooked the obvious. *Am I really smitten? Is it possible?*

As they closed up the mercantile, she glanced across the street at Kaufman's Barbershop. Through the window, she saw Georg working. He looked her way, but instead of smiling and waving, he turned back to tend to a customer.

Perhaps Hilde was right. Maybe she was hurting Georg. But what could she do about it now? This train was already barreling down the track. How could she possibly stop it now?

Walking home from the store, she couldn't seem to avoid the couples. They were everywhere. She passed by Sonnets and Bonnets—the renovations now nearly complete—and said hello to James and Corabelle. The reverend and Marta Schuller offered up their greeting as they walked toward the restaurant, holding hands. Katie Sue and Bucky hollered out hellos as she passed by the gristmill.

Yes, couples were truly everywhere. And she had no one to blame but herself.

When she walked through the front door of her home, she found Mama and Papa in a warm embrace and giggling like school kids. Was no place safe? Looked like everyone in Poetry was happily matched.

"All but me, Lord," Belinda whispered as she headed up to her room. "All but me."

Chapter Fourteen

The following Sunday, Belinda managed to put all thoughts of Georg Kaufman out of her head and focus on the events of the day. On this particular morning, Reverend Billingsley and Marta Schuller took their place before the congregation to tie the knot.

Belinda stood up for Marta, of course, as did Katie Sue and Prissy, who had just returned from her honeymoon in Dallas. Sarah Jo played the "Wedding March" on the piano, though her version sounded a bit more like a barroom ditty than the traditional piece. A visiting pastor from Terrell performed the ceremony. The whole thing was short but sweet, garnering a bit of laughter and even a few tears. Belinda especially loved the scripture Reverend Billingsley read from the Song of Solomon. She'd even noticed a twinkle in his eye as he shared the words:

"'My beloved spake, and said unto me, Rise up, my love, my fair one, and come away. For, lo, the winter is past, the rain is over and gone; the flowers appear on the earth; the time of the singing of birds is come, and the voice of the turtle is heard in our land.'"

Indeed, the reverend's season of mourning had passed. The winter was over, in a sense. Marta's entrance into his life had changed absolutely everything. And Belinda couldn't help but feel such joy at that realization—and all the more, when she thought about the fact that she had played a role in bringing Marta here.

Why, she could hardly believe the way things had turned out. Nearly every one of her clients was happy now. Well, all but Georg, of course. But, he would be, once Adeline arrived. For some reason, thinking of Georg caused a strange twisting in her heart. It hurt to know she'd disappointed him in some way. That had never been her intention, of course. Her intentions were...well, she wasn't completely sure what just yet. But she truly longed to make him happy, and fulfilling her promise to bring him a bride seemed to be the most logical way to accomplish that.

She glanced across the room at Myles Lott. There sat another man who wasn't exactly thrilled with her services. Not yet, anyway. She sighed as she looked at the somber look on his face, wondering if she would ever find his perfect match. If not, would she have to refund his money? Probably.

And then there was Sarah Jo. The boisterous woman hadn't exactly settled down, either, though she had certainly kept her focus on Peter Conrad. She'd even managed to wriggle her way into the pew next to him just after the service began. Either Peter had thrown in the towel or he was actually getting used to her wily ways. He never even flinched as she took her seat.

Sarah Jo had affected the town in other ways, as well. The groundbreaking for the new opera house had taken many by surprise, but not Belinda. No, with Sarah Jo at the helm, she felt sure the building would be grand, indeed. And every time she thought about how the town was changing—new shops going in, a fresh influx of women—Belinda got even more excited. Before long they would rival Dallas, for sure.

After the service, Belinda walked the church grounds and visited with several friends and neighbors. When she came upon Katie Sue and Bucky, she paused to praise the wedding cake, which Katie Sue had baked for the ceremony.

"Katie Sue, that cake was divine, to say the least. I've never tasted anything like it. Was that a strawberry jam between the layers?"

"Indeed. And the frosting is my own secret recipe."

"Well, it was scrumptious. Best cake I've ever eaten. Everyone is saying so."

Katie Sue's cheeks flushed pink. "Thank you. I've always loved baking, and Bucky seems to enjoy my homemade goodies, so I'm a happy girl."

"I've put on weight since our wedding," he said, rubbing his belly. "Not that I'm complaining. I've always loved sweets, so I'm doubly blessed in marriage." He gave Katie Sue a kiss on the cheek and she blushed.

"Have you thought about making cakes professionally?" Belinda asked. "We have several other weddings coming up, you know."

"Really? Who's getting married?" Katie Sue asked.

"We are!" Two voices laced with vibrato rang out from behind Belinda. She turned to see the widow Hanson standing there, her arm linked with Samuel Bromstead's.

"You are?" Belinda looked at the elderly couple, more than a little stunned. Her instincts about the two of them had been right all along!

"Yes, it's true!" Samuel said with a nod. "I asked her just this morning, and she has agreed."

"So, you two are... I mean, you really are..."

"We are indeed." Samuel looked at her with a smile. "And we have you to thank. You really opened my eyes to the possibilities, Belinda. Why, when I think that I almost missed the very woman who'd been right there in front of me the whole time..." His eyes welled. "Well, I'm just grateful I finally woke up and saw the light." He gave his bride-to-be a kiss on the tip of her nose and she blushed.

"And when will the wedding take place?" Katie Sue asked. "If I'm to bake the cake, I'll have to plan ahead."

"Three weeks from today," Samuel said. When Belinda gasped, he added, "At our age, what would be the sense in waiting?" He laughed long and loud at that one.

The two lovebirds turned and walked away arm in arm, but Belinda's thoughts were elsewhere. Samuel's words about almost missing what had been in front of him the whole time had reminded her of what Aunt Hilde said just yesterday.

Coming to attention, Belinda turned to Katie Sue. "Looks like we've got another wedding cake in our future. And that's not even the one I was talking about."

"It sounds like I'm going to have my hands full! Who are the others?" Katie Sue asked.

"Well, let's see...Doc Klein's wife-to-be is arriving on tomorrow's train, though I don't have a clue if or when they will marry, of course. One can never be too sure about these things."

"Obviously." Katie Sue laughed. "What sort of woman is she?"

"A nurse. Isn't that ideal?"

"Sounds too good to be true," Katie Sue responded with a thoughtful look on her face. "However did you manage to arrange such a thing?"

"Just the Lord, I guess. He seems to be in the details. I'm just following His lead." She paused for a moment and then said, "Mostly, anyway."

"I think you've done a fine job," Bucky said, drawing his wife even closer. "No complaints on this end."

"Nor from me," Katie Sue said with a contented smile. "Now, tell me who else I'll be baking for. Don't leave out a thing."

"I'm expecting a young woman from Charleston for John Ogilvie, as well," Belinda said. "No telling how long before either of these couples wed. Could be a few days. Could be a few weeks. Are you up to the task? That will be three wedding cakes in all."
Four, if you count Georg and Adeline, but I won't mention that one just yet.

"I suppose I'm up to it," Katie Sue said with a shrug. "I've never been one to balk at hard work."

"You know, I just had the most wonderful idea," Bucky said, snapping his fingers. "You need your own bakery, Katie Sue. One with a real kitchen. You could bake wedding cakes and other pastries. And your pies would be a big hit with the locals. Why, the shop would be filled morning to night with townsfolk."

"Do you really think so, Bucky?" She gazed up at him, her eyes sparkling with joy.

"I do. That blueberry pie of yours is enough to make me want to write another love poem."

"Then I'll bake one tonight." Katie Sue gave him a coy smile. "But really...you would do that for me? Build a bakery?"

"For you, I would sail the seven seas. I would climb Mt. Everest. I would..."

Belinda never heard the rest. She found herself wondering what it would be like to have someone she loved say such silly and romantic things to her. What would it be like to bake pies for one's husband? To have his undying love and devotion, as well as his support with business ventures?

She would never know.

"We will have to think of a name for this bakery," Bucky said, tapping his chin with his index finger. "That might take some work. But I'm sure we can come up with something. What do you think?"

Katie Sue's eyes brimmed over. "I think it's the most marvelous idea I've ever heard in my entire life, that's what I think. And I think I'm the most grateful woman ever!" She stood on her tiptoes and attempted to kiss him. When the deed could not be accomplished— Bucky being at least a full foot taller—he leaned down and swept her into his arms. If things got any mushier, Belinda thought she might start feeling nauseated.

On the other hand, she had to admit that they made a darling couple.

When the kiss ended, Katie Sue let out a little gasp and Belinda looked her way. "What is it? Is everything all right?"

"Yes." Katie Sue twittered. "I just thought of a name for the bakery, that's all."

"What's that?"

"Couplets." Katie Sue looked up at her husband once more, the tears starting to flow. "Don't you see? A couplet! That's the type of poem you wrote to woo me here, remember?"

"Oh, um, yes, I, um..." Bucky stumbled all over himself. Clearly, he hadn't yet told Katie Sue that Peter had penned the couplet. Belinda wondered if he ever would.

But what did it matter, really? Katie Sue would get her bakery, and the townspeople would get their pastries, pies, and cakes. Sounded like a sweet deal for all involved.

* * *

Georg looked across the church grounds to find Belinda engaged in conversation with Katie Sue and Bucky. Looked like they were in it up to their eyeballs. He wanted to speak with her, but he wasn't sure what to say. For, while his feelings for Belinda were ever-growing, they were somewhat masked by the anxiety of knowing a young woman was on her way to Poetry...intended for him. What could he do about it? He didn't want to lead the poor woman astray, and yet he couldn't fathom seeing past Belinda to even give this young woman a second thought.

"Georg, you're mighty quiet, standing there." Reverend Billingsley drew near with his new bride at his side. "Deep in thought?"

"Mm-hmm." He collected his thoughts then turned to the reverend and Marta with a smile. "But I'm back now. Just have a lot on my mind."

"I know what that feels like." The reverend Billingsley smiled. "Been a little preoccupied myself lately. But a nice preoccupation, all the same." He gave his wife a shy smile, and she leaned in to peck him on the cheek. Georg couldn't help but think about how the Lord had arranged their meeting. Indeed, He'd been in on it from the start, just as He had arranged the other couples.

"I daresay, married life will suit me just fine," the reverend said. "And did you hear?"

"Hear what?"

"I'm starting a Sunday school for the children." Marta smiled broadly. "We will meet before service every Sunday. I'll teach Bible stories and memory verses and so on."

"Isn't that wonderful?" the good reverend said, beaming ear to ear. "Marta can put her teaching skills to work, and the church's children will benefit as a result."

"Yes, and that way I can have my weekdays free so that we can spend every minute together." Marta leaned over and placed her head against her husband's. "I'm so excited about the days ahead."

"As am I." Her husband gave her a little squeeze and then looked at Georg. "So, what do you think of the transformation of our little town, Georg? It's something to see, isn't it?"

"Indeed." He looked to his left just as Sarah Jo handed a glass of lemonade to Peter Conrad. "It is something to see all right."

"The Lord moves in mysterious ways, that's all I've got to say." The pastor's voice drifted off as he and Marta moved on to greet the rest of the congregation.

Georg had no trouble believing that the Lord moved in mysterious ways. He did have to wonder, however, if the Lord took his marching orders from Belinda Bauer. He glanced across the church lawn, finding her engaged in conversation with John Ogilvie and Doc Klein. Preparing them for their new brides, more than likely.

She turned and caught Georg's eye and gave him a little wave. Seconds later, she drew near with a smile on her face. "God's in His heaven; all's right with the world."

"Beg your pardon?"

"Oh, I'm just saying everything is going well. According to plan. Both of those men are happy as larks that their new brides arrive tomorrow. I've never seen John so excited about anything."

"I see." Georg wanted to say more. Wanted to say that he wasn't as happy with his situation, but he didn't. No, something about seeing the relaxed smile on Belinda's face put his heart at ease, if only for the moment. Incoming bride or not.

Belinda began to tell him about Katie Sue's plan to open a bakery, and Georg found himself, as always, falling into easy conversation with her. At one point she paused and gazed into his eyes. For a moment, time stood still. Georg could hear his own heartbeat in his ears. Then, just as quickly, Belinda dove back into the story.

She could have been talking about the moon, for all he cared. All that mattered was standing here, listening to the sound of her voice and sensing her closeness. For tomorrow, once Adeline arrived, all of that would change.

How it would change, he had no idea. Still, he couldn't help but think it wouldn't be for the better.

POETRY
1904
LEY

Chapter Fifteen

....

Early Monday morning, the train brought yet another bride—the lovely Rebecca Morgan from Virginia. Doc Klein, less stoic than usual, sat tall and straight in the wagon beside Belinda, the sunlight reflecting off the bald spot on the top of his head. The tips of his ears were red in anticipation. Looked like the forty-something bachelor was nervous. Not that Belinda blamed him. This had to be nerve-wracking. It turned out, Rebecca—who looked to be in her late thirties—was tall and slender with a comely physique. Her style of dress was plain but practical. Her shoes, sensible. She greeted them with a warm smile, but Belinda could sense her nervous anticipation, as well.

Doc Klein scrambled into action, fetching her bags and loading them into the wagon. As he did so, he managed to keep a lively conversation going.

From the moment Rebecca met Doc face-to-face, Belinda sensed at once that these two were a bona fide match. They talked about medicine and medical procedures all the way back to Poetry, continuing as Belinda dropped them off at the restaurant. In fact, Belinda couldn't remember ever hearing so much chatter about surgical instruments, boil lancing, and the like. Not exactly the stuff romantic unions were known for, but the two clearly had a lot in common. More than any couple she'd ever met, in fact.

She barely had time to contemplate this fact, however, because John Ogilvie's bride was set to arrive at the station at one o'clock on the dot. Adeline would arrive less than an hour later on a train from Boston.

Belinda headed back to Terrell with the wagon, this time taking Greta along for the ride. They were thrilled to find Cassie Bly an intelligent young woman with great zeal for life. Surely she would find John Ogilvie her perfect complement. Belinda hoped so, anyway. The two would meet in a few hours. Right now, they had to stay at the depot to wait for Adeline's train.

As they waited, the three women gabbed about all sorts of things, primarily Cassie's plans for the future. It turned out she had a lot of them.

"I've been sewing since I was a little girl," Cassie said. "Folks have always brought their mending to me, and every woman in our town who ever wanted a wedding dress came to me, as well. I've been gifted with a needle and thread for as long as I can remember, and I love coming up with patterns. Folks say I'm quite creative, though I consider myself calculated, not free-spirited."

"Well, sewing is a fine occupation," Greta said. "You will surely have your hands full with making wedding dresses in Poetry."

"Oh, I hope so! I'm planning to open my own dress shop someday," Cassie announced. "What do you think of that idea?"

"Dress shop?" Belinda paused, offering up a smile. "Sounds lovely." Corabelle would find it a wonderful idea, no doubt. In fact, she would probably insist that the shop go into the empty lot next to Sonnets and Bonnets. Belinda could just picture the women in Poetry scurrying in and out. Surely Sarah Jo would love the idea. She would probably commission Cassie to make her seven new dresses, each in a different color to match her new hats.

"I think our town is growing by leaps and bounds and can use a dress shop," Greta responded. "We've got a new hat shop. Just opened, in fact."

"Perfect!" Cassie looked as happy as a lark.

Belinda wanted to join in the conversation but found herself distracted. She knew that Adeline was due to arrive anytime now. For whatever reason, whenever she thought of the woman she'd brought to marry Georg, her heart felt as heavy as lead. Perhaps—oh, joy!—perhaps this would be an ill-fated match. Maybe Adeline had a houseful of rambunctious, ill-mannered children. Perhaps she was ugly. Maybe her nose was long or her ankles heavy. Perhaps her waist was thick or her eyes too close together.

Yes, the more Belinda thought about it, the more she envisioned the young woman to be quite ugly indeed. Hadn't Sarah Jo said as much? Didn't she mention that women who placed advertisements were prone to exaggeration where their looks were concerned? And, knowing Georg, he would never agree to a passel of children. She simply couldn't imagine it.

Now in a more relaxed frame of mind, Belinda waited for the train to arrive. It came on time, the grinding of brakes nearly deafening them. Belinda, Greta, and Cassie drew near to watch the passengers disembark.

"Looks pretty crowded," Greta observed. "I hope we can figure out which one she is."

Belinda looked about but couldn't see anyone who matched the description of the woman in the advertisement. *Maybe she missed the train. Or changed her mind.*

Finally a young woman exited the car, gingerly taking a couple of steps down and forward. She held a parasol in one hand, which she opened as soon as she stepped out into the sunlight. Belinda's breath caught in her throat. She had never seen such a beautiful woman in all of her life.

The exquisite blond was like something from a catalog. Her perfectly trim waistline was pinched tight in a dress unlike anything Belinda had ever laid eyes on. Oh, how the bright blue fabric brought out the color in her big blue eyes. Why, oh why, did she have to have eyes the color of bluebonnets? On top of that disaster, the woman didn't have a freckle or blemish on her ivory cheeks. No, everything about her—from the top of her coiffed hair to the tips of her delicate button-up shoes—was the very picture of perfection.

Belinda groaned inwardly, plastered on a smile, and greeted the woman with the most pleasant voice possible under the circumstances. "Adeline! Welcome."

"Oh, I'm so thrilled to be here." The woman flashed a smile so genuine and heartfelt that Belinda at once realized her charm. She reached for Belinda's hand and gave it a squeeze. "You must be Belinda Bauer."

"The very one."

"Oh, Belinda, I'm so glad to be here." Adeline's eyes sparkled. "I've waited and prayed for this day for such a long time now. You know, I had no idea what kind of a man would answer my advertisement. Oh, but the Lord knew! And isn't it fascinating to think that He has known all our lives who we would marry and where we would live? It thrills my heart to know I can trust Him so!"

"Yes, well…" Belinda tried to think of something to say, but could not.

Thankfully Greta interrupted, making introductions for her and Cassie. Within minutes they were all acquainted, and by the time the porter loaded Adeline's bags onto the wagon, they shared an easy and pleasant conversation.

Belinda made the drive to Poetry in silence. Greta made up for it from her seat in the back, so no one seemed any the wiser. Still, as Belinda peeked out of the corners of her eyes at Adeline, who sat beside her on the front seat, she couldn't help but think she'd made a huge mistake by bringing her here. Something about all of this just felt wrong.

"Belinda, how can I thank you?" Adeline said. "You have been such an answer to prayer. You found my advertisement, wrote to me...and all because you sensed the Lord's leading. I'm forever in your debt."

"Yes, well..." Belinda sighed.

"And I can hardly wait to meet Georg." Adeline sighed. "I even dreamed about him last night."

"You did?" Belinda found that quite ironic, in light of the fact that she'd dreamed about him, as well.

"Yes." Adeline's expression shifted to one of pure excitement. "I dreamed about the house we will one day live in. It was quite lovely, with two bedrooms and indoor plumbing. I made little curtains to hang in the windows, and Georg built our furniture with his own hands."

Greta laughed at that one. "I can hardly imagine Georg building furniture. Still, I feel sure you will one day have a home just like the one you described, especially if Georg falls head over heels for you, like I know he will."

"Don't be so sure, Greta," Belinda interjected, her heart now thumping madly. "I have it on good authority that Georg enjoys living at home with his parents. It is somewhat likely he will stay close to his mother after he weds."

"Oh?" Adeline shifted nervously. "Well, that would be one possibility, of course, though it would be nice to have a place of our own." She paused for a moment and appeared to be deep in thought. "Still, I must admit, the idea of having a mother and father nearby sounds divine, too." Dabbing at her eyes, she whispered, "I lost my parents a year ago."

"Oh, Adeline, how awful. I'm so sorry." Belinda hardly knew what to say next. Suddenly she felt like giving herself a good swift kick.

"I have a younger sister," Adeline continued. "She's twelve. If Georg and I marry, she will come to live with us, of course. That is why I worded the advertisement as I did. If I ended up with the wrong man—say, a fellow who didn't love children—it would be problematic. My sister depends on me for everything, you see."

Aha. So there are children involved. Or at least one child. Belinda pondered this fact, realizing that she had neglected to mention to Georg that Adeline wanted a man ready for a family. Would that be a problem? Belinda sighed as the truth registered. Surely, if he fell for this lovely young woman, he would take in her sister, as well. Why, Georg was the kindest man in the world. He would bend over backward to accommodate, especially if he genuinely cared about the person in need.

Still, the idea of him caring for Adeline caused Belinda's heart to twist. This new revelation both frightened and thrilled her, though she couldn't decide which emotion to entertain first.

Cassie, who'd been quiet till now, interjected her thoughts on the matter. "I say if the man doesn't tend to the needs of both you and your sister, you should give up on the idea of matrimony immediately. Don't waste your time on someone who doesn't appreciate and sympathize with your situation."

"I suppose you're right," Adeline said, looking a bit defeated. "Though I would hope to convince him over time, should the need arise. And my sister is quite easy to live with. Very compliant."

Cassie continued. "Still, make sure before you agree to marry him. Men these days are quite modern in their thinking, at least the men I know. They understand that a woman's needs are different than they were, say, a hundred years ago. So, if Georg is the man intended for you, you will know it beyond a shadow of a doubt, because his thoughts will correspond with yours. That's not to say you will agree on every detail, but in general you will be compatible on issues such as children and the like."

Adeline smiled. "What a sensible way to look at things. Our thoughts will correspond. I like that image. You've given me a lot to think about, Cassie. Thank you for that. I will pray about this and get the Lord's perspective on it. He will show me what to do, should any problems arise." She shifted her gaze to the blue skies overhead, sighing. "Oh, but what a perfect place to contemplate life's greater mysteries. You have such lovely weather here. I can't believe it's this warm in September."

"Warm?" Belinda debated, tugging at her collar. "Why, it's absolutely hot. Of course, our autumns are often unbearable, though not as awful as the summertime." *Okay, Belinda. Perhaps that was a bit much.*

Greta snorted. "Belinda, what in the world are you talking about?"

"Is it really this warm every September?" Cassie sounded nervous, and Belinda realized she'd better rethink some of her comments, lest she scare both women away. She opened her mouth to say something sensible, but Adeline interrupted.

"Oh, I love the warmth," the lovely young woman said, contentedly. "In Boston I'm chilled to the bone all of the time. Here I can bask in the glow of the sun...and my future husband's love." She giggled. "Sorry if I sound a little silly, but I'm so excited."

"Who can blame you?" Greta said. "And who wouldn't love you? Why, you're about the sweetest thing I've ever met in my life."

Adeline blushed and whispered a shy, "Thank you."

"Yes, who wouldn't love you?" Belinda whispered. She turned her attention back to steering the wagon toward town and hoped the *clip-clop* of the horse's hooves drowned out the sound of her anxious heart.

"You are far more romantic in nature than I am, to be sure, Adeline," Cassie proclaimed. "I tend to look at life practically. For you, I would imagine the dream of a happily-ever-after is always at the front of your mind."

"Of course." Adeline blushed. "Is it not the same for you?"

"I don't think of happily-ever-afters in the same way as most, I guess. I'm more scientific in my mind-set."

"As am I!" Belinda looked back at Cassie, stunned. "I've always said a perfect match is a matter of both science and faith and that if either is missing from the equation, the relationship is doomed to fail."

"I agree completely," Cassie said. "Though I daresay romance sounds good in theory."

Adeline laughed. "You two are so funny! I've never once thought of love and marriage as being scientific at all. Why, to me it's all a matter of feelings."

Feelings. Hmm. Belinda paused to push those away as they arrived in town. For now, she'd better keep her feelings—whatever they might be—to herself. She slowed the pace of the horse to a slow trot so that the women could get a good look at Poetry in all its glory.

"Why, speaking of feelings, this town gives me such a good feeling," Adeline said, looking about. "It's such a darling little place!"

"Growing like a weed, too," Greta chimed in. "We even have an opera house going in. It will be finished in time for a Christmas production. I can't wait for you to meet Sarah Jo, the woman in charge of it. She's such fun."

"I love a good theatrical," Adeline said with a nod. "I'm happy to hear about the opera house. What about Georg? Does he like the theater?"

"Surely not," Belinda said, shaking her head. "I can't picture it."

Greta mumbled something indiscernible, and Belinda knew she'd have to give an explanation later regarding her odd behavior.

"I love the idea of the opera house, too," Cassie spoke up. "In fact, I find the whole town absolutely charming. I'm sure Mr. Ogilvie and I will lead a very nice life here. If we are suitably matched, I mean." She paused for a moment, looking at the stores. "How do you think he will feel about me putting in a dress shop, though?"

"Oh, I've already told him you are interested in working after marriage," Belinda said. "He's quite busy at the butcher shop and appreciates the fact that you can fill the hours doing something you love."

"Perfect. Why, I can see my dress shop going in right over there." She pointed to an empty lot next to the post office. "Oh, but you will have to help me come up with a name in keeping with the town. That will take some doing." She paused then snapped her fingers. "No, I have it! What about this? Metric Patterns!"

"Metric Patterns?" Adeline glanced back at her with confusion. "What does that mean?"

"Life is very much like the patterns I use for sewing," Cassie said. "Everything calculated. Measured. A poem is much the same, each line carefully thought-out. So I've merged the two together in my mind and come up with that name. What do you think?"

"I think it's a perfect idea," Belinda said. She turned to Adeline. "Are you hoping to open some sort of business like so many of the other ladies?"

"Who, me?" Adeline shook her head. "Heavens, no." Her cheeks turned pink. "I'm hoping to marry and raise a family. I wouldn't want anything to get in the way of my relationship with my husband. Georg will come first. No doubt about that."

"I see." Belinda sighed once more.

She pulled the wagon up to the front of Poetic Notions, and Georg appeared at once from the barbershop door. She watched as his gaze shifted back and forth between Cassie and Adeline, as if trying to figure out which one was meant for him. To put him out of his misery, Belinda made quick introductions once he crossed the street.

"Georg, this is Adeline Jewett. Adeline, this is Georg Kaufman, my..." She started to say "best friend" but stopped herself. No, after he married, they could no longer go on being best friends, could they? She would have to take a giant step backward. Oh, if only she could convince her heart that it was the right thing to do. Then all would be well.

* * *

Georg stared in silence at the lovely young woman in the wagon. When she rose, he extended a hand and helped her down. She responded with a smile so genuine that it warmed his heart.

"Adeline." He spoke the word softly, and it sounded like music as it slipped between his lips.

"Actually, I go by *Adeline Rose*," she said with a girlish smile. "*Rose* is my middle name."

"Adeline Rose, welcome to Poetry." Her hand lingered in his as they gazed into the other's eyes.

"For now, *Adeline* will do," she said. "Until we know one another better."

"Of course. Adeline, then."

"Georg, I'm so happy to make your acquaintance at last." Her long eyelashes batted, though he sensed she didn't do it on purpose. "I've been so excited, I could scarcely think of anything else for days."

"O-oh?" He found himself enraptured by her bright blue eyes and intricately styled hair. Truly, Adeline Rose was the most beautiful woman Belinda had brought to town thus far. And she was meant... for him?

In that moment, he very nearly lost control of his senses. For, while he considered himself a practical man, there was nothing practical about this kind of beauty. It defied the odds. It sent the mind reeling. It gave one hope to believe he could actually attain the unattainable.

"We—we are thrilled to have you in our fair town," Georg managed. He attempted a smile but thought it felt a little cockeyed. What was it about this woman that made him nervous? Even his hands were shaking. Could it be that Belinda had been right all along? Perhaps he'd been so enraptured with what was right in front of him that he'd ignored the possibilities of something else coming along. Well, he would weigh his options over the upcoming days and weeks and ask the Lord's opinion. Surely the circumstances would not be terribly painful, not with such an exquisite woman to consider.

Two exquisite women. He turned to Belinda, for the first time noticing the look of pain in her eyes. What had caused it? He offered a smile and she returned it, though her eyes still reflected something he couldn't quite discern. Was she upset at him? Had he done something wrong? Surely not. He had played along with her plans and not complained a whit. Why would that bother her now?

"Can I get your bag, Adeline?" he asked, coming back to his senses.

When she nodded, he reached for her things and carried them across the street and into the hotel. Once they were all inside the lobby, Belinda turned to Adeline, her voice quite businesslike as she spoke. "Be careful not to speak to strangers, Adeline."

"O–oh?"

"Yes. I don't believe I've mentioned it before, but there is an insane asylum in Terrell, just six miles away." Belinda spoke with an all-too-serious look on her face. "I often wonder if we are at risk, living so close."

"Oh my." Adeline began to fan herself.

Georg looked at Belinda, curious about both her demeanor and the direction the conversation was heading. He hadn't heard her mention the insane asylum since their days in school, when they would tell scary stories about it. Why today, of all days? He stared at her, wondering about the somewhat frantic way she spoke. Maybe all of this matchmaking was finally getting to her. She was acting mighty strange.

And scaring Adeline, from the looks of things. Unfortunately, he never had a chance to address it. Belinda kept right on going, surprising him with her next words.

"Now, Adeline, be on the lookout for tornado warnings."

"Tornado warnings?"

"Well, yes," Belinda said, with an all-too-serious expression on her face. "Did I forget to mention that the entire town was devastated by a tornado fourteen years ago?" She paused and shook her head. "I was sure I mentioned that. Sorry."

He made an attempt to interrupt, trying to bring some sense to this conversation. "Belinda, what in the world are you—?"

"Just listen for the sound of howling wind," Belinda said, her eyes narrowing into slits. "It's a terrible sound. Kind of like a train coming through town. Terrifying, really."

Adeline's eyes widened. "Oh my. I had no idea."

Georg shook his head. "Adeline, you have nothing to worry about. This town hasn't seen a tornado in years."

"Still." Belinda nodded, as if that settled the whole thing. "You never know."

Georg gave her a "What are you trying to accomplish here?" look, and Belinda shifted gears immediately. She turned to their new guest with a winning smile.

"Adeline, Georg was wondering if you would like to go to dinner at the restaurant tonight."

He turned her way, stunned, and mouthed, "I was?"

When she nodded, he turned to Adeline. "I would be thrilled to escort you to dinner tonight, Miss Adeline. If you would be so kind as to accompany me, I will meet you at seven o'clock in the hotel lobby."

"Indeed." She smiled. "I would be honored. In the meantime, I must check into my room and freshen up. I must look simply awful."

"Certainly not." He couldn't help but smile. The young woman clearly had no idea just how beautiful she was. He found himself captivated by her, in fact.

"I look forward to our evening together." She gave him a shy smile then followed on the bellman's heels toward her hotel room. Georg turned back to Belinda, who still had the same pained expression on her face.

"What?"

"Nothing." She shook her head. Her eyes flooded, and he reached to take her hand.

"I'm at a loss to know what to say here, Belinda. Truly."

"Why? Are you unhappy with Adeline? She disappoints you in some way?"

"No, of course not. It's not that. She seems quite wonderful, in fact."

"Well, then," Belinda said, her businesslike voice taking over once again. "It looks like I was right this time. You two *are* a match made in heaven. You are destined to be together." After a brief pause, she turned. "I'd better be getting back to the store. Aunt Hilde has done without me all day. I suppose I will see you later, then."

"Belinda..." He drew near and took her arm. She turned to him, a lone tear trickling down her cheek. He brushed it away, and she reached up to take his hand.

"Yes?"

"I just wanted to say..." He shook his head, realizing others had stopped to watch. "Well, thank you for all your hard work on my behalf. I'm grateful."

"You're welcome, Georg. You know, you are still my best friend in the world. Next to Greta of course. There's nothing I wouldn't do for you."

"And you are mine as well," he said, gazing into her tear-filled eyes. "I feel exactly the same."

"Well, then..." At that, she hiked her skirt and took to running across the street in the direction of Poetic Notions. Georg fought the urge to follow her. If he did, it would only complicate things further. Instead, he turned back toward his shop, the thoughts in his head moving in a hundred different directions at once.

Chapter Sixteen
....

A couple of weeks after the newest batch of ladies arrived in town, Belinda found herself facing a dilemma of major proportions. It centered around Rebecca Morgan and Doc Klein. As much as she had hoped to happily match them, they did not take to each other as she'd planned. Oh, they had much in common. Perhaps too much, as Georg had once insinuated. So when Rebecca paid Belinda a visit at home on a windy Thursday evening, she wasn't particularly surprised to see her.

Belinda greeted her at the door. "Come in, Rebecca. Please." She ushered her inside, out of the dismal rain, and gestured for her to sit in Papa's favorite rocker. Belinda swallowed hard as she took a seat across from her.

"I think you can guess why I'm here, Belinda." Rebecca twisted her hands together in her lap. "These past couple of weeks have been very trying for me. I feel as if I've made a mistake by coming here."

"You have?" Belinda sighed. "I'm so sorry, Rebecca."

"It would have been worth it, I suppose, if I'd fallen in love. But the truth is, I'm simply not enamored with Doctor Klein. I've tried ever so hard to think of him as husband material, but I can't seem to do so. We are compatible as friends or even coworkers, but not as romantic partners. Not at all."

"We've plenty of other available men in town," Belinda offered. "So if you're interested in a different sort of match, perhaps something could be arranged."

Rebecca shook her head. "I don't believe so, though I thank you for the offer. I would love to go back home. The sooner, the better."

"Ah." Belinda drew in a deep breath. So it had finally happened after all. One of her brides had chosen to leave. That meant someone had to pay for her train ticket. That someone would apparently be Belinda. She couldn't very well charge Doc Klein, now could she? No, and in fact, he would likely ask for his money back for Rebecca's original ticket, as well. So this would be quite a financial loss for Belinda's business. "You cannot be persuaded?" she asked, trying to sound hopeful.

"I cannot."

Belinda pushed back a sigh and forged ahead, looking as sympathetic as possible. "Then I will arrange for your ticket tomorrow morning. When would you like to leave?"

"I believe there is a train out of Terrell on Saturday morning, and I'd like to be on it." Rebecca's eyes filled with tears. "I want you to know that I am ready for marriage. There's no doubt in my mind about that. I waited for years for the right man to come along, and when he didn't, my desperation drove me to place that advertisement. I came to Poetry with the highest hopes. But Doctor Klein isn't the man for me, and I wouldn't be true to my heart if I married him."

"Oh dear."

"I feel badly about this, Belinda. I got the man's hopes up. And yours. But I can't go through with it. I simply can't."

"Of course you can't," Belinda said with a sympathetic nod. "I'm sad, of course, but I understand completely."

"You have no idea how difficult it is to give up everything—

the people you love, your church home, your familiar surroundings—
to come to a place where you know no one. Can you imagine how
you would feel, were the shoe on the other foot?"

"No, I must admit, I cannot. I would imagine it's a lonely venture."

"Especially when you're hoping to find love but only end up with,
well, with a mismatch."

"No sparks at all with the doctor, then?" Belinda asked.

"None. I thought about lighting some fireworks underneath
him to see if that would help." Rebecca offered up a shy smile. "But
I stopped short of doing it."

"Probably for the best."

"I was swayed by his poem, to be sure," Rebecca said, confusion
registering in her eyes. "But it's the oddest thing. The man I found
upon arrival didn't seem at all the same romantic who penned those
beautiful words. Don't you find that strange?"

"Strange? Oh, well, I..." Belinda's words trailed off. "I suppose
it does seem a bit odd." *Perhaps because he never wrote that poem.
Peter did.*

Belinda eventually bid her guest farewell, promising to buy
her ticket first thing tomorrow morning. Rebecca would be on the
Saturday morning train out of Terrell, no matter the cost.

As she sat alone in the living room, Belinda reflected on all
she'd heard. For the first time, she began to contemplate the fact
that the poems Peter had written to the various ladies were, in fact,
somewhat deceptive. She'd never thought about it from that angle
before, but the women were bound to expect their husbands-to-be
to have the same romantic flair in real life as on paper. And surely
a man like Doc Klein—stoic and a bit cold at times—wasn't capable

of such glowing words in person.

Really, the only man in town who might pull off a real love poem—next to Peter, of course—was Georg. Perhaps he was finishing his now. For Adeline.

Belinda headed into the kitchen to have a talk with her mother.

Mama turned from washing the dishes as she walked into the room. "Problems on the matchmaking front?"

"Yes." Belinda sighed. "I don't know where I went wrong with that one." Her mother handed her a plate and a dish towel. Belinda went to work, drying as she talked. "I was absolutely sure the doctor would be enamored with Rebecca and she with him. But I was wrong."

"Sometimes life is nonsensical," her mother said. "Things that appear to be obvious are anything but."

"As I am learning." Belinda sighed and put away the dry plate. "Can I ask you a question, Mama?"

"Sure." Her mother looked up with a smile, handing her another plate.

"How did you know that Papa was the one for you?"

Her mother stopped working and gazed at her. "I've never told you that story?"

Belinda shook her head, never losing her grip on the plate, which she continued to dry. "No."

"Well, your father was actually the last man I'd ever thought of marrying, if you want the truth of it," her mother said with a hint of laughter in her voice. "You'd never seen two more different people. I was outgoing; he was shy. I was the first to volunteer for every church committee; he was content to work quietly in the background. But there was something about that man I could not deny."

"What was it?" Belinda put the plate in the cupboard and focused on her mother's story.

Mama shook her head and smiled, a wistful look on her face. "There's really only one way to describe it, honey. Our souls were connected. They still are. I know that man inside and out, and he knows me. We were destined by the Lord to marry. There's no doubt in my mind about that."

"So you think God knows in advance who we're going to marry, then?" Belinda asked.

"Why, He must," Mama said. She offered a comforting smile.

"Then why doesn't He just come out and tell us?" Belinda said with a sigh. "Give us some sort of sign or something?"

"Sometimes He works like that," Mama said with a shrug. "But if you'll notice, the Lord rarely reveals everything at once. No, He tends to move in our lives...well, much like a poem. One stanza at a time."

Belinda nodded. "I think you're right. Oh, but don't you ever wish you could read the whole poem at once? What if you're at the end of one line and you're aching to know what's coming next?"

"Then you trust, honey. You trust. And you believe that whatever is coming next—whether it rhymes with the line before it or not—will work to God's glory. And that the whole poem, once completed, will speak of a life completely devoted to Him, even during the hard times."

Belinda sighed. "Mama, how did you get to be so smart?"

Her mother laughed. "Must be my sixth-grade education shining through. But believe me, sweet girl, there are some things you can't learn in books. They are the lessons of life, meant to be learned by living."

"I think I will be learning for the rest of my life, then." Belinda grimaced.

"Then you are in good company," her mother said. "For we all go on learning till the day we die."

Belinda gave her mother's words a lot of thought as she continued helping with the dishes. And later that night, as she settled into bed a good two hours earlier than usual, she chewed on them a bit more. She closed her eyes and offered up a prayer, asking the Lord to show her the next verse of her poem—but only silence permeated the room. If He knew, He wasn't saying.

Then again, maybe she didn't need to know, either. Maybe half the adventure was, as Mama had said, in finding out one line at a time.

* * *

Georg sat across from Adeline Rose in the restaurant at Stanzas, hanging onto her every word. There was something about her voice, the way she pronounced her words, that he found charming. Of course, he found just about everything about her charming, especially the way she batted her eyelashes when she got excited about something, which seemed to happen a lot. These past two weeks had been a blur, moving far too rapidly. It seemed every time he prayed the clock would slow down, it sped up instead. And though he felt he was getting to know Adeline, he still struggled to know her from the inside out.

The beautiful young woman now sat across the table, talking about her younger sister. "I'm quite anxious to bring Catherine here," she said. "I know she will love this town. Why, what's not to love?"

"I agree completely." He paused, not sure what to say next. Over the past couple of weeks, he'd heard about Catherine in detail. Surely the child would love Poetry. But was he ready to take on both a wife and a child? He had smiled and nodded his way through many conversations about her but didn't feel settled about it in his heart. Not yet, anyway. Still, how could he say no to anything Adeline might ask? The woman was sheer perfection, and her love for both the Lord and people came shining through in everything she did. He would be blessed to have her as a wife. Blessed beyond belief.

"Did you hear that Rebecca Morgan is leaving on the Saturday morning train?" Adeline said, interrupting his thoughts.

That certainly got Georg's attention. "No. Are you sure?"

"Very. She stopped me in the hotel lobby this afternoon on her way back from Belinda's house to tell me. I could tell she had been crying, poor thing."

"So, it didn't work out with the doctor." He pursed his lips and leaned back in his chair, thinking that one through. The doctor wasn't the easiest person in the world to get to know. He had a stiff demeanor at times.

"Apparently not," Adeline said. "I daresay, some of these matches are harder than others."

"Clearly." He nodded and then took a swig of coffee, deep in thought. Every time he turned around, someone was getting hurt. And yet this whole thing was a bit like a snowball coming down a hill. The farther it went, the faster it moved. And the faster it moved, the bigger it got. Heaven help the person standing at the bottom of the hill. Surely that man—whether it was the doctor or Myles Lott or Georg Kaufman—would be buried alive, if he didn't watch himself.

Oh, how easily he could get swept away by this snowball. After all, Adeline held every charm. He found her giggle to be light and airy. Her conversation compelling. Her flattery sincere. Every word she spoke was laced with kindness, and her heart for others remained evident, especially when talking about her sister.

She was truly the most perfect woman he'd ever known. Not that any woman could truly achieve perfection, but she certainly came close. He turned back to her with a smile and continued their conversation without interruption. No point in causing any pain on her end. She needn't be aware of any internal struggles he might be having. Not yet, anyway.

On top of that, the scent of her perfume pulled at him. It was different from the fragrance Belinda wore. What was that called, again? Ah yes, lemon verbena. This had a sweeter smell.

Adeline continued talking, oblivious to his thoughts. Georg eventually jumped back in, paying attention to every word, lest she find him inattentive. Before long, they chatted about the upcoming campground meeting.

"Oh, I'm so excited to hear about this!" Adeline said. "Camp meetings are my very favorite. When my papa was alive, he would preach at our local camp meetings. He was quite the preacher." She dabbed at her eyes with her hankie. "Sorry, I miss him so much."

"Please don't apologize." Georg reached out to grasp her hand, giving it a squeeze. As he stared into her beautiful tear-filled eyes, the strangest sense came over him. He felt such a strong need to protect Adeline from life's many storms. She'd been through so many already.

"I think you will enjoy the preaching at our camp meetings," Georg said. "Pastors come from all over the county to converge upon the campground at the north end of town. You've never seen anything like it. Folks camp out, share meals together, and sing hymns and other rousing choruses. It's very invigorating."

"I can hardly wait. When is it again?"

"Mid-October."

A cloud seemed to come over her. "I do hope Catherine is here by then. That would make it even better. The longer I'm away from her..." She brushed away a tear then offered a weak smile. "There I go again, talking about my sister. I do hope you will forgive me."

"There's nothing to forgive."

They were several minutes into the conversation when Georg noticed Myles Lott enter the restaurant. There were no tables to be had. Considering all the circumstances, Georg felt terrible for the man.

"Would you mind?" he asked Adeline. "I'd like to ask him to join us."

"What a kind gesture," she said. "I think that would be wonderful."

Moments later Myles sat at the table with them, sipping a cup of coffee and waiting on his dinner. Somehow, with Myles there, Georg could relax and be himself. There was no pressure to do—or be— anything he was not with another person at the table.

"So, you are a schoolteacher?" Adeline asked, turning to Myles.

"Yes. Have been for quite some time now." He drew in a deep breath and grew silent.

"What is it, Myles?" Georg asked.

"Oh, I was just thinking about the many children who've come through my classroom. They have made up for the lack of children in my own life. And many have grown into fine men and women. Take you, Georg. Why, you're all grown up and ready for a family yourself."

"Y–yes." Georg stumbled over the word as he reached for his coffee cup. Perhaps it would be better to shift gears. "The new school year has started up again, hasn't it? Any rambunctious students?"

"Oh, yes. I have a handful of girls around age ten or eleven who tend to squeal a lot. Sometimes their high-pitched shrieks catch me off guard."

"I remember that age." Adeline smiled and her eyes took on a faraway look.

"These girls are quite a handful," Myles said with a nod. "Never stop talking."

"My sister, Catherine, is twelve and will be a student at your school...should we decide to stay in Poetry." Adeline's cheeks turned pink, and she dabbed at her lips with the edge of her napkin. "It would be nice for me to meet some of the girls her age so that proper introductions can be made once she arrives."

"You are welcome to stop by the school midday whenever you like," Myles said with a nod. "I'll be happy to introduce you to the children. Tell me a little more about your sister."

The two dove into a lengthy conversation about Catherine, and Georg relaxed. Thankfully, he could leave this one in Myles's capable hands. For once, it was nice just to sit on the sidelines and listen. Of course, with a woman like Adeline, he could pretty much sit and listen all day. The sound of her voice was akin to water running over river rocks. Soothing. Comforting.

Yes, indeed. He might just learn to love this.

Chapter Seventeen

....

Belinda arrived in church on Sunday morning with her mind still reeling from the past few days. Just yesterday morning she and Papa had driven Rebecca Morgan to Terrell to board the train. She'd left with the promise to write, though Belinda secretly wondered if she would ever hear from her again. Likely not. And perhaps that was for the best. Belinda still had other clients to tend to, after all. The doctor, of course. And Myles Lott. And Sarah Jo. All of these were surely in need of encouragement.

She arrived at the church earlier than usual and was stunned to find Cassie Bly seated not next to John Ogilvie, but to Doc Klein. Surely there had been some mix-up in the communication. Belinda drew near the doctor, who was grinning like a schoolboy as he listened to Cassie talk about her plans to build a dress shop. On and on she went, talking about her dress designs, the patterns she planned to sell, and even the types of fabrics. As if the man cared one whit about fabrics. Still, he sat gazing into her eyes as if she'd cast some sort of spell on him.

"Doc?" Belinda gave him a warning look. "Could I have a moment of your time?"

"Perhaps after the service, Belinda," he said, shooing her away. "I am otherwise occupied at the present."

"Indeed you are." She shook her head then took a few steps, looking for Greta. Maybe she would know what to make of this.

Greta was apparently looking for her, as well. She rushed to Belinda's side and grabbed her by the arm.

"Do you see what's happened?" she whispered.

"It would be hard to miss."

"Doc Klein and Cassie met in town yesterday," Greta added. "You're not going to believe it, but she took a fancy to him right away. Turns out they both have family in South Carolina. Mutual friends, even."

"Are you serious?"

"Never more so. And what do you think about this? Cassie is telling Doc Klein all about her plans to make costumes for the new opera house. Before you know it, she'll be volunteering to make bandages for his practice. Why, he's absolutely mesmerized by her. Spellbound."

"What about John?" Belinda asked, looking around to find him. "Is he brokenhearted?"

"To put it mildly. He's pacing at the back of the church with a pained expression on his face. I've never seen him so upset."

"Oh dear. My heart goes out to him. Oh, what a mess this has turned out to be!"

Belinda went to speak to him, hoping he would hold his temper in check. She took Greta along for safe measure. She arrived to find him pacing and glaring...at Doc Klein.

Belinda drew near, whispering her opening line. "John, I understand there's been a mix-up of sorts." She reached to touch his arm, but he pulled away quickly.

"I don't believe I would call it a mix-up. It's clear what's happening here." He turned to face her with anger emanating from his eyes. "Doc Klein has stolen my woman."

"Well, *stolen* is a harsh word," Belinda said. "I think it's clear neither of them set out to fancy one another. But sometimes our hearts have a way of tricking us." She paused to think about what she'd just said. Yes, it was true. Even her own heart had deceived her at times.

"So what am I to do?" John asked. "Become the laughingstock of the town, like Myles Lott? Be known as the man who was ditched by a mail-order bride? Or traded in for an older model?"

"Surely people will see this for what it is," Belinda said.

"I can see it plain as day," he said. "And I also see that someone owes me some money. I paid a retainer fee and covered the cost of Cassie's ticket from Charleston. If she ends up with the doc, he'd better pay me back."

"Well, that's where things get tricky," Belinda said. "He paid for Rebecca to come, after all, so in essence, he paid for one bride and ended up with another. I think that means I'm square with Doc Klein, should he really take a serious interest in Cassie."

"Well, you're certainly not square with me. I paid for one bride and got nothing in return." A sour look crossed John's face. He crossed his arms over his chest and stared at Belinda. She wondered if he might take to sparring with her right there in the house of the Lord.

"Come now, John." Greta intervened, taking him by the arm. "Let's go outside for a walk. We will try to calm ourselves." She patted his arm. "I think you can rest easy in the fact that the Lord obviously never intended for you to marry Cassie in the first place. Think of the pain you have been spared by avoiding such a hasty and uneventful marriage. Why, who knows what you might've had to endure."

He exhaled loudly and then gazed at Greta and shrugged. "I suppose. I never thought about it from that angle before. Perhaps

I have been spared a greater pain."

"Well, you've never been in this situation before," she said, patting his hand. "How are you to know what to do? That's why you need the counsel of another woman. Come with me, and we will talk this through."

Belinda could have hugged Greta right then and there. She'd managed to calm the storm before it took the building down.

As soon as Greta and John headed off for their walk and she entered the sanctuary once more, Belinda discovered Adeline sitting with Georg's family. Mrs. Kaufman talked nonstop with the young woman. Clearly, she had taken to her. Why that thought bothered Belinda so much, she did not know. Wasn't that the goal, after all? For Adeline to fit in with Georg, his family, and the town? Belinda started to walk over there, to say hello, but decided against it. Somehow it just felt wrong.

The service was just minutes from starting when Myles Lott approached Belinda. She managed to dodge him by ducking behind her mother and slipping into the pew. Once settled, she reached for a hymnal and pretended to be reading it. Surely the man wouldn't bother her in church with her nose in a hymnal.

He paused at the end of her row and gave her a glance but didn't say a word. Oh, she knew he wanted to. The somber schoolmaster probably wanted to know why she hadn't fetched a second potential bride for him. To be honest, she didn't feel like it. In fact, she didn't feel like pairing up anyone these days. She felt rather deflated whenever she thought of it, in fact. The fun had all frittered away. Sure, the town was filled with happy couples, but it seemed there were more discontent than content. She had no idea how to fix this.

A few minutes into the service, the back door of the church opened and Peter Conrad slipped inside. Funny, he was never late. Funnier still, he made his way up the aisle and settled into an empty seat next to Sarah Jo, who beamed like a Cheshire cat.

Belinda swallowed her astonishment and focused on the reverend, who asked the congregation to open their Bibles to the story of Isaac and Rebecca. She hadn't thought about that story in ages. She listened with interest as he talked about the emotional needs in Isaac's life after losing his mother and how Rebecca had entered his life at just the right time. Funny, she'd never thought about that before. But God's timing was always perfect.

Hmm. Perhaps that warranted a bit more thought. If one got ahead of God, did it interrupt His perfect timing? And if one lagged behind, did it throw the Almighty off course? She pondered these things as the message continued, even spending some time in prayer about it as the congregation prepared to sing the final hymn.

Afterward, the reverend got everyone's attention. "We'll be having another wedding in a few minutes, as most of you are aware. Samuel Bromstead and Ella Hanson have invited all of you to stay and join them for their nuptials on the church lawn."

Another wedding. Instead of celebrating the fact, Belinda found herself feeling a bit apathetic. Oh, she was happy for the bride and groom, of course. And happier still that she'd somehow played a role in bringing them together. But every time she thought about weddings, she pictured Adeline and Georg and wondered what their big day would be like. Would Adeline carry wildflowers or roses? Would she wear a new dress? If so, what would it look like? Would Georg's eyes pop as he saw her marching down the aisle?

With a sigh, Belinda focused on Samuel and Ella. There would be plenty of time to think about Georg and Adeline later. If she chose to think of them at all.

* * *

Georg watched the marriage of Samuel Bromstead and the widow Hanson with a smile, wondering what was going through Belinda's mind. Surely she was responsible for this match. No one else had quite believed it when she suggested the two start courting, but they did indeed seem to be well suited.

And speaking of people being well suited, Georg looked around for Belinda. He could hardly wait to get her take on the latest debacle. Cassie and Doc Klein appeared to be interested in each other, much to John Ogilvie's chagrin.

"Is everything all right?" Adeline asked, taking Georg by the arm.

"Oh, yes. I'm just looking for..." He glanced through the crowd. "Looking for someone."

"Oh?" Adeline stared into his eyes, and he practically melted. What was it about this woman?

Just then, Belinda happened by. She looked his way, but as their eyes met, she shifted her gaze. Strange. Georg lifted his hand to wave at her, but she quickly ducked through the crowd and headed off to the far side of the lawn. If he didn't know any better, he would say she was avoiding him. But why? Had he done something to hurt her feelings?

The thought of hurting Belinda struck a deep chord. He could hardly bear the thought of injuring her in any way. "You should sit awhile," he said to Adeline. "Would you like me to fetch a glass of punch? I hear it's quite good."

"Yes, please." She opened her parasol and held it over her head to block the sun. "I would be grateful, Georg. And I do believe I will sit. The heat is bothering me." She looked at him with a warm smile. "Not that I'm opposed to the heat, mind you. It's just going to take some getting used to. Boston is already facing autumn's chill, you know."

"I understand." After getting her settled into a lawn chair near his mother, Georg went in search of punch. He went in search of something else, too. He had to find Belinda, had to get to the bottom of this. If he had hurt her, he needed to make it right. Somehow.

Off in the distance, he saw her talking to John and Greta. Perfect. He could slip through the crowd and get to her just in time....

No, just as she saw him coming, she slipped away, heading off to talk to Doc Klein and Cassie. Georg paused to talk to Greta, hoping she would offer a hint about Belinda's strange behavior. Unfortunately, he found Greta and John engaged in an eye-to-eye chat about heartbreak. Unwilling to interfere, he backed off and continued his search for Belinda.

"Ah. There she is." She glanced up and met his gaze. For a moment, he saw a hint of sadness in her eyes. He waved and then took a few steps in her direction. For whatever reason, she hiked her skirt to her ankles and began to sprint in the opposite direction.

Georg stopped in his tracks. No point in pursuing her if she didn't want to talk to him. But what had he done to warrant such unusual behavior?

"Everything all right, son?"

Georg turned when he heard his father's gentle voice.

"Oh, yes, sir. I..." His voice trailed off.

"I understand you've gone in search of punch for the ladies." His father gave him a curious look. "Mighty odd, since the punch bowl is on the opposite side of the church lawn."

"Oh, yes. Well, I was just trying to..." Again his words failed him. Georg gave his father a wistful look, hoping he would let it go. Fortunately, his father simply nodded and patted him on the back.

"You know, son, I've learned that some things are worth waiting for."

"Sir?"

"It's kind of like a cup of cold punch on a hot afternoon. The longer you have to wait for it, the more satisfying it is to finally get it. If you get my meaning."

Though he wasn't completely sure, Georg nodded. It would be better not to ask for a full explanation. Still, he couldn't help but wonder if his father had somehow seen right through his skin into his very heart. How else could he know that Georg had been waiting not for Adeline, but for Belinda Bauer?

Turning in the direction of the punch bowl, Georg forced a smile. Suddenly, a cup of cold punch sounded mighty good.

Chapter Eighteen

....

Belinda spent much of Sunday afternoon dodging Georg Kaufman. If she stopped to talk to him, her heart would surely give her away, and that would never do. Not now, with Georg and Adeline so happily matched. She managed to chat with everyone in the congregation, bouncing her way from one spot on the church lawn to another. Finally, when exhaustion settled in, she decided to sneak into the church for a few minutes of peace and quiet.

Once inside, she settled into the back pew and reached for a hymnal. As always, the words of the songs brought comfort. She searched from page to page until she found exactly the right one, a hymn by Horatio Spafford—one of her favorites. She hummed as she read the familiar words.

> *When peace, like a river, attendeth my way,*
> *When sorrows like sea billows roll;*
> *Whatever my lot, Thou has taught me to say,*
> *It is well, it is well, with my soul.*

A noise at the back door startled her, and she dropped the hymnbook. In that moment, Georg slipped into the pew beside her.

"I've been looking for you."

"O–oh?" She looked his way only for a second and then scrambled to pick up the hymnal, her hands trembling.

"Belinda, I've done something to hurt you. You've got to tell me what it is so I can make it right."

"Hurt me?" She lifted the hymnal and put it back into its spot on the back of the pew. "Whatever do you mean?"

"Belinda." He reached to take her hand. "Please."

She closed her eyes and squeezed back the tears that threatened to erupt.

"You're trembling."

"I am?"

"Yes." He gazed into her eyes. "Something has happened."

She managed a nod.

"Something to do with me, or are you just upset about the way things are going with John and Cassie?"

Oh, if only she didn't have to answer that question! If only she could avoid it altogether. After a lingering pause, she whispered, "Well, I am sorry to hear that Cassie broke John's heart, to be sure. And I'm concerned about how I can make this right. But, beyond that..." Her heart thumped in her ears as she tried to work up the courage to tell him what was really bothering her.

She never had a chance to finish. The back door of the church swung open and Sarah Jo entered with Adeline on her arm.

"Well, there you are!" Adeline said, as she saw Georg. "I was getting worried."

"Poor thing couldn't find you, so I told her I'd help her look." Sarah Jo glanced at Belinda, then back at Georg, clearly unsure of what to do next. "Well, I will leave you to your own devices, then. Er, I'll leave you alone." She headed out the door, leaving Adeline standing in the aisle of the church.

"Do—do you need me to leave?" she asked.

"No." Belinda rose and scooted past Georg. "We were just finishing up. Georg and I..." She wasn't sure what to say next, so instead she darted out the back door and ran toward home as fast as her legs could carry her.

* * *

Georg had a hard time sleeping on Sunday night. He rose from his bed around one in the morning and slipped on his shoes, convinced that a walk outside would settle his troubled thoughts. All day long he had wrestled with the Lord over what had happened with Belinda in the church earlier today. She'd started to tell him something, but what?

On top of this, Georg still found himself struggling over something else, too—his feelings toward Adeline Rose, or lack thereof. She was a remarkable woman, to be sure. And she'd been mighty patient with him these past couple of weeks, likely waiting for him to state his intentions. Oh, if only he knew what they were, then he would voice them. Until then, it made more sense to say nothing, even if his lack of response troubled her.

Georg grabbed a lantern and headed outside, deep in thought. He went to the one place he always found solace when troubled— the barn. His family didn't own much of a farm, just a few acres and a couple of dairy cows, but he always managed to find the barn a place to voice his thoughts to the Lord. And the cows. Daisy and Milly didn't seem to mind. They always heard him out without complaint. Surely tonight would be no different.

Georg eased his way across the yard, careful not to wake his parents. Unfortunately, Buster, the family's coonhound, got spooked and let out a howl. Georg quieted him right away then kept walking. "C'mon, boy," he whispered. "We've got some business to do."

He entered the barn and hung the lantern, his eyes adjusting to the space. Then he began to pace, as always. His mind went several directions at once, but he finally managed to collect his thoughts into a sensible prayer.

"Lord, I don't want to get ahead of You. You know me, Lord. I'm sensible. Practical. I'm not the sort to jump ahead of the pack. I'm more calculated than that."

Suddenly the barn door swung open and a voice rang out. "Son, do you mind if I ask what you're doing out here in the middle of the night?"

Surprised, Georg turned to face his father, who stood in the doorway bleary-eyed with a lantern in hand and his thin wisps of hair askew. "I'm sorry I woke you," Georg said. "I've just got a lot on my mind and needed to clear my head."

"Female troubles?" Thomas Kaufman asked, taking a seat on a bale of hay and running his fingers through his hair to tame it.

"I guess you could call it that." Georg sat next to him with a shrug. "Strange how I lived my whole life without giving much thought to women, and now..."

"Now you're having to give the fairer sex some thought?" His father laughed. "Son, let me tell you something. They're worth giving thought to. In fact, the more thoughtful you are about any decisions you might make, the better. I've known many a man to marry impulsively and then regret it later. I would only ask that you move thoughtfully and carefully."

"I am. No doubt about that. I just have to wonder if I'm ready to marry at all."

"Well, I can tell you from experience—having married the best woman in the world—that getting the right one is the key thing. To be mismatched while courting is one thing. To be mismatched for fifty years as husband and wife is another altogether. I've known a few of those couples in my day. Not a pretty picture, for any involved."

"So you think Adeline and I are mismatched?" Georg asked. "You can be honest with me. I'd be grateful."

His father paused before responding. "I'm not saying that. It's not my place. I'm simply saying that you don't need to rush into a decision because you're feeling pressured in some way. It's better to take your time and choose wisely than to act impulsively and find yourself married to someone before you're sure it's *God's* someone. Does that make sense?"

"Perfect sense." Georg rose and began to pace once more. "I just don't want to lead Adeline on if I'm not going to ask her to be my wife. That would be cruel."

"You're not leading her on. You're getting to know her. There's a difference. And who knows... She could very well turn out to be God's best for you. So don't discount the possibility." His father paused. "On the other hand, my heart tells me that you're torn because you are interested in someone else. Am I right about that?"

Georg groaned. "I didn't mean for this to happen. To be honest, I didn't even know until recently that I was—" He stopped short of saying "in love with Belinda."

His father gave him a sympathetic look. "Son, the Lord knows your heart. And He alone knows the future. You can trust Him with this."

Georg continued to pace. "Adeline is a wonderful young woman. She's come such a great distance and has plans for the future. She also has a younger sister who needs a home. A good home. I could give them that. I would build her a house by the creek, and we could live out our days there together."

"Live them out as a match made in heaven, or live them out as a match conceived on earth?" His father's voice was gentle but firm.

Georg had no answer for that one. The match had been conceived on earth, no doubt about that. And conceived by someone who... Georg sighed as he thought about Belinda. Conceived by someone with the kindest, sweetest heart of anyone he'd ever known. Someone who still caused his heart to flip whenever she walked in the room. Someone who had taken a piece of his heart with him when she fled from the church earlier in the day.

He sighed, trying to make sense of it all. Maybe he'd better wait before declaring his intentions to Adeline. Looked like he had a little more thinking to do before then.

"I'm just saying to pray it through before deciding." His father rose and stretched then reached for his lantern. "That's the only way to know for sure."

"That's what I'm doing in the barn at one in the morning."

"Well then, I'll leave you to it." He slapped Georg on the back. "You're a good man, Georg. You come from a long line of good men. And you will do the right thing, no doubt about that. Just listen to the voice of the Lord, and don't take a step until He's given the word."

"Yes, sir."

Georg spent the next half hour praying things through then sat on the bale of hay and waited. For what, he wasn't sure. For the Lord to speak in an audible voice? For the jumbled thoughts in his head to cease? For his twisted heart to rest easy?

After some time, he drew in a deep breath and released it, finally ready to head back to the house. Really, there was only one sensible thing to do. Stay the course. Pray it through, day by day, minute by minute. The Lord had an answer, and it would surely come. Georg decided he was willing to wait, even if waiting meant causing discomfort between himself and Adeline. It would be better, as his father had said, to hurt her feelings than to marry her if she wasn't the one God had for him.

With a heavy heart, Georg made his way back to the house. Once there, he tumbled into bed and fell into a deep sleep.

1904

Chapter Nineteen
....

Monday morning seemed to come earlier than usual. Belinda arose feeling exhausted and somewhat frustrated. She needed to get to the mercantile and look through the newspapers for someone for John Ogilvie. And quickly, before the man turned on her and demanded his money back. Her finances were strapped enough already, what with having to pay for Rebecca's train ticket.

She'd barely made it through the doors of the store when Mayor Mueller met her there. He stammered all over himself as he explained the reason for his visit.

"I, um...well, I've been watching all of these marital conundrums with interest, Belinda."

"Oh?"

"Yes, well, see, I am widowed myself, as you are aware, I'm sure."

"Of course." Belinda had known his wife as a child, but she'd been gone for so many years now that the memories were foggy.

"I thought I'd settled into a life as an old bachelor—like Peter— but seeing all of these happy couples makes me wonder if, perhaps, there might not be another woman out there for me."

"Oh?"

"Here's the truth of it, Belinda," he said with a crooked smile. "I'm itching to be hitched."

"Yes, I have heard that phrase before, to be sure. In fact, I might just embroider it on a sampler and hang it about the door." She swallowed the laughter and reached for the newspaper.

"Now that the opera house is going in and business is booming, I find myself looking for someone to share the joy with. I can think of no better person than a wife. Someone who could help with my many projects and who could spend time with the townspeople when I am otherwise engaged. A helpmeet, as it were."

"Yes, the idea of having someone to share your dreams is a lovely one." Belinda drew in a deep breath, trying to decide what to do. Finally an idea came to her. "Well, then, let's do this together, Mayor. I'm tired of my many mismatches. Let's go through the advertisements as a team and see if we can't find a potential mate. Agreed?"

"Agreed."

"Surely we can find someone to fit the bill."

They spent the next hour doing exactly that, finally settling on an older woman from Maine who longed to live in the South. Her name—Rena—made Belinda smile. She liked Rena even before meeting her and prayed the mayor would, too. Still, she was reluctant to send a letter. Not just yet, anyway. With all that had happened, she needed to pray about it first.

"I am willing to wait, Belinda," the mayor said upon leaving. "Everything in the Lord's time. That's what I always say."

"I agree completely."

After the mayor left, she turned her sights to finding someone for John Ogilvie, just in case. The doctor hadn't yet made any declarations about Cassie, but Belinda could sense it coming and wanted to be ready. After thumbing through several ads, she tossed the paper aside, unable to think clearly. Perhaps finding a bride for John could wait for another day. She rose and walked to the front window, gazing outside. Closing her eyes, she tried to remember what the town was like before all of the women started arriving.

After a while, a voice rang out. "Belinda, what are you doing?"

"Hmm?" She turned away from the window to look at Greta. "What do you mean?"

"You've been standing there for over ten minutes. Who are you staring at?" Greta drew near, squinting to see past the glare. "Ah. I see."

Belinda sighed. So, Georg and Adeline happened to be taking a walk together. So what? It meant nothing to her. She had other things to concern herself with, after all. She peered through the glass, trying to get a better look. What was he doing outside the barbershop in the middle of the day, anyway? Spending so much time with Adeline would eventually hurt his business, if he didn't watch out.

Just then Georg looked her way, and she ducked, not wanting to be seen.

"Greta, hand me a rag, will you?" Belinda turned to her cousin, an idea settling in. She took the proffered rag and pretended to be cleaning the glass. That way no one would question why she happened to be standing at the window for so long.

Before long, she realized the window actually was dirty and took to cleaning it with a vengeance. Somehow hard work eased her anxious heart. It did not, however, prevent Adeline and Georg from walking directly in front of the store. When they reached the spot opposite the glass from her, Adeline gave a little wave, which Belinda returned out of politeness. She then marched across the store and into the back room, where she plopped down on one of the barrels and battled her emotions.

After a few moments, Greta joined her. "Are you all right, Belinda? I'm worried about you. So is Mama."

"I'm sure I will be fine. I don't know why, but I have a tightness in my throat today. Maybe I'm coming down with something. Doc Klein says there have been a couple of cases of influenza in Terrell this week. Maybe I'm getting sick."

"Mm-hmm."

"What?" She rubbed at the back of her neck, ready to be rid of the headache that now consumed her.

"Oh, nothing." Greta took a seat near her. "I can see that you're not well, but I'm not convinced it has anything to do with your health."

"What do you mean?"

"I've just been concerned about you these past few days. You are not yourself, and that worries me. Your problems are more internal than external, I believe."

"Are you concerned about my work, because—"

"No, no." Greta put her hand up. "It's not that. You always manage to work your way through everything. No, it's your heart I'm concerned about. That and the somber expression on your face this week."

"I'm sure it will pass. I just have a lot on my mind." *To say the least.*

"About Georg and Adeline?"

Belinda sighed. "Perhaps." She looked at her cousin with tears in her eyes. "Oh, I don't know, Greta. Truly, I don't. I wanted to find a wife for Georg because he deserves someone very special. And now I've done it. I've found the perfect woman for him."

"Only you're unhappy with her."

"Who could be unhappy with Adeline? She's very nearly perfect in every conceivable way. I don't blame him for taking to her. And her with him. It's just that..."

"You wish you hadn't done it?" Greta said tenderly. "You wish you could roll time backward and not bring Adeline to Poetry in the first place?"

Another lingering sigh slipped out. "Is that awful, Greta? I'm a terrible girl. What must the Lord think of me? I've somehow been playing with Georg's emotions and didn't even realize it. Till now, I mean."

"So you do have feelings for him."

Belinda grew quiet but slowly nodded her head. "Oh, I try not to, honestly! In the mornings when I see him go into his shop, I try not to think about his kind heart or his dashing smile. And when he comes into the store to fetch supplies, it takes everything within me not to think about his brown eyes and the soothing sound of his voice. When I see him at church on Sunday sitting next to Adeline, I try not to think about how I want to pull out every hair in her head." She clamped a hand over her mouth and then pulled it away. "I cannot believe I just said that out loud." She looked around to make sure no one else had heard, releasing a sigh when she realized her secret was safe with her cousin.

Greta erupted in laughter. "Belinda, you're in love with Georg."

"I—I am." She shook her head. "I am in love with Georg. And I'm completely and utterly miserable."

"Oh, but don't you see, this is great news!" Greta sprang to her feet and began to pace the room. "You just have to let him know. The Lord will work out the rest, of course."

"How do I go about that when he's fallen for Adeline? And who am I to compare with such a beauty queen? She's slender and pretty and…have you seen those eyes? She has the prettiest eyes of anyone I've ever seen. And that voice? That Boston accent sways Georg. I can sense it whenever she speaks." The intensity in Belinda's voice increased, and her throat felt tighter and tighter. "Oh, I want to stop her from speaking at all sometimes but don't know how to go about it. Then I realize just how terrible that sounds, and I repent. But my repenting goes out the window when I see them walking arm in arm. Is that terrible? Am *I* terrible?"

"Well, actually—"

Belinda's words sped up, until she was speaking at a frantic pace. "The Bible says that jealousy is a sin. I've honestly tried to repent for what I'm feeling. But I'm not sure these feelings will go away, and that's what scares me most. Not that I even knew I cared about Georg Kaufman till now. I didn't." She groaned. "Oh, maybe I did, but I couldn't admit it to myself. How can I blame myself for something I didn't know? Or didn't know that I knew? Does that make sense?" Belinda finally paused, and tears filled her eyes. "Greta, what if they actually get married and I go on feeling like this for weeks or even months into the future. What then?"

Greta laughed long and loud. "You are so funny, Belinda. And while I'm sure you need to repent for some of your thoughts, you cannot deny what is motivating them. You are in love. You have nothing to be ashamed of. It's perfectly natural."

"I am in love." As Belinda repeated the words, the tears flowed. "But it is hopeless. I'm in love with someone I can't have."

"Let's not be too hasty to say that," Greta said. "You need some time alone with the Lord. Share your heart. He will fix any broken places. Just remember, Belinda, this is something only He can tend to, not you."

"I—I know." Belinda paused, thinking about her cousin's words. "I brought my lunch from home. Would you mind if I went for a walk and ate down by the creek?"

"Of course not. Will you be all right? Do you need me to come with you? I can ask Mama."

"No, I need to handle this on my own. It's not just Georg I'm upset about. It's Rebecca. And Myles Lott. And John Ogilvie. I've hurt so many people."

"In the process of *helping* so many people," Greta was quick to remind her.

"Yes, but does the good outweigh the bad? With so many broken hearts, I have to wonder." She stood and began to pace the room. "Truly, much of this is my own doing. I get myself into so many messes and need to figure a way out of them on my own. Just me and the Lord, I mean."

"I understand." Greta took her hand. "But, Belinda, remember, we all get into messes. You're not alone. Your messes are just more...well, more visible than others."

Belinda shook her head. "I know."

"It's only because you do so much for so many," Greta assured her. "Those who do little for others make few public mistakes. Those who do a lot..."

"Don't say it." Belinda waved her hand in Greta's direction and then reached for her lunch pail. "I will be back in an hour, I promise. In the meantime, if any of the men come in looking for wives, tell them to look for themselves. The newspapers are on my desk."

"I'll do that." Greta nodded. "Now get on out of here. Go spend some time with the Lord."

"That's exactly what I plan to do." With resolve building, Belinda turned toward the door.

* * *

Georg was in the middle of trimming John Ogilvie's mustache when he caught a glimpse of Belinda scurrying past the front window of the barbershop. With razor still in hand, he sprinted to the window. Though it took everything within him not to step outside and call her name, he restrained.

"Um, Georg?" John looked up from the barber's chair. "Did you forget something?"

"Oh, no, I..." He shrugged and walked back over to John. "Sorry about that. Just needed to..."

"Mm-hmm."

"What?" He smeared lather on John's face and started shaving, his emotions now keyed up.

"Ow!" John took his hand and pushed the razor away. "If you're going to kill me, I think I'll ride over to Terrell for a shave from now on."

"Sorry." Georg slowed his pace and used a lighter stroke. "My mind is elsewhere."

"No doubt about that. But would you mind focusing before you hit my jugular vein? I'm a young man. Not quite ready to meet my Maker yet, if you don't mind."

"Sorry." Georg paused and pulled back the razor. He stood there not saying a word, for a good minute or two, working all the while. Perhaps once John left, Georg could have the place to himself, to do a little business with the Lord about what he was feeling.

"So how's it going with that pretty young thing from Boston?" John asked.

"Oh, fine, I guess." Georg thought he saw a woman's reflection in the window and headed that way for another glance outside. Unfortunately, it was just that new woman, Cassie, walking with Doc Klein toward his office. Georg prayed John wouldn't turn his gaze this way and see them together. He'd already had an earful about Cassie Bly today and didn't need to hear any more.

"Everything all right over there?"

Georg quickly returned to John's side, wiping the shaving cream from his face. "Sorry. I have a lot on my mind this afternoon."

"I guess you do." Now clean-faced, John stared at his reflection in the mirror. "I have to tell you, my world was a lot less complicated without women in it."

"Amen to that."

"Why do we try so hard to win them, when they only bring us heartbreak?" John raked his fingers through his hair and sighed. "Not that I'm complaining. Cassie didn't seem like my match, anyway, so it's best that it didn't happen."

"Oh?" Georg sat in the chair next to him and gazed at him intently. "How do you know if someone is the right person for you? I mean, how do you really, really know it?"

"Can't answer that." John shrugged. "I can only tell you that when it's not right, you'll have an uneasy feeling about it. I should've picked up on that uneasiness from the start with Cassie, but I think I was just swept away by how pretty she was. Or *is*, rather. She's a beautiful woman, no doubt about that."

"That she is." Georg glanced out of the window once more,

watching as Cassie and the doctor crossed the street arm in arm. He diverted the conversation. "Well, I must say, the town is now filled with blushing brides and confused grooms."

"To say the least." John rose and pulled off the apron. "But if I'm being honest here, I'd have to say I still want that."

"Want what?"

"Want a blushing bride." John shrugged, and an embarrassed look came over him. "Is that too much to ask?"

"No." Georg shook his head. "It's not too much to ask. And I'm sure God has the perfect woman out there. Perfect for you, I mean. My father once told me that God is in the business of bringing the right woman to the right man. So I suppose sometimes it's just a matter of waiting."

"Yep." John dropped a handful of coins on the counter. "I think you're right. And who knows...maybe I won't have to go very far to find what I've been looking for." He glanced across the street in the direction of Poetic Notions then turned back with a suspicious smile. "Maybe she was right here all along."

The clean-shaven butcher reached for his hat, gave Georg a nod, and headed for the door.

Chapter Twenty

....

Belinda set off from Poetic Notions ready to do business with the
Lord about her aching heart. She carried her lunch pail in one hand
and her heart in the other. At least it felt that way. As she passed
Stanzas, she nodded at Cassie Bly and Doc Klein, seated in the
restaurant. They waved from the other side of the glass. Then, as she
happened upon Rhyme and Reason, she glanced inside and found
Peter arranging books. He nodded in her direction. She happened by
Sonnets and Bonnets, resisting the urge to go inside to look at hats or
to gab with Corabelle, as she was wont to do. No, Belinda had other
things to take care of today, things that could not wait.

She rounded the corner past the lot where the walls were now
going up on the opera house. One day it would stand glorious, but
today it was a reminder of all the changes of late. Though they had
seemed good before, today those changes just felt...wrong.

Belinda made her way south then east, knowing she would feel
better as soon as she landed at the creek. Somehow being near water
always made things right. She thought of Adeline, living in Boston.
Wondered what it would be like to live so near the sea, where the
waves pounded away every trouble. Oh, how wonderful that sounded.
How glorious! If Belinda closed her eyes, she could almost envision the
sound of the waves. Taste the salty seawater. Feel the pull of the tide.

On the other hand, if she kept her eyes open, she might just make
it to the creek in one piece. Stepping off the street, she picked up

speed, eventually kicking up her heels and running. Oh, how many times had she done this as a girl—run all the way home from town. She'd been called a tomboy for it, no doubt, but Belinda didn't care. In fact, she'd rarely given much mind to what others thought of her.

My, how times had changed. These days, she worried nearly every day that folks would think she was off her rocker. *Lord, am I off my rocker?*

Her pace slowed as she neared the creek. By the time she got there, Belinda was breathless and ready to eat. She consumed the sandwich in short order and ate the apple as well. Then she leaned back and closed her eyes, ready to pray. Trying to get her mind still was a different matter altogether.

After a few moments, her troubled thoughts settled, and she rose to her feet, pouring out her heart to the Lord. She told Him how sorry she was for barging into people's lives, and for the pain she'd caused Myles and some of the others. Then she got to the nuts and bolts of her conversation with God: Georg Kaufman.

"Lord, how was I to know? I didn't! I had no idea that I..." Belinda paused. "That I care for him. I'm as surprised as anyone. Maybe more so." She thought about those words a minute, realizing just how true they were. She picked up the pace, her feet now moving in time with her heartbeat. "It's not like I did this on purpose, Lord. I would never hurt him. I don't want to hurt Adeline either, Lord. Oh, but if You could see fit to sending her back to Boston, that would be lovely."

She stopped pacing and exhaled. "I'm sorry, Lord. That's not my business. Of course, I'm the one who brought her here in the first place, so here I go, trying to intrude again. Trying to tell You what to do." She groaned and her mind began to wander. "Oh, maybe You did bring her here on purpose, Lord. I am not clear about all of that yet.

Maybe she's supposed to be here and I'm just not seeing it. Either way, I ask You to show me what to do. I need your help, Lord! More than ever!"

She told the Almighty all of her feelings, good and bad, as she continued to pace. After some time, she settled onto the grass, exhausted. Wrestling with God was taxing, to say the least. And though she hadn't yet heard Him answer in an audible voice, Belinda did feel somewhat better for getting her feelings—her true feelings—out in the open.

She thought once again about that hymn, "It Is Well with My Soul." How could she get to the place where all of this felt well when it clearly was not? The words ran through her mind once again and she gave herself over to them:

> When peace, like a river, attendeth my way,
> When sorrows like sea billows roll;
> Whatever my lot, Thou has taught me to say,
> It is well, it is well, with my soul.

Belinda pondered those words at length, finally ready to let go. Ready to give her heart fully to the Lord, regardless of the outcome. Finally, blissfully, peace fell over her like a comforting cloud. Her anguish seemed to roll away, much like the sea billows in the song. Her mind could rest easy in the words, "It is well with my soul," which she now whispered.

As the anxiety lifted, Belinda grew sleepy. Her eyes drifted closed and she relaxed, drawing in a breath of fresh air. Resting under the shade of her favorite oak, Belinda found herself whispering a prayer for forgiveness.

"Lord, I am so sorry. Truly. I don't want to hurt anyone else, especially not Georg. Or Adeline. She's done nothing to deserve my censure. And she's certainly been through enough pain in her life without experiencing any at my hand. Forgive me, Lord, please. And if I am to marry Georg..." She paused, feeling a smile begin. "If I am to marry Georg, You will have to take care of the details, Lord. Just show me what to do, Father."

Belinda closed her eyes and rested. After some time, she jolted and realized she'd fallen asleep. With a gasp, she sat up, believing it must be well after one o'clock. She scurried back into town, her empty lunch pail clattering at her side as she ran.

Once in town, she headed in the direction of Poetic Notions. However, just as she reached the bookstore, she took note of Georg and Adeline coming out of the restaurant across the street. She quickly darted into Rhyme and Reason to avoid them.

Inside, it took a moment for her eyes to adjust to the dim lighting. She contemplated what she would tell Peter, should he ask why she'd stopped by. Just as quickly, she knew how she would remedy this. She needed a poem. A love poem. One sure to win the heart of the man she loved. Peter wouldn't have to know who it was for. He knew so little of love, anyway, being an old bachelor and all. Still, he knew poetry and would be the best to advise her.

Belinda heard a giggle coming from the back of the store. A suspicious giggle. She stood as still as a mouse, hand clamped over her mouth. Oh, how she wanted to bolt out the door—but at just that moment, Georg and Adeline passed by on the boardwalk, arm in arm. She ducked down to avoid being seen through the glass, her heart thumping madly.

She heard another giggle behind her. Now her curiosity was duly piqued. What in the world was going on here? She heard soft words being spoken and was reminded of the time when she'd stumbled upon Mama and Papa alone in the parlor, whispering words of love to each other. Oh, how embarrassing that had been!

A few seconds later, Belinda recognized a familiar female voice speaking in a soothing tone. "Why, Peter Conrad, I haven't been kissed like that since I was a girl!"

Belinda clamped a hand over her mouth to keep from laughing aloud. Sarah Jo Cummings! A few more giggles erupted and Belinda did her best to reach for the door handle...but in doing so, she managed to drop her lunch pail, which went clattering across the floor. She scrambled down to pick it up, somehow falling flat on her belly, her skirts twisted in a knot.

Peter appeared a few seconds later, staring down at her with a stunned expression on his face. "B–belinda. I, um...I'm so sorry. I didn't hear you come in."

Clearly. "Oh, I, um..." She tried to stand but got twisted up in the fabric. The lunch pail fell once again, making a terrible noise.

"May I help you?" The tips of Peter's ears were as red as could be, and he wore a suspicious smile.

"Oh, no," Belinda said, rising to her feet. "Actually, I just stopped in to..." She looked around the shop, finally noticing a book of poetry by John Keats. "I've been meaning to buy this book for some time now, you see. I've been wearing you out with writing love poems, and I thought the classics might be of help to me. So, would you put this on my account, please?"

"Indeed." He took the book and walked to the register. "Will that be all?"

"Mmm, yes." She nodded, anxious to be on her way.

At that moment, Sarah Jo appeared with an armload of books. She placed them on the front shelf and began to arrange them in a colorful display.

"Well, hello, Belinda," she said with a suspicious smile. "I didn't realize we had a guest. Peter and I were just..." She bit her lip and then said, "Talking about poetry."

"Oh?"

"Yes, I am his apt pupil." Sarah Jo's eyes twinkled merrily.

"Um, yes." The tips of Peter's ears turned even redder, though Belinda hadn't thought that possible. "We were talking about the great Robert Browning and his views on poetry, to be sure."

"And what were his views?" Belinda turned her question to Sarah Jo, who paled.

"Gracious, I can't remember. You tell her, Peter."

He nodded. "Browning said, 'God is the perfect poet.' Truly, only the Lord can compose a life. And he does it in perfect rhyme, perfect meter. His ways are vastly beyond our own."

"Ah. Lovely." Belinda fought to think of how she could escape before making a bigger fool of herself.

Sarah Jo sighed. "Is he not the most brilliant man you have ever met in your life? Peter, I mean. Not Browning."

Belinda couldn't help but smile. "Indeed he is. Not to diminish Browning's intelligence, of course. I've found that all poets are quite witty."

"Truly." Sarah Jo gave Belinda a curious look. "Why did you say you came in again, honey?"

"Oh, to buy this book," Belinda said, trying to keep her voice steady. "It's something I should have purchased ages ago." She began to ramble about the book, and before long her words sounded silly even to her own ears. Still, she dared not speak about what she'd just overheard coming from the back room. Surely her laughter would get the better of her.

"We got a new shipment today," Sarah Jo said, gesturing to the books in front of her with a smile. "So there will be many more to look at once I get these shelved. Thank you for stopping by."

"Y-you're welcome." Belinda stumbled out of the store, wondering how and when Peter and Sarah Jo had finally fallen for one another. Obviously Sarah Jo had known all along, but Peter had not.

Or had he? Maybe his vehement denial of feelings for Sarah Jo was really nothing more than a ruse, a way to convince himself otherwise.

No one could deny the feelings between the two now. And it looked as if Sarah Jo had gone to work for him, filling both his shelves and the empty space in his heart. Would wonders never cease?

"Oh, Lord, this is blissful news!" she whispered to the heavens. "Truly, You are the best poet of all! Thank You so much for accomplishing what only You could accomplish. You knew all along!" No doubt about that, at least now. God brought Sarah Jo all the way to Texas to be with Peter Conrad. The Lord had an amazing sense of humor.

Thinking of happy couples caused Belinda's thoughts to shift to Adeline and Georg. She looked this way and that, making sure they were nowhere in sight, then sprinted up the boardwalk to Poetic Notions. Once inside, she leaned against the wall to catch her breath.

"Belinda, are you all right?" Aunt Hilde drew near, a look of concern on her face. "I was so worried. We were about to send out a posse to search for you."

"I'm fine." Belinda gasped for breath. "I...just...I just had to spend some time alone."

"You look as though you've seen a ghost," Greta said, drawing near. "Has something happened?"

"I'm not sure you would believe me if I told you," Belinda said. "But suffice it to say, Sarah Jo Cummings was, indeed, supposed to come to Poetry, Texas. She is here for a reason, to be sure, and that reason includes both loving and being loved."

"Ah." Aunt Hilde grinned, and her eyes narrowed as she pondered Belinda's statement. "I suspected as much. So, all's well that ends well, then?"

"Apparently so." Belinda walked into the back room and reached for her apron, which she quickly tied around her waist. Could the day possibly get any stranger?

* * *

Georg closed up shop for the day and walked across the street to Rhyme and Reason. He needed to see a man about a poem, and it wouldn't wait.

The door was open, but the shop appeared to be empty. Perhaps Peter was in the back. Or maybe he'd already headed home for the day but had forgotten to lock up the shop.

"Anyone here?" Georg called out. When no one responded, he tried again. "Hello! Anyone here?"

He had just turned to leave when Sarah Jo came from the back room, carrying a stack of books. "Well, hello, Georg. What can I do for you on this fine day?"

He looked at her, a bit startled to see her there with her arms full. Was she purchasing them, perhaps, or had she taken to working in the bookstore? Recovering quickly, he said, "Oh, I'm looking for Peter. I need help with..." He shook his head, not wanting to finish. No point in letting Sarah Jo know what he was up to.

Peter arrived at that moment and nodded in Georg's direction. "Good to see you, Georg. What brings you here this time of day?"

"Actually, I..." Georg shook his head. "I suppose it can wait."

Sarah Jo looked at him thoughtfully, placing the books on the glass case near the register. "No, you two men go right ahead and talk. I need to get back to the hotel, anyway. Cassie and I are going to have dinner together, and I need to freshen up a bit first." She gave Peter a girlish smile and a wave then disappeared out of the door, humming a happy tune.

"So, what can I help you with, Georg?" Peter asked.

Georg reached into his pocket, pulling out the poem he had started weeks ago for Corabelle. "Well, I hope you don't think I'm crazy."

"Impossible. You are one of the most levelheaded men in all of Poetry."

"Hmm." *Debatable.* "I've been working on a love poem, but I can't seem to finish it. I meant to ask for your help with it ages ago, but, well, my situation changed. I no longer needed it."

"And now you do?"

"Perhaps."

"Would you mind if I took a look at it?" Peter asked.

"No, that's why I'm here, in fact," Georg admitted with a shrug. "I need your help."

He handed Peter the poem and listened as his friend read it aloud:

Oh, lady fair
With golden hair
And winsome smile
You've crossed the miles
To meet me here
And now, my dear,
I offer you
My heart so true...

Peter looked up with wrinkled brow. "If you don't mind my asking, who did you write this for?"

"Well, that's just it." Georg sighed, nervous about admitting the truth. "Originally I wrote it for Corabelle. Then I decided to rework it to give to Adeline. I've spent the last two weeks trying to change it up, but nothing sounds right. Now, well, now I'm not so sure a poem is even a good idea. Seems like no matter what I try, the poem just sounds...ridiculous. Like I'm trying too hard."

"Maybe you are. Why don't we go into the back room where we can sit and talk this through?"

"Sounds good." Georg followed Peter until they reached the small office at the rear of the shop. He'd never been back here before and was astounded at the clutter. Everywhere he looked, there were books and more books.

Peter gestured for him to sit and he did, but he had to move several books to accomplish the feat. Once Peter was seated, he read the poem again, this time silently. Afterward, he looked at Georg.

"I'm going to ask you some hard questions, Georg."

"Fine." He took a deep breath and waited.

"You know what the great Anton Chekhov said, don't you, son?"

"Um, no, sir."

"He said, 'Don't tell me the moon is shining; show me the glint.'"

"Ah." Georg scratched his head, trying to make sense of what he'd just heard.

"That's what's missing here," Peter said, shaking his head. "The glint."

Georg had to agree, but he wasn't quite sure what to do about it.

"Talk to me about your feelings for Adeline." Peter looked over at him, lips pursed. "Forget what you've written here. Let's start from scratch. What do you feel when you're with her?"

"Well, I..." He shrugged. "I feel like she's a wonderful person. I really like her a lot."

"Hmm. Not exactly the stuff love poems are made of." Peter rose and paced the crowded room. "When you see her face, what comes to mind? Does it make you think of a Greek statue, perhaps, or maybe the Mona Lisa?"

"Not really," Georg said.

"Some other great work of art, then? Something more abstract?"

Georg shook his head. Though he tried to think creatively, his thoughts were jumbled.

"Let's talk about her hair," Peter said. "What does it put you in mind of?"

"Well, as you can see, I've mentioned her golden hair," Georg said with a shrug. "Do you think I should say something else about it?"

"You've mentioned that it's golden, yes, but you haven't shared what happens to your heart when you see it." Peter shook his head.

LOVE FINDS YOU IN POETRY, TEXAS

"When you see her walking down the lane, does that golden hair inspire you in some way? Does it affect your heart? Are you a better man for having seen it?"

Georg responded with a shrug. "Perhaps if I think on that, something will come to me."

Peter shook his head. "I see a potential problem here, Georg. You're missing the most critical part of the equation."

"O–oh?"

"Yes. The feelings. It is impossible to write a poem without feelings. They are the driving force, in fact."

Georg groaned. "I guess you're right. But what can I do about it? You're good with words, Peter. Surely you can come up with something flattering."

"Flattering, yes, but if the feelings aren't there, the poem will sound stilted. There's nothing I can do to fix a love poem that was never meant to be." Peter sat and folded the paper, passing it back to Georg. "I'm sorry."

"So what do you suggest? A poem from a book? Would that do the trick?"

"Georg, let me ask you a question." Peter stared at him intently. "I hate to ask in such a blunt manner, and it's really none of my business. But do you love Adeline?"

"Well, I'm only just getting to know her. I don't suppose I..." He sighed. "I don't suppose I do, to be completely honest, though the idea of having a woman like that holds some appeal."

"You know, of course, what the great Henry David Thoreau had to say on the subject, do you not?" Peter crossed his arms over his chest, his eyes narrowing.

Georg could feel the sweat on his brow as he responded. "Um, no, actually."

"He said, 'How vain it is to sit down to write when you have not stood up to live.' I do not believe anyone could have said it better. You have not lived what you hope to write. Therefore, you should not write it. You don't even know your own feelings. Or the lack thereof." Peter shook his head, clearly frustrated.

"But how do I know what I'm feeling, anyway?" Georg asked with a sigh. "I've never been very good with words on paper."

" 'Put the argument into a concrete shape, into an image, some hard phrase, round and solid as a ball, which they can see and handle and carry home with them, and the cause is half won.' "

"I beg your pardon?" Georg looked at him, confused.

"Those were the words of the great Ralph Waldo Emerson. Writing a poem is the equivalent of putting your argument—what you're trying to say—into concrete form. That way, people—in this case, Adeline—can see it, taste it, feel it. Does that makes sense?"

"Oh, sure. Well, why didn't you just say so?"

After a brief pause, Peter gave him a pensive look. "As long as we're being completely honest, let's steer this ship in a different direction. Let's use Belinda Bauer as an example."

"Belinda?" Her name caught in Georg's throat.

"Yes." A hint of a smile crossed Peter's face. He took out a clean sheet of paper and reached for a pen. "Now, tell me what you think when you see Belinda coming into the mercantile each morning."

"Well, if I must."

"Just as a demonstration, you understand." Peter stared at him intently.

"Fine." Georg raked his fingers through his hair. "Well, my heart doesn't seem to beat right until I see her. I find myself standing out on the front porch, scrubbing bugs off the window, just so I can catch a glimpse of her. Does that sound crazy?"

"Maybe. But crazy isn't necessarily a bad thing where poets are concerned." Peter scribbled a few words. "And then? What about when she walks into the room? When you see her for the first time face-to-face?"

"Oh, that's easy." Georg nodded. "The rhythm of my heart comes back into alignment. I can breathe again. It's almost like she brings order to my life."

"Could you be more specific?"

Georg closed his eyes and tried to picture it. "I think it's her smile. Her smile lights up the place and strengthens me, especially on days when I'm down. And there's something about the sound of her voice that puts one in mind of angels singing. There's really no way to describe it accurately without sounding ridiculous."

"Let me be the judge of that." Peter scribbled a few more words. "Now, tell me about her hair."

"Her hair?" Georg grinned, leaning back in his chair. "To be honest, it has plagued me since she was a girl."

"Plagued you?"

"Yes. Those long pigtails were always such a temptation. I can't tell you how many times they tormented me."

"Oh?" Peter wrote something down then looked over at him. "How so?"

"When I sat behind her in class, I wanted to dip them in the inkwell." Georg laughed. "I reached for them at least a hundred times but never could go through with it."

"Why not?"

"Because I knew it would hurt her feelings, and I couldn't do that." Why, just the thought of hurting her brought pain. "Sometimes I sat on my hands just to avoid the temptation. Isn't that ridiculous? But I could never hurt her. Never."

"Mm-hmm." Peter scribbled something else. "And why is that?"

"Well, because she was my friend. *Is* my friend." Georg shook his head, now overcome with emotions. "That's not completely true. We're not friends these days, and frankly, I don't know what to do about it. I think maybe I've lost her friendship."

"How does the idea of losing it affect you?" Peter asked.

"It's killing me, if you want the truth of it. Every day I go without speaking to her, I feel like I'm losing air. If I go any length of time like this, I'm going to shrivel up and..."

"And die?" Peter gazed into his eyes.

"Sounds overly dramatic, but yes." Georg rose and began to pace. "Can we go back to her hair for a minute?"

"Of course."

"When I see those loose wisps around her face, I see a woman who is so concerned about the needs of others that personal vanity is swept aside. She cares more about others than fussing. Not that her hair doesn't look nice. On the contrary, there are times when the sun picks up three different colors in the strands of her hair."

"Is that so?"

"Yes. I've never seen such a beautiful contrast of colors. If you look closely, you'll find strands of deep gold and soft yellow. There are even tiny slivers of brown running throughout. In the summertime, the lighter colors are even more pronounced. They remind me of the wheat in Samuel Bromstead's fields."

Peter continued to scribble. "And if you had to describe her personality, what would you say?"

Georg paused and smiled. "That she could win over a total stranger with her enthusiasm for life and for people. That her outgoing nature is like a church bell on Sunday morning, calling people to service. That, at times, her heart is an open book begging to be read, and at other times, she is a mystery novel pleading to be solved. And that I could go on reading that book for years and probably still not scratch the surface of who she is, because there is such depth to her."

Peter scribbled a few more words then looked over at Georg, his eyes narrowing into slits. "You've given me the foundation for a beautiful poem, Georg." He folded the piece of paper and put it into his coat pocket. "I will work on it over the next few days." He paused then looked into Georg's eyes. "Just one thing."

"Yes?"

"Promise me you will give it to the right person when the time comes. This is a piece of your heart, after all. You don't want to be dishonest."

Georg managed a nod but couldn't speak a word. He couldn't get past the images of Belinda he'd just painted with his words. Her face. Her smile. Her hair. Her personality. Coming up with fodder for a love poem came easily as long as he focused on her. Perhaps that was because having Belinda in his life kept everything in a steady flow, in perfect rhyme.

Without her...well, without her, everything was off-kilter.

Georg rose and shook Peter's hand. "I can't thank you enough. I daresay this poetry lesson was as enlightening as a sermon. Maybe more so. You've helped me put things into perspective."

"That's what poets do, Georg," Peter said, gripping his hand. "That's what poets do."

Chapter Twenty-one

....

Belinda and Greta closed up shop later than usual that day. After all of the chaotic events that had taken place, it took a bit longer to get back into the swing of things. And with more folks in town these days, the shop stayed filled with customers until the CLOSED sign went up.

Afterward, Belinda got busy sweeping up and organizing the back room. She owed Greta and Aunt Hilde that much, considering her disappearing act earlier in the day. As she gave the store one last glance, something caught her eye. Or rather, *someone* caught her eye: John Ogilvie, on the other side of the glass, peering through.

She opened the door and called out to him. "Something I can do for you, John?"

"Oh, no." He shrugged then took a few steps in her direction. "Just killing time."

"I see." She paused, wondering if, perhaps, he was lonely. "I did a bit of looking for another bride for you, John. Haven't found anyone just yet. I do hope you will forgive me for the mess I've made of things. I certainly never meant to hurt you in any way. I hope you know that."

"Don't worry about it." He gave her a funny look, one she could not interpret. "In fact, it's very likely I won't need you to search for anyone at all." Now a smile curled up the corners of his lips, and he gave her a wink. "I do believe the Lord has other ideas. I'm beginning to think I have been searching far and wide when I should have looked a bit closer."

"O–oh?" She drew in a deep breath, unsure of what to do next. Was John Ogilvie making advances? If so, what could she do to dissuade him?

He walked to the window and peered inside, smiling as he saw Greta working. "She's a fine girl, isn't she, Belinda?"

Ah. "Indeed. The finest."

"A man would be someone mighty special to win a girl like that."

"True." Belinda stifled a grin. "Though I daresay, a fair maiden such as Greta could be won if the right man came along."

"You think?" He grinned.

"Perhaps. And I have it on good authority that she loves yellow roses, especially the ones Ella Bromstead is growing in her front garden."

Belinda gave him a nod and then stepped back inside, clamping a hand over her mouth to keep from chuckling. Another peek out the window revealed John sprinting down Main Street. Belinda laughed for a moment and then quickly stifled it, not wanting to draw attention.

Greta gave her a curious look from across the room. "What's happened, Belinda? Something has you tickled. Is Sarah Jo up to her tricks again?"

"No, it's not that. And I'm not really tickled so much. Just have a lot on my mind." Belinda cleared her throat and tried to remain calm. "Greta, something rather odd has been happening of late. I don't know if you've noticed it or not."

"What's that?" Greta looked up from her work with a wrinkled brow. "Something I need to be concerned about?"

"Perhaps." Belinda grinned. "It's John Ogilvie. He's been hanging around the mercantile a suspicious amount of time. Have you not noticed?"

"What? Hmm? Noticed John who?" Greta looked down, her cheeks slightly flushed. "Not sure what you're talking about."

"Mm-hmm. Sure, you're not." Belinda grinned. "Why, Greta! I can't believe you kept this from me. Are you—"

"I'm nothing," Greta responded, turning back to her work. "Nothing whatsoever. Don't have a clue what you're talking about. Let's just stop this before it gets out of hand."

"Methinks she doth protest too much," Belinda said, fighting back a grin.

Greta shrugged. "I cannot control what you are thinking. I can merely say that the man is coming around because he's lonely. He doesn't know what else to do with his time, so he spends it here." She paused and then looked up with tears in her eyes. "Look at me, Belinda. I'm not a pretty girl, and I'm as round as a butterball. What man is going to want me, especially a fellow like John Ogilvie? He's nice-looking. And...trim. I'm anything but."

"Greta!" Belinda gasped. "Don't you ever let me hear you say that again! You are the prettiest girl I know, and your heart is prettier still. If you don't believe that, just ask the Lord. He will convince you that you are created in His image. He doesn't make anything less than perfect."

Greta chuckled and dabbed at her eyes. "All right, all right. I'm just saying that I don't usually turn men's heads. So, if John Ogilvie has his head turned...or if he's spending an exorbitant amount of time at the mercantile, he's probably interested in someone else, not me." She gave Belinda a knowing look.

"Are you saying he's interested in...me?"

"Well, yes," Greta rolled her eyes. "Obviously. It's the only thing that makes sense. I'm surprised you haven't thought of it before now. John isn't the first man to look your way, and he certainly won't be the last." She went off on a tangent, talking about Belinda's assets—her beautiful hair, her contagious smile, her curvy physique. After several moments, Belinda interrupted.

"Greta, have you ever heard the term 'poetic justice'?"

"I believe so." Her cousin shrugged. "Why?"

"In every great, classic story—the really good ones, anyway— good is ultimately rewarded and vice is punished."

"Right." Greta nodded. "What does this have to do with anything? I'm not following you."

"You are the finest person I know, and you will be rewarded in the greatest of ways. That is how poetic justice works, both in literature and in real life."

"I cannot deny that I am ready for something wonderful to happen," Greta said with a smile. "Though I would hardly call it poetic justice. If anyone deserves her happily-ever-after, it's you."

"Thank you." Belinda smiled. "I hope you're right, though I'm not sure I need to be rewarded for anything."

"Well, of course you do. Look at all the happy couples who have benefitted from your services."

Belinda chuckled. "All right, all right. I am happy they are all so happy." She sighed. And I suppose, for the first time in my life, I'm ready to admit that I would like to be married, too. I do not claim to know how the Lord will accomplish this, only that He will...in His time and His way."

In that moment, something served to distract them both. Belinda looked up and smiled, noticing John Ogilvie, who stood several feet in front of them with a fistful of yellow roses in his hand.

"This is not about me, Greta," Belinda whispered. "I daresay, a certain man is not headed *my* way with those flowers; he's coming straight to you."

"Oh my goodness." Greta fussed with her hair then turned to Belinda with a frantic look in her eye. "He really is, isn't he?"

"Mm-hmm."

"What do I say to him?"

"Oh, I'm sure you'll come up with something. Just speak your heart."

Belinda headed to the other side of the store to give John and Greta some privacy but kept a watchful eye on them, all the same. Her heart was so broken after her cousin's emotional outburst that she hardly knew how to respond. Did Greta really see herself as unlovable? Did she think there were no men out there for her? And why would she compare herself to Belinda? Had she fretted over these comparisons for long?

For whatever reason, thinking about Greta's love life reminded her of Georg. Thinking about Georg caused tears to rise in her eyes. Oh, what she wouldn't give for Georg to come marching through the door of Poetic Notions with flowers in his hand...for her. She would dab on a whole bottle of lemon verbena to draw him in, if that's what it took.

No, she wouldn't, either. She would sit back and wait. And wait. And pray. And do absolutely nothing unless the Lord instructed. If she'd learned anything at all over the past few months, it was this: walk at least one pace behind the Almighty, never in front. With that formula firmly in place, all would be well. Where He led, she would go.

And if He didn't...well, she didn't want to think about that.

* * *

Georg's heart grew heavier with each step away from Rhyme and Reason. *I can put this off no longer. I know what I have to do.* The Lord had spoken very clearly through Peter, though in a roundabout sort of way. Georg now had his answer. He did not love Adeline. Never had and never would. And he could not marry her. To do so would be deceptive. Perhaps Belinda would never care for him the way he cared for her, but marrying the wrong woman would not make that situation any better. And it would not honor God. No, there was only one thing to do now. He had to let Adeline know—and the sooner, the better.

He thought about what his father had said that night in the barn, about how it would be better to walk through a bad courtship than a bad marriage. How many people married only to discover they did not love the person after the fact? Well, he was not going to be one of them. Georg could not marry a woman he didn't love, and he could not be convinced to love Adeline when he did not. And no matter how hard he prayed, the Lord would not deliberately send him into the arms of the wrong woman.

True, from all external appearances, they were perfect for one another. And they even shared a like faith, something critical to a couple's survival. Still, when he gazed into her eyes, he didn't get that gripping feeling in his heart that he expected to have. He didn't wake every morning thinking only of her. He didn't fall asleep every night with her name on his lips.

In short, he didn't love her. Oh, maybe he could learn to, in time. He was certainly attracted to her, after all. But love? No, love was something so much deeper. Love was what he felt for Belinda Bauer, and it couldn't be traded for anything in the world. In fact, he wanted to share his heart with anyone and everyone who would listen. He wanted to stop the stranger passing by and tell him about Belinda's blue eyes. He wanted to climb to the rooftop at Stanzas and holler his feelings to the masses. In short, he wanted to make his feelings known, regardless of the cost. For only in making them known would he be completely honest...with himself and with Belinda.

The things he'd just said to Peter now stared him in the face. He was in love with Belinda, and there would be no turning back. Every step would be calculated and carefully prayed through. Surely the Lord had his future planned out. *I know I can trust You, Lord.*

As he drew near the school, Georg caught sight of Myles Lott on the front steps with an armload of books. He called out to him. "Myles? Need some help with those?"

Myles looked up. "Actually, yes. I saw you coming and decided to bring them out to you."

Georg laughed. "My learning days are over, Myles. At least, classroom learning."

"Oh, the books aren't for you." The schoolmaster smiled. "I've been putting together the books and lessons Adeline's younger sister will need when she arrives. I thought it might be wise to go ahead and get these to Adeline now so that she can tutor Catherine as soon as she gets here. The earlier, the better; otherwise, the child will lag behind the other students. She will feel out of place."

"Ah, I see." Georg stopped cold. "Well, about Catherine..."

"Yes?"

Georg sighed. "Myles, I'm not altogether sure she will be coming after all. In fact, if I had to guess, I would say it's not going to happen."

"Really?" To his credit, Myles didn't ask any questions. However, Georg could see the curiosity etched in his brow.

"Yes. I, um...well, I have not yet declared my intentions to Adeline," Georg said. "And, in fact—"

"Oh, I spoke with Adeline just this morning," Myles said with a perplexed look on his face. "So don't fret over that. She has told me that Catherine is to arrive Friday on the train, just in time for the camp meeting this weekend. She knew you would be thrilled to meet her. She will start class the following Monday."

"W–what?"

"Apparently she's been quite lonely for her sister. I don't blame her. I'm sure it's difficult to be apart. So Adeline sent for Catherine and the governess. They will arrive on Friday, as I said. At that point, the governess will stay a few days to freshen up before returning to Boston."

"And Adeline?"

"Well, I assume she will stay on with her sister and...well, marry. Isn't that the idea?"

When Georg responded with a sigh, Myles placed the stack of books on the railing and turned to face him. "I sense a problem, Georg."

"Yes, a large one." Georg shook his head, unsure of what to say next. "To be quite honest, I have decided not to..." He raked his fingers through his hair. "Oh dear. I can't do it, Myles. I can't marry her. It would be deceptive. I'm not in love with her."

"Georg, I'm sorry." Myles paled. "I feel as if I'm somewhat to blame. I told Adeline that Catherine would fall behind if we didn't get her into the classroom in short order. It's so difficult for a child to get caught up when they miss the first month or two of school. But I never dreamed this would happen."

"It's fine." Georg reached over and took the books, his heart heavy. "Sooner or later I'm going to have to tell her. I—I can't marry her, Myles. It would be wrong."

"Well, let's do this..." Myles took the books from him, offering up a sympathetic look. "You just go on home and pray about how you're going to do that. I will take the books and talk with her as if everything were moving forward as planned. The Lord will show you what to do. You're a good man, Georg, and you will do the right thing."

"Yes. Though I've often wondered why the right thing to do is usually the hardest thing to do." Georg sighed. "But go ahead. Take the books to Adeline. I plan to talk with her this weekend, anyway. And it sounds like Catherine is already on her way, so nothing I could say at this time would change that."

"True." Myles pursed his lips and released a sigh. "If I've learned anything over the past few weeks, it is this: life is filled with hard choices. And some of them can have disastrous results. To marry the wrong person..." He shook his head. "To do so would be a crime against the heart."

Georg nodded. So Myles had recovered from his near miss with Marta Schuller. Perhaps he wasn't as embittered as folks thought. In fact, he looked downright peaceful about the whole thing.

Then again, people who followed the leading of the Spirit usually had peaceful looks on their faces, didn't they? Georg smiled, realizing just how true that was. No matter how difficult, he would follow the leading of the Lord. He would tell Adeline the truth. Somehow... someway...God would honor it. And peace would surely follow.

1904

Chapter Twenty-two
....

The following Saturday, people came from all over Kaufman County for the annual camp meeting. Folks arrived in wagons, in buggies, and even on horseback to set up camp for the big event.

This was always Belinda's favorite time of year, one she looked forward to. It was so nice to see folks from the various churches—Baptist, Presbyterian, Methodist, and so on—come together, laying all differences aside. Women, men, and children converged upon Poetry, ready to meet the Lord in a new and different way. He never failed to disappoint! Year after year, as believers met together, the Spirit of the Lord fell on the group. Tears. Repentance. Joy. Followers could find a little of everything at the camp meeting, and all of it straight from heaven. Truly, Belinda found these meetings to be among the most invigorating of her life, and she wouldn't trade them for anything.

On Saturday evening, the festivities got underway on the grounds with singing and lots of food. Samuel Bromstead pulled out his fiddle and played a toe-tapping version of "When the Roll Is Called Up Yonder," one of Belinda's favorite hymns. Ella sang out in a voice so pure, Belinda felt closer to heaven than ever. After that, several sang in groups, entertaining the crowd until the sun went down. Belinda sat with her family, of course, paying particular attention to Corabelle, who seemed a bit off-kilter this evening.

"Are you not well, Corabelle?" she asked, growing concerned when her sister-in-law refused to eat.

"Oh, I'm fine. I'm just..." She shook her head then focused on the singer.

Belinda turned to James. "I'm worried about her, James. She hasn't been herself lately."

"Well, perhaps she's overworking herself at the hat shop, then," Belinda's mother said. "I've been concerned that it might be too taxing to care for both a business and a home. I have given my thoughts on this from the beginning, and I won't mention it again after tonight. But I have to wonder if a woman was meant to do so many things at once. Caring for a husband and children was always plenty time-consuming for me."

"Ah. Perhaps you are right." James nodded and gazed tenderly at his wife. "We have given some thought to asking Sarah Jo if she would help out at the shop, provided that she's willing. Corabelle will need to trim back her hours." The corners of his lips curled up, and eventually his whole face lit into a smile.

"Why?" Belinda asked, a hint of suspicion now creeping in. "What is at the root of all this?"

"Oh, well..." Corabelle grinned.

"I'm going to be a father," James said with a twinkle in his eyes.

"Are you sure?" Mama clapped her hands together and let out a squeal.

Corabelle nodded, her cheeks now duly flushed. "Very sure. Went to see Doc Klein yesterday. I was feeling a little under the weather and suspected...well, anyway, my suspicions were true." She giggled. "We're going to have a baby."

Belinda's heart practically sang at the news. "Oh, Corabelle, this is wonderful! I'm going to be an auntie!"

"And I'm going to be a grandmother!" Her mother looked thrilled at the prospect. She leaned Belinda's direction and whispered, "Do I look old enough to be a grandmother?"

"No. Not even close," Belinda whispered in response. In fact, her mother looked finer than most in their late forties.

"Oh, we have to get busy, Belinda. We need to help Corabelle set up the nursery. There are booties to knit, samplers to embroider, little dresses to smock." On and on her mother went, talking about the various things the baby would need.

Corabelle beamed and Belinda watched her, mesmerized. So, they were going to have a child. What would that be like, to discover you were going to have a baby with the person you loved? To nurture and care for that little one together, raising him—or her—to love the Lord and to love their neighbors as well?

Her heart twisted at the very idea. She looked at Corabelle with new eyes, seeing her for the first time not just as a beautiful young woman, not just as James's wife, but as a mother.

"You *are* going to need help at the shop," she said, coming to life. "I wonder if I could cut back on my hours at Poetic Notions so that I could be available to you part-time."

"I doubt Hilde could manage without you these days," Mama said. "Now that the town has grown like wildfire, the mercantile is filled to overflowing most of the time, is it not?"

"Yes." Belinda chewed on that idea. "Asking Sarah Jo is the perfect solution. She's particularly thrilled with the hat shop, so she will likely be tickled with the proposition." She did have to wonder, though, if Sarah Jo would sweep in and take over the place.

Mama rose with a smile on her face. "I'm going to visit with a few friends. Corabelle, do you mind if I share the news, or would you like to do that yourself?"

"Oh, I don't mind a bit." Corabelle offered up a shy smile. "You're going to be a grandma! This is a big moment for you."

"I am! I'm going to be a grandma!" Hannah Bauer scurried through the crowd, stopping to tell folks.

Belinda sat with Corabelle, still thinking about Sonnets and Bonnets. Soon another thought came to mind. "Oh, I know how you can rectify the situation with your store! Cassie Bly! She wants to open a sewing shop, where she will make dresses for the ladies. Why not combine forces? Let her take the empty spot next to Sonnets and Bonnets and open a wall between the two. That way you could have two stores in one. Dresses and hats go hand in hand, after all."

"Wonderful idea!" Corabelle said, looking pleased at the suggestion. "I'm surprised I didn't think of it myself. That is the perfect solution." She paused for a moment and then said, "Of course, I would still need someone to help with my side of the store. Asking Cassie to handle both would be too much in the end. I've given some thought to asking that lovely young woman, Adeline, to help me."

"W–why?" Belinda looked at her, stunned. "I can assure you, she will not be interested."

"Oh?" Corabelle gave her a curious look. "How do you know?"

"She told me all about her plans, and they do not include running a shop. She is quite old-fashioned in that respect." Belinda peered through the crowd until she saw Georg and Adeline seated with his family. "I do not think she will ever merge love and shop-keeping." In that moment, Belinda saw someone unfamiliar sitting next to Adeline. A girl, probably eleven or twelve. A pretty little thing. *Who is that?* She squinted to get a better look. *I don't recognize her.* "Hmm. That must be Adeline's sister over there."

"Oh, yes, it is." Corabelle nodded, a smile now lighting her face. "Have you not met her? Her name is Catherine."

"No. When did she arrive?"

"Just yesterday," Corabelle explained. "Georg and Adeline fetched her from the train depot yesterday afternoon. She will start school on Monday, I hear."

In that moment, Belinda's heart sank to her toes. "So, it's true. Adeline is staying."

"Well, of course." A look of concern came over Corabelle at once. "Does this trouble you?"

Belinda pushed aside the tears that threatened to rise and turned her head. Oh, if only she could speak the truth. If only she could tell Corabelle all of the reasons why she'd secretly hoped Adeline and Georg would sever their relationship.

She happened to glance across the campgrounds and caught a glimpse of Georg passing a cup of cider to Adeline. The beautiful young woman looked up at him with such tenderness that Belinda at once felt overcome, both with jealousy and guilt.

Lord, forgive me. I can't let my mind wander like that.

"Oh, Belinda...," Corabelle whispered, drawing near. "I'm sorry. I didn't know."

Belinda shook her head and shushed her sister-in-law at once. No point in alarming James or the others. Her secret would be safe with Corabelle, surely. She strained to see through the crowd, to see Georg's face. She had to know what he was thinking about Adeline's sister coming to Poetry. Did the idea of settling in with a ready-made family excite him? Had he forgotten all about his friendship with Belinda? Moved on to greener pastures?

Obviously he had made his intentions known to Adeline; otherwise her little sister would not be here. With those intentions clearly stated, Belinda could not now—nor ever—bother with wondering what he might be thinking or feeling. It simply wasn't her business. And yet... *Lord, I'm going to need Your help with this. I don't know if I can get past this without it. In fact, I know I can't.*

At this point, several fiddlers stood and made their way to the front, where they began to play another rousing hymn. Everyone rose to their feet, clapping their hands and singing along.

Belinda looked out across the crowd, determined to remember why she'd come—not to fret over Georg, but to focus on the Lord. To get His perspective on the details of her life. To hear whatever messages He might speak to her this fine weekend. How could she do that if her thoughts were otherwise engaged?

She drew in a deep breath, intent on listening only to the voice of the Lord, not her overactive imagination. Surely this latest bout with envy was unwarranted. It was just a sudden reaction to the idea—however skewed—that Georg was intended for her. This silliness had lasted long enough. If she wanted to maintain her status as a skilled matchmaker, it was important to see Georg and Adeline succeed as a couple. And surely if the Lord had any matrimonial plans for Belinda, He would reveal them in His own time and in His own way.

Somehow, this revelation lifted a load from her shoulders. She offered up a silent prayer, asking the Lord to forgive her for going so far out of her way to discourage Adeline during those first few days—complaining about the heat, mentioning the insane asylum, and, oh, so much more. These things all seemed so foolish now, but what could she do about it, short of asking the Lord to forgive her?

As the lively music drew to a close, one of the singers from Terrell stood and began to sing one of the great hymns by Fanny Crosby, a melody quite familiar to Belinda. Still, she could not help but draw parallels as the mighty chorus of believers began to sing together:

> *Jesus, keep me near the cross;*
> *there a precious fountain,*
> *free to all, a healing stream,*
> *flows from Calvary's mountain.*

Belinda closed her eyes and listened to each word, thinking about how far she'd wandered from the Lord's leading of late. How she'd gotten ahead of Him on so many occasions during the past few months. Still, He somehow, mercifully, made all things right again, turning her blunders into something beautiful. Weren't Corabelle and James a fine example? And what about the Reverend and Marta Schuller? Weren't Prissy and Charlie Grundy a delightful couple? And who could argue the fact that Bucky and Katie Sue were blissfully in love? Yes, the Lord had certainly taken her messes and straightened them out just fine.

With her heart and mind renewed, Belinda now sang the chorus with great abandon.

> *In the cross, in the cross,*
> *be my glory ever;*
> *till my raptured soul shall find*
> *rest beyond the river.*

That last line, of course, made her think of the hours she'd spent at the edge of the creek, pouring her heart out to the Lord. He alone saw her deepest cries. And He alone knew her recent struggles. How she'd wrestled with her feelings for Georg. How she'd struggled to get past feelings of envy toward Adeline.

Belinda closed her eyes and listened as the next verse was sung.

> *Near the cross, a trembling soul,*
> *love and mercy found me;*
> *there the bright and morning star*
> *sheds its beams around me.*

She whispered a prayer, thanking the Lord for His mercy in her life. Again, her voice rang out, this time louder than before.

> *Near the cross! O Lamb of God,*
> *bring its scenes before me;*
> *help me walk from day to day*
> *with its shadow o'er me.*

The final verse was sung quietly, prayerfully. Belinda kept her eyes closed, still reflecting on the words.

> *Near the cross I'll watch and wait,*
> *hoping, trusting ever,*
> *till I reach the golden strand*
> *just beyond the river.*

As the chorus repeated, Belinda felt like lifting her arms to the skies and turning in circles. Perhaps folks would think her daft, but she didn't care. She'd made such a silly fool of herself already, what did it matter? And here, with the evening shadows falling, no one would be the wiser, anyway. Wasn't that what these camp meetings were all about, anyhow? To encourage followers of the Lord to express their love to Him in a deeper way than before?

There, in the dark, with stars just beginning to twinkle overhead, Belinda knelt on the quilt and poured out her heart to the Lord as never before. Yes, she spoke to him of her wounded heart, but beyond that, she offered herself to Him afresh.

* * *

As the service progressed, Georg wrestled with feelings of guilt. Every time he attempted to tell Adeline that he would not be asking for her hand in marriage, she turned her attentions to her sister. Clearly, his news would devastate her. And yet he could no longer string her along. To do so went against everything he believed, particularly on days like today, when he was gathered with fellow believers to lift up the name of the Lord.

Lord, I have to tell her, but I'm going to need Your help to know how. And when. Give me wisdom, Father.

Georg wrestled with his emotions in part because he hated the idea of hurting Adeline. After all she had faced in her young life— losing her parents, leaving her sister behind for a spell to seek out a new life—he hated to cause her any unnecessary pain.

The musicians took a break so that folks could fellowship. At that moment, Myles Lott appeared. He smiled down at Catherine, who sat on the quilt eating a plateful of food. "So, our new student has arrived at last."

Georg rose to make introductions. "Miss Catherine, this is your new schoolmaster, Mr. Lott."

The youngster looked up with a contented smile. "I've come all the way from Boston, sir," she said politely. "And I'm so excited. I will be there Monday morning with bells on."

Myles nodded. "I look forward to getting to know you." He turned his attention to Adeline. "Would you mind bringing her early? I would like to show her around and administer a brief test to see where to place her. If that doesn't inconvenience you, I mean."

"Of course." Adeline nodded then reached across the blanket to embrace her sister. "I cannot tell you how happy I am to have my baby sister here at last. Our family is complete." She smiled. "Oh, how good that sounds." She looked over at Georg with a shy smile, and his heart lurched.

"I understand there's a new opera house going in," Catherine said, with a bright smile following.

"Indeed," Myles responded. "Do you like to attend the theater?"

"Oh, I do." Her eyes sparkled. "Our parents used to take us all the time. When Adeline told me, I was quite excited." She smiled. "I fancy myself a singer, and I often perform theatricals for my sister to pass the time."

"She is quite good," Adeline added.

"Do you think they will let me audition?" Catherine asked. "I can think of nothing more exciting than to be upon the stage in front of the masses." She spoke the words dramatically, causing all to chuckle.

"No doubt Sarah Jo will put you to work immediately." Myles grinned. "She will give you the starring role and folks will come from all over the county to hear you sing."

"Oh, she has the loveliest voice you ever heard," Adeline chimed in. "Like an angel."

Catherine blushed. "That's a bit of an overstatement, sister." She smiled at Myles. "Though I do love to sing. And to perform."

"Sounds like you were born for the stage." He gave her a nod. "And I can't wait to see you up on that stage."

Georg watched this exchange with great curiosity. Looked like Catherine would fit right in.

Just then Myles looked his way, clearing his throat. "Um, Georg, I wonder if you would allow me the privilege of taking Adeline and Catherine for a walk. Several of my students are here at the camp meeting, and I would like to make introductions. I believe things will go smoother for Catherine on Monday should she get to know her fellow students in advance."

"Of course."

"So your students are all churchgoers?" Adeline asked in a voice sweeter than honey.

"Most of them, anyway." Myles nodded. "And trust me, if anyone needs to hear the gospel message, those little hooligans do." He grinned. "You know, of course, that I'm exaggerating. They're not really hooligans. I love them dearly. Just have to remember that God is still forming them into the people they will one day be."

"Indeed," Georg said. "I believe He's still doing that with me, as well."

Adeline smiled. "Me, too. We are ever growing into the people we are to become." She laughed. "That sounded silly."

"Oh no." Myles shook his head. "On the contrary. I found it to be quite accurate. And I have it on good authority—my mother—that I was a little hooligan once myself. I daresay I grew up all right, though."

"Truly, you did." Adeline's cheeks flushed.

Georg watched the two of them and then extended his hand and helped Adeline rise. After straightening her skirts, she took her sister by the hand and they began to walk with Myles.

"Thank you, Georg," Adeline called back with a smile. "We won't be long, I'm sure." She took Myles's proffered arm, and they set off in search of his students. Georg watched them, grateful for the reprieve.

Just a few feet away, Myles paused to introduce Catherine to one of his students, a rambunctious boy named Bruce. Within minutes, they were all laughing and talking about something that Bruce had done in class last week.

Georg smiled as he looked on, happy to see them fit in so well with those they met. Hopefully everything today would go as smoothly, particularly the part where he shared his heart with Adeline...and told her that he could not marry her.

Something Myles said must have embarrassed Adeline, for she giggled and her gaze shifted to the ground. She was such a pretty young woman—eyes that sparkled merrily whenever she was tickled by something, which seemed to happen a lot. Cheeks that flushed crimson at happy news. Yes, nearly everything about Adeline was perfect...just not for Georg.

As they walked away, he turned to his mother. "Myles has changed a lot since my days in the classroom."

"How so?" she asked, gazing at him with curiosity.

"He's softer now, I believe. I don't mean that in a bad way. He was never harsh. He was just always a little lonely. Kept to himself. Now he seems to have opened himself up to life and to people. I like the transformation I see in him."

"Indeed. He is a very nice man." His mother smiled. "And a wise one, too."

"Oh?"

"Yes." She nodded. "He handled that situation with Marta very well, don't you think? It took a lot of wisdom to realize he had the wrong woman. And a lot of grace to watch her marry someone else. He kept his emotions in check and didn't make a fool of himself, as many would have done."

"Yes." Georg shrugged, not sure where she was headed with this.

"I daresay, a man with wisdom like that could go a long way in life." She gave him a wink and shifted her gaze.

Georg looked at his mother, now catching the meaning of her words. She wasn't talking about Myles Lott anymore. Oh, no. She'd gone to talking about someone else.

Georg smiled. "I have a lot to learn from Myles."

"You've always been an apt pupil." His mother's lips turned up and she gazed into his eyes. "It's never too late for learning, son. Life itself offers many lessons."

"Like now, perhaps?"

She nodded. "Mm-hmm."

"You are a wise woman, Mother, and I appreciate you." He scooted over to sit next to her, wrapping an arm around her shoulder. "Myles Lott isn't the only great teacher in Poetry. Both of my parents seem to do a fine job of it, too."

"Thank you, son," she whispered. She planted a kiss on his cheek.

At this moment, Belinda's mother appeared, her face flushed. "Did you hear our news?" she asked.

"News?" Georg's mother looked up. "No, what is it?"

"I'm going to be a grandmother. James and Corabelle are expecting a baby!"

The two women took to talking, but Georg was distracted. He looked through the crowd until his gaze fell on Belinda, seated next to Corabelle. They were thoroughly engaged in conversation. Then, in a moment too special for words, the throng of people seemed to part just as Belinda looked his way. She gave him a shy smile and a little wave, and his heart leaped into his throat. Both his mother and Belinda looked over at him a few seconds later with knowing looks on their faces. Strange how everyone seemed to be able to read his heart these days.

Then again, it appeared to be an open book. One filled with new and exciting possibilities.

Chapter Twenty-three

....

As the camp meeting progressed, Georg looked around for Adeline. She and Myles had been gone for some time. As the musicians played their final toe-tapping number, they finally appeared, arm in arm, with Catherine at their side.

"Oh, I had such a wonderful time getting to know the children," Adeline said, a look of pure joy on her face.

"I'm glad." Georg rose to greet them.

"I'm sorry that took so long, Georg," Myles said. "Catherine hit it off with Nellie Johnson. Looks like they're going to be fast friends. The girls have much in common."

"Yes," Catherine agreed with a nod. "I think I'm going to like it here." She slipped her arm around her sister's waist and gave her a warm smile. "Thank you so much for bringing me here, Adeline. We're going to have a wonderful new life."

Adeline nodded, and Georg noticed a hint of moisture in her eyes.

"Are you all right?" he whispered.

"Yes." She nodded. "Just thinking about Mama and Papa... wondering what they would have thought of this lovely place. I think my mother would have fit right in with all of the ladies. She always had such a way about her. And Papa..." She dabbed at her eyes. "Well, I daresay he would have been up there with his fiddle, playing with the others. Don't you think, Catherine?"

Her sister nodded and then gave her another tight hug. "This will be a place for new beginnings. I can just feel it!"

"Yes, I agree. It is so fascinating to see what the Lord has done," Adeline said, gazing back and forth between the schoolmaster and Georg. "How He's brought us from halfway across the country to this strange and wonderful new place. I feel a bit like one of the Israelites, crossing over the Jordan into the Promised Land."

"I can see how you might consider Poetry the Promised Land," Myles said, gazing into her eyes intently. "This has been a place where I've found myself again. And a place where people love the Lord and each other."

"Indeed." She gave him a shy smile. "The perfect combination."

Georg watched this exchange, his interest piqued.

"Georg, what did you think of the service?" Myles asked, looking his way.

"I think it was the best by far. Can't wait for tomorrow. It's going to be a wonderful day."

They progressed into a conversation about the upcoming events, but Georg's thoughts had already shifted. He needed to talk to Adeline... alone. Thankfully, Nellie Johnson showed up just then. She, Catherine, and Myles began an excited conversation about the opera house. Before long, they were speculating about the first performance and giggling up a storm. Georg didn't know when he'd ever seen a happier bunch.

"I wonder if I could have a moment of your time, Adeline?" he whispered, drawing near.

"O-oh. Of course." She looked a bit flustered as she responded.

"Could we take a little walk, then?" he asked.

"Certainly." She turned to Catherine. "Would you mind waiting here, sweet girl? I won't be long."

"No, I don't mind." Catherine went back to chatting with Nellie. Georg felt sure the child wouldn't miss them. Not much, anyway.

He and Adeline took a few steps away from the crowd, toward the old cemetery. At first, neither said a word. In spite of his thumping heart, he finally managed an opening line. "Adeline, there's something I need to tell you."

"Really?" She paused and turned to look him in the eye. "There's something I've been needing to talk to you about, too. I've put it off for days, but I can do so no longer."

"Well, then, you go first," he offered.

"No, you." Adeline reached to take his hands, and for the first time he noticed they were trembling.

"Fine." He rose and paced the area, praying for just the right words. How did one go about breaking things off with a girl, anyway? He'd never faced this problem before. "You are a wonderful girl," he said at last. "I've been so blessed to get to know you. Truly, I don't deserve someone like you. You are beautiful inside and out. The love of the Lord radiates from you, and it's clear you love Him and others in the most unselfish way imaginable."

"Why, thank you so much. I'm embarrassed to hear such flattery." She batted those eyelashes again, and he looked away, lest they tempt him.

"Don't be embarrassed," Georg said. "You are truly wonderful. I don't deserve you, to be sure. Though, I must admit that I have been flattered by the very idea that you might one day be mine."

At this point, Adeline began to cry. When he tried to console her, she put her hand up to stop him. "Georg, please. I cannot let you say another word. In good conscience, I cannot."

"W–what?" He stared at her, confused. "Why?"

Adeline began to pace. "Oh, I am so sorry, Georg. So sorry."

"Sorry? About what?"

She shook her head then turned to him with tears streaming down her face. "I'm sorry, but I cannot marry you."

"W–what?" Had she taken his words as a proposal?

"No." She then began to pace, finally stopping and turning his way. "There is no other way to say it than to just say it. I cannot marry you because I have given my heart to another."

"Y–you have?" He shook his head, dumbfounded.

"I didn't mean for it to happen." She drew near, her words now coming quickly. "I fought it at first, especially with the gap in our ages. Oh, but Georg, I've found him to be the most amiable man, suited to me in every respect. He has taken an interest in my sister and in me. Oh, and have you seen his eyes? Are they not the prettiest eyes in town? And his face...is it not the most handsome?" She continued talking about the physical and spiritual attributes of the man she'd fallen head over heels for—only she never mentioned a name.

"Are we, by chance, talking about Myles Lott here?" Georg asked, dumbfounded.

"Yes." She turned to him, her brow wrinkled. "Oh, Georg, I'm sorry. I knew this would be hard to hear. That's why I've put off telling you."

"Has Myles declared himself to you?" Georg suddenly found himself swallowed up by a mixture of emotions—good and bad. He wondered if perhaps the schoolmaster had taken advantage of the situation in some way. No wonder he had been so willing to carry the schoolbooks into town. He wanted to spend time with Adeline.

Hmm. On the other hand, Georg's actions had been somewhat questionable, too. Had he not led Adeline along over the past couple of weeks, letting her think he would one day propose?

Adeline shook her head. "No. Myles has said nothing," she whispered. "He's a true gentleman. In fact, he doesn't even know of my feelings." Her cheeks flashed pink. "And maybe I'm childish to hope. Oh, but I pray I'm wrong about that. He is in every way my equal. We are perfectly matched, and it is only a matter of time before he sees it." She drew near and took Georg's hands in her own. "Georg, I am so sorry to have hurt you. I knew this news would be hard to hear. You've had your heart set on marriage and family, and I've pulled the rug out from under you. Can—can you ever forgive me?"

He stared at her in silence and then doubled over—not in pain, but in laughter. Before long, others were looking their way. Still he could not help himself. On and on the laughter came. The whole thing was just too...too funny.

"Georg, are you all right?" Adeline asked, sniffling back the tears. "You must be in shock. Have I wounded you for life?"

He contained his laughter, rose, and looked her in the eyes. "I must admit, your news surprises me," he said. "But I am not devastated, Adeline. And I cannot help but admit the truth. I, too, care for someone else. Deeply."

Her mouth rounded in a perfectly formed O, and she smiled. "What a conundrum." She grinned. "What a silly mismatched pair we've been, Georg! Oh, but God is good to show us that sooner rather than later. Is He not?"

"He is indeed." *And my papa said as much.* Georg took her hand and kissed it then gave her a wink. Off in the distance, he caught a glimpse of Myles talking to Catherine and Nellie. The three were engaged in a rousing conversation that involved plenty of laughter. Georg felt sure that Adeline's future would be filled with much of the same, should Myles ask her to marry him.

"I am not devastated," he whispered. "I am grateful...for your time, your company, and your kind spirit. My life is better for having known you."

"I feel the same." She reached up and gave him a warm hug. "Oh, Georg, aren't we silly?" She turned as Myles's laughter rang out.

"Yes." Georg nodded. "But why are you standing here talking to me, anyway? If I were you, I would set my sights in a different direction." He gestured toward Myles, and Adeline's face lit into a smile.

"Yes." She ran her fingers through her hair and dabbed at her eyes. "I must look frightful."

"Not at all," Georg said, turning her to face Myles. "Now go and fetch your fella, Adeline, before I drop down on one knee and propose right here."

"You wouldn't dare!"

"No, I wouldn't dare." *Nor had I ever planned to.* "But go now. I think you have some learning to do." He gave her a playful wink then watched with a grin as she hiked her skirt and sprinted across the campground, stopping at Myles's side. The schoolmaster looked his way and waved.

Georg returned the wave, his heart completely free. Now there was just one thing left to be done. He had to find Belinda...right away.

* * *

Belinda looked across the campground, searching for Georg. He and Adeline seemed to have disappeared. After a bit more looking, she caught a glimpse of them standing hand in hand at the edge of the cemetery. They faced each other, their expressions quite serious. Belinda's heart felt as heavy as lead. Then she watched as Adeline threw her arms around Georg's neck and gave him a warm hug. He returned it, the smile on his face growing wider by the minute. After that, he took her hand and kissed it. Belinda's heart twisted at the sight of this romantic exchange.

Unable to watch any more, she turned to her mother. "I'm tired. Are we going soon?"

"Yes, let's get these things loaded up into the wagon and head home. I'm exhausted and need to get a good night's sleep so I'm fresh for the service tomorrow morning."

Moments later, Belinda, Mama, Papa, and the twins had the wagon loaded and were about to head home. Off in the distance, she thought she saw Georg Kaufman coming her way. Belinda deliberately hid behind her brothers, who had taken to scuffling in the back of the wagon. Tears welled up in her eyes, and she didn't even try to stop them. In that moment, she realized she would likely go on hiding from Georg and Adeline...for the rest of her life.

Chapter Twenty-four

On Monday morning Belinda walked the road to town, moving at a snail's pace. Truth be told, she was in no hurry to see Georg and Adeline together. Though she tried to quiet her heart on this matter, it would not be still. Seeing them together yesterday still haunted her in some ways, though she did not know what to do about it except leave the matter in God's hands.

Why was it that leaving things in God's hands was such a tall order? Seemed like the right thing was always the hard thing. Trusting the Lord, for instance. Rarely did she find it an easy thing to do.

Belinda arrived at the store and was stunned to find John Ogilvie already there, talking with Greta. Every day the truth grew clearer, both to Belinda and to Greta, who had stopped trying to pretend she did not notice his advances. In fact, Belinda now thought she saw amazing possibilities of a future with these two. Eventually, anyway.

"Belinda." John turned to face her as she walked in the shop. "I slipped away from the butcher shop to tell Greta the news."

"News?" Belinda's hands began to tremble, wondering what he might say. "What news?"

"There's been a wedding." John waggled his brows as he leaned in close to whisper, "In secret."

Belinda's heart quickened and her breath caught in her throat. "Wedding?"

"Yes, after the service yesterday. I happened to come back to the campground because I lost my pocket watch. When I arrived, I saw Reverend Billingsley performing a ceremony. You will never guess who."

At once, tears sprang to her eyes. "No." She put her hand up. "Do not tell me. I—I—" She ran to the back room, overcome. She couldn't bear the news. Not today, anyway. Maybe tomorrow. Or the day after that. Or the week after. But certainly not today.

Greta followed on her heels. "Belinda! Are you all right?"

"No. Yes. I—I don't know. But this news will ruin me."

"Ruin your reputation, you mean?" Greta looked confused. "I doubt it, Belinda. People see the hand of the Lord at work here. Don't fret over that."

"So you think this is the Lord's doing?" Belinda looked up with tears in her eyes. "I am surprised to hear that. I thought you, of all people, would understand my plight. Do you not see it? Have I not made it plain?"

"I'm not sure." Greta looked more confused than ever. "And I thought you, of all people, would find this delightful news, all things considered." She took a seat on one of the barrels and stared at Belinda. "I'm perplexed. I mean, I know you were keen on Cassie marrying John, but his heart is not broken over this news, so why should yours be?"

"W—what?" Belinda dabbed her eyes and looked at her cousin, trying to make sense of everything. "Are we talking about Cassie here?"

"Why, yes. Who did you think we were…?" Greta clamped a hand over her mouth. "Oh, Belinda! You thought John and I were talking about Georg and Adeline? You thought they were married?"

"Y–yes!" Belinda drew in a couple of deep breaths, trying to calm down. Oh, how wrong she had been. How blissfully, gloriously wrong! At once her spirits lifted. She paced the room. "Oh, I feel so foolish. Crying over the wrong wedding." She stopped to dry her eyes. "Are you telling me, then, that Cassie and Doc Klein have married? Really and truly?"

"Really and truly." Greta giggled. "And I have it on good authority they plan to leave later this week for a honeymoon in Dallas." She leaned in close and whispered, "They spent last night at Stanzas. Isn't that romantic? And doesn't it all just sound wonderful?"

"Yes. Oh, Greta!" Belinda flung her arms around her cousin's neck. "This is the best news I've heard in my entire life."

"It is?" Greta hugged her back. "Well, I'm glad you're happy about it." She released her hold on Belinda as she gave a little laugh. "To be perfectly honest, it's the best news I've ever had in my life, too. Want to know why?"

"I think I can guess." Belinda gazed at her cousin with joy. "But tell me anyway."

"John has declared his intentions." Greta's eyes filled with tears as she whispered the words. "He has asked to court me, and I have agreed. Mama is all for it, so I am now officially being wooed by a man I care deeply about. Can you believe it?"

"Oh, I can! I can! And I'm delighted." Belinda reached to embrace her. "When did this happen, Greta? Tell me everything!"

"At the camp meeting. He went to Mama personally." Greta grinned. "I wish you could've seen the look on her face."

"No doubt she liked the idea."

"Very much. Turns out she's known for some time that John was interested in me. Or hoped, anyway. So she was quite happy for the confirmation."

"Oh, this is the happiest news in the world! I want to celebrate, to shout it from the rooftops!" Belinda let out a cry of sheer delight, which John must have taken as a cry of fear because he came running. She impulsively threw her arms around his neck. "Oh, you dear, dear man! I could just kiss you right here and now!"

He backed away immediately, his eyes wide.

"I think not." Greta slipped her arm around John's waist. "If there's any kissing to be done, leave it to the two of us, all right?"

"Oh, of course! I didn't mean..." Belinda began to giggle. "I'm sorry, John. But Greta just told me...well, you know."

"Ah." He drew Greta close and planted a kiss on her forehead then turned back to face Belinda. "I take it you're fine with our news, then?"

"Oh, I'm more than fine with it. I'm ecstatic." She turned to John with a smile. "Isn't it funny, how God works? You came to me looking for a match, and your perfect match was right here all along."

"Interesting how we sometimes miss the obvious," he said, gazing into Greta's tear-filled eyes. "But I'm so glad we figured it out. I wouldn't want to waste another moment."

Belinda dropped onto one of the barrels, overcome with relief. "I'm delighted for the two of you." She paused a moment, deep in thought, and then looked up with a grin. "So, Cassie and Doc Klein are married."

Greta nodded. "Indeed. And I daresay she will open that sewing shop in short order. What do you think of that?"

"I think it's marvelous." Belinda smiled. "I do hope she and Corabelle can work something out. Corabelle's in the family way, you know."

"Oh, yes! Everyone in town knows." Greta laughed. "Your mother is beside herself."

"Yes, she's going to become a grandmother for the first time. It's all she talks about now."

John pulled his pocket watch out and held it up. "I found my watch, by the way, in case you were wondering." He glanced at it then looked up. "Ladies, I must go. I have a busy day ahead of me at the butcher shop." He pressed the watch into his pocket and took Greta's hand in his and kissed the back of it, causing her cheeks to turn bright pink.

"Come to see me on your lunch break," Greta whispered. "I've brought sandwiches from home."

"I wouldn't miss it for the world."

As John and Greta made their way to the front of the store, Belinda watched in dazed curiosity. So, those two were in love after all. Oh, what joy that brought to her heart! And how delightful!

Minutes later, the store filled with happy customers. At one point, Belinda gazed over at her desk, staring at the words MARRIAGE BROKER. Perhaps this would be a good time to close up shop, so to speak. To put an end to her matchmaking days. Sure, the mayor still wanted a wife—they'd talked about sending off a letter. A handful of other fellows wanted wives, too. But what did the Lord want? She pondered this as she waited on folks right and left.

Around ten in the morning, Prissy came into the shop, bubbling over with what appeared to be anticipation. She drew near to Greta and Belinda and whispered, "Have you heard the news?"

"About Cassie and Doc Klein?" Greta said. "Yes, isn't it wonderful?"

"Indeed. But that's not what I'm talking about." She looked around to make sure no one was listening in. "I meant the news about Adeline Rose."

Belinda's heart flip-flopped. So, it had happened after all. Georg and Adeline had tied the knot. They had secretly married.

"Has she decided to leave?" Greta asked, her eyes wide.

"No, on the contrary," Prissy said. "She is completely smitten. In love. Beside herself. I could hardly make sense of her words just now, but she is definitely planning to stay. Forever, I mean. And she's particularly thrilled because her sister has started school. They will have a whole new life here."

Belinda began to weep at once, and Prissy reached for her hankie. "Oh, I know! The news is all good today, isn't it! Overwhelming, in fact. Well, you go ahead and cry those tears, Belinda. Tears of happiness are nothing to be ashamed of. I have it on good authority that Myles Lott shed a few tears himself."

"Myles Lott?" Belinda looked up, stunned. "Myles...crying? W–why?" She shook her head, perplexed. "In what way does this affect him?"

"Why, in *every* way!" Prissy stared at her, clearly stunned. "He is in love with Adeline and will take on a fatherly role with Catherine. So he is in every way affected."

"Wait." Belinda put both hands up, completely confused. "Are you saying that Myles Lott and Adeline are..."

"Courting?" Prissy asked. "Well, yes. That's what I've been saying all along. I'm sorry if I didn't make it clear. I thought you would be thrilled with this news."

In that moment, Belinda felt like her heart came dancing out of her chest just as Greta let out a whoop and hollered, "Praise the Lord!" Belinda wanted to sing. She wanted to shout. Adeline and Myles Lott...were a couple! That meant Georg was... The minute she thought about Georg, tears sprang to her eyes.

"Oh, I'm sorry, Belinda." Prissy clamped a hand over her mouth. "I see the dilemma now. You are concerned about how this will affect your business. Are you worried about what people will think?"

"No!" She spoke the word triumphantly. "Never again will I worry about what others think, trust me. From this moment on, I focus only on what the Lord thinks. He, alone, matters. The opinions of man—or woman—do not."

"Well, I am convinced the Lord is behind these most recent unions," Greta said with a nod. "It appears as if the pieces to the puzzle are coming together for our little town."

"Much like the rhyme in a poem," Prissy said. "Interesting, eh?"

"Indeed." Belinda nodded.

"What did you call it again, Belinda?" Greta asked. "Poetic justice?"

"Yes. Poetic Justice." She smiled. "Each gets what he deserves, right or wrong." She paused, wondering just where that left her. Only time would tell. But one thing was sure and certain. She would see Georg this afternoon and tell him how she felt. She would cross the Jordan into the Promised Land.

* * *

"Everything all right today, Georg?" Charlie Grundy asked.

"Yes." Georg continued to peer through the barbershop window.

"Looking for something. Or...someone?" Charlie asked.

"Not exactly."

Charlie cleared his throat. "Listen, I heard about Adeline and Myles Lott. That's rough news, my friend. I'm sorry for your broken heart."

"My broken heart?" Georg turned to him with a broad smile. "Oh, no. My heart is not broken, I assure you. I am the happiest man in Poetry today."

"I feel sure there are many other happy men here, as well," Charlie countered. "But what has motivated such happiness on your end?"

"I am a man transformed!"

Charlie nodded, looking at his reflection in the mirror. "Now that I understand." He turned and looked at Georg. "But you seem the same as always to me. Externally, anyway."

"The work has taken place here." Georg laid his hand over his heart. "And trust me, you might not see it on the outside, but the transformation is complete all the same. I am in love, Charlie Grundy. I am head-over-heels-could-write-a-poem-about-her-wish-I-could-sing-but-can't-carry-a-tune-in-a-bucket in love!"

"Whew!" Charlie looked at him, stunned. "Well, that is something, though I might dispute the 'can't carry a tune in a bucket' part. Do you mind if I ask who the lucky girl is?"

"The same one I've loved for years." Georg nodded at Charlie and then went back to the window, staring out onto the street. In that moment, he noticed something rather odd. The Reverend and Marta Schuller stood in the center of the street, talking with Cassie. Ah, they must be discussing last night's wedding ceremony.

Or something else entirely. Corabelle entered their circle and they all stood in the center of the street in a huddle, whispering together.

"What's all that about?" Georg asked. Something was surely underfoot. He could sense something coming but couldn't quite put his finger on it.

Charlie dropped a couple of coins into his palm. "Perfect day," he said as he headed to the door. "Yep. It's a pert near perfect day in Poetry."

Georg pondered that last statement. To be sure, Charlie wasn't exactly a poet. Still, his words had a certain rhythm to them. And the words were dead-on. This *was* the perfect day in Poetry...the perfect day to tell a certain woman just exactly how he felt.

Chapter Twenty-five

....

Just before noon, Belinda found herself overwhelmed with customers at Poetic Notions. With so many women in town, the workload was higher than ever, for with women came the need for things like bolts of fabric, canned goods, cleaning supplies, and so forth. Not that Belinda minded. She would rather fill her days ordering these goods than pipe tobacco and shaving mugs.

With most of her orders made and the customers taken care of, she stepped out onto the front porch to shake out several of the rag rugs. As she snapped them, the dust pieces floated through the air, catching on the breeze. She glanced across the street at the barbershop, where Georg was wiping down his front window. At just the right moment, he turned to face her, as well, from his side of the street. Oh, how she wanted to cross the Jordan and run to meet him, especially with the news about Adeline and Myles Lott.

In that moment, Belinda's heart quickened. Georg gave her a shy smile and she returned it, not moving an inch. Though they didn't speak a word, her heart felt as if it might burst. She longed to run straight into the middle of the street, to cross the great divide, and run directly into his arms.

She giggled, thinking of how brazen that would be—to declare your love for someone in such a public way. And yet she couldn't help but think that was exactly what it might take to get the deed done.

Otherwise, the two might be destined to spend their days staring at each other from opposite sides of the street.

Just then a loud banging noise caught Belinda's attention. It came from the south end of the street. She peered off in the distance, trying to figure out what the noise was, but could not decipher it. The banging grew nearer. And nearer. Before long, it was so loud that Greta came out of the shop to see about it. Aunt Hilde joined her. From across the street, Georg stopped his work, put down his rag, and stepped into the street, gazing in curiosity.

Minutes later, folks poured out of Stanzas, all with eyes wide to catch a glimpse of whatever might be happening. Corabelle came out of the hat shop, carrying something in her hand. Something white. Belinda couldn't be quite sure what it was.

In that moment, Cassie arrived on the street, panting. "Just in time."

"Just in time for what?" Belinda asked.

"You'll see. But don't go back inside, whatever you do."

Belinda, now fully engaged, watched as the noise grew nearer. She gasped as she laid eyes on Peter and Sarah Jo, coming down the street with cooking pots and metal spoons in hand. They used the spoons to beat the pots, creating that loud rhythmic banging.

Belinda gasped as she looked at Sarah Jo, who was done up in the most beautiful white dress she'd ever seen. And Peter was dressed like something from a storybook, in a suit and, of all things, an ascot. His hair, what was left of it, anyway, was immaculately combed. And the smile on his face spoke of mischief.

Aunt Hilde began to laugh at once. "I don't believe it. I simply don't believe it."

Belinda watched in awe as Corabelle met Sarah Jo in the middle of the street and pinned on the tiny white cap with a long veil attached. She gasped as the picture was complete. "Oh, Greta, look. Have you ever seen anything so beautiful?"

Cassie drew near and whispered, "I made the dress last week. Talk about a short order! What do you think?"

"I've never seen anything like it," Belinda confessed. "Your work is the best I've ever seen." She gazed at Cassie with new eyes. "And by the way, I understand that congratulations are in order."

"They are." Cassie grinned. "Oh, it's the best news in the world. And I'm the happiest woman ever!" She pointed at Sarah Jo and Peter and chuckled. "Looks like I'm not alone, though. The whole town is filled with happy couples."

She gave the cousins a little wave and disappeared into the crowd, likely in search of her new groom.

By now, people had come from all corners of the town. They lined Main Street. Every shopkeeper. Every hotel guest. Every worker from the outlying areas. The banging of the pots and pans had drawn them all.

Peter stood in the center of the street, looking quite dapper. He removed his hat and gave a sweeping bow then gestured to his bride-to-be, who gave a silly little curtsy.

"Ladies and gentlemen," Peter shouted. "Fine friends of Poetry, Texas—we have an announcement to make."

A couple of the men from the barbershop let out piercing whistles and the crowd grew silent.

Peter's face was lit in a smile. "For some time now, I have claimed that the life of an old bachelor was the life for me, but that is no longer the case."

"You've been bit, haven't you, Peter?" one of the older men hollered out.

"Yes, I'll be the first to admit it," Peter said with a grin. "I've been bit. And I've never been happier in my life." He drew near to Sarah Jo and took her hand. "I am the happiest man in the world, and I want to share it with the people I love. This woman—Sarah Jo Cummings—has done me the honor of agreeing to marry me."

A loud whoop went up from several of the men, and the women began to cheer, including Belinda and Greta. Aunt Hilde looked on with tears in her eyes.

"Well, it's about time," she whispered. "I daresay, it's about time."

"Because our love story has been a bit unorthodox, we felt the ceremony should be, too," Peter said. "So we made up our minds to get married in the middle of Main Street on a weekday, when no one was the wiser. Hope you don't mind giving up a few minutes away from your businesses to celebrate with us."

At this point, even more people appeared. It looked like the word had spread, because Mama and Papa rounded the corner with Elisha and Elijah not far behind.

"Before we get hitched, I just want to say one thing." Sarah Jo looked through the crowd until she clamped eyes on Belinda. "I wouldn't even be in this town if it weren't for a certain young woman."

"Oh dear." Belinda shook her head and tried to scoot behind Greta and Aunt Hilde, but they nudged her forward.

Every eye turned Belinda's way, and she felt her cheeks turn warm. Through the crowd, she caught a glimpse of Georg beaming from the opposite side of the street.

"If this darling girl hadn't listened to the Lord, I wouldn't be here now." Sarah Jo nodded. "O'course, she brought me here to marry someone else, but that's all water under the bridge now. The Lord knew what He was doing. And what she was doing." Sarah Jo laughed and everyone joined her.

"It's only fitting that we ask Reverend Billingsley and his wife, Marta, to join us," Peter called out.

At this point, the reverend and Marta made their way up the street, arm in arm. The reverend carried his Bible and wore a smile brighter than sunshine. Belinda grinned as she watched them approach a very anxious Peter and Sarah Jo, who now turned toward each other and clasped hands.

"I don't believe it," Greta whispered. "They're really going to do it. They're getting married in the middle of the street on a Monday afternoon!"

Belinda laughed. "Well, of course they are! What else would you expect from Sarah Jo and Peter?"

Marta took her place next to Sarah Jo, fussing with the bride's veil. Then the reverend began the ceremony. The whole town stood silent as the words were spoken. Well, silent, at least, until a man on a wagon tried to pass through town—but he was quickly stopped at the corner and sent in a different direction.

The reverend had chosen his passage from the Song of Solomon. Ironic, Belinda thought. Thankfully, he chose with great discretion. As the words of love were read, the crowd fell into a holy hush. They might as well have been in church, for the spirit of the Lord hung heavy over the congregation. In fact, Belinda felt as surely as if the camp meeting had begun all over again.

Reverend Billingsley finished his reading and paused.

"Now I have something I'd like to read to my bride," Peter announced for all to hear. "I know you all fancy me a poet. I've fancied myself one, as well."

Sarah Jo punched him in the arm. "You are a poet, Peter Conrad. And the best I've ever heard, to boot."

"Still, for an occasion such as this, I can only quote the best. And the person whose poems far exceed mine is a woman." He chuckled. "I have recently determined that only a woman can truly capture the essence of love in words, though I will surely give it my best from this day forth. I want to recite a piece by Elizabeth Barrett Browning. For a woman like Sarah Jo, only the best will do."

With a voice like honey, he began to quote the words from memory:

" 'How do I love thee? Let me count the ways. I love thee to the depth and breadth and height my soul can reach, when feeling out of sight for the ends of Being and ideal Grace. I love thee to the level of everyday's most quiet need, by sun and candlelight. I love thee freely, as men strive for Right; I love thee purely, as they turn from Praise. I love thee with the passion put to use in my old griefs, and with my childhood's faith. I love thee with a love I seemed to lose with my lost saints!—I love thee with the breath, smiles, tears, of all my life!—and, if God choose, I shall but love thee better after death.' "

When the poem ended, there wasn't a dry eye on Main Street. Belinda reached for her hankie then dabbed at her eyes. Through the crowd, she once again caught a glimpse of Georg. At this point, her tears came freely. Who would know the difference, anyway? Let them think she was moved by the poem.

She *was* moved by the poem, after all. It had spoken to her heart in a dozen different ways, for she had those same feelings...for Georg.

She loved him with a childlike faith. She loved him with a love that seemed to surpass anything else—smiles, tears, even the very breath she took. She loved Georg Kaufman...and, oh, how she hoped he loved her, too!

When the people stopped clapping, Reverend Billingsley made his pronouncement. "And now, fine folks of Poetry, I'm thrilled to announce that Peter and Sarah Jo are now husband and wife. I give you Mr. and Mrs. Peter Conrad." As the crowd roared with delight, Belinda could barely hear the reverend's closing words: "What God has joined together, let no man tear asunder. You may kiss your bride, Peter!"

Peter swept Sarah Jo into his arms and planted a kiss on her that made several of the womenfolk blush. Belinda felt sure it made them a wee bit jealous, too. For while Peter was enthusiastic in approach, there could be no denying his love for the woman in his arms. And what woman wouldn't want to be swept away in such a fashion? To be told in front of her friends and neighbors that she was adored? To be kissed with such fire?

A shiver ran up Belinda's spine as she thought about all of those things. Oh, how she wanted them, too! How she longed to be told that someone loved her with such a love. The words of that poem touched the deepest places of her heart.

"I spent so much time fooling myself," she whispered.

"What?" Greta drew near. "What did you say, honey?"

"I spent years fooling myself." Belinda sighed. "All this time I've been saying I didn't want that. Didn't want love. Didn't need to be married. And yet..."

She looked out across the street to Georg, whose gaze never left hers. He watched her with such tenderness that her heart gravitated to her throat. Turning back to Greta, she whispered, "For the first time in my life, I know exactly what I want."

"Then what are you waiting for?" Greta whispered. "For the Red Sea to part?"

"Mm-hmm." She gazed at the ever-growing throng of people in front of her, now unable to see him. Surely Georg was still over there somewhere. And when she found him...she would never let him go.

Chapter Twenty-six
....

Georg watched the wedding with his heart in his throat. He'd never seen such an outward display of affection between a man and a woman, and it jarred him. In a good way. He wished for the courage to make a similar proclamation. Instead, he watched in silence. Sure, he paid attention to the ceremony, but beyond that, he kept his focus on the beautiful young woman across the street, the one he longed to sweep into his arms. Would he ever have the courage?

Georg listened as the reverend invited everyone to Stanzas for a wedding lunch. Looked like Peter and Sarah Jo had planned this thing well, for Katie Sue came scurrying down the street with a wedding cake in hand, which she proceeded to deliver to Stanzas with a smile.

Yes, they'd surely planned this for a while but had somehow managed to keep it a secret.

Funny how secrets could be kept. How big news could be kept under lock and key till just the right time. Oh, but when God turned the key in the lock and the appropriate moment came, what a difference it could make!

Georg looked across the crowd once more, seeking out Belinda's face. She gazed at him with a hint of a smile on her face. And were those...tears in her eyes? He took a step into the street, determined to talk to her. If he didn't, his heart would burst from his chest. Unfortunately, he ran smack-dab into Katie Sue and the wedding cake. She jolted, almost dropping it. Georg made a thousand quick apologies then helped her regain her footing. "So sorry!" he said.

"You need to be more careful, Georg," Katie Sue said, shaking her head. "You almost caused a calamity."

"Indeed, I almost did." He took his first step across the Jordan, pushing his way through the mob, past Reverend Billingsley and Marta, beyond Mr. and Mrs. Grundy, past Corabelle and James, to the boardwalk in front of Poetic Notions. For some reason, when he finally stepped foot onto the Promised Land, Belinda could not be found. "What in the world?"

He gazed through the packed street and now found her on the opposite side. "I don't believe it." She looked at him through the crowd, offering up a shrug. Had she crossed over to meet him? The very idea sent his heart a hundred different directions at once. If she'd crossed over to meet him, that spoke a thousand words. All good words.

"Belinda!" he called out her name and she stepped forward, eyes wide.

"I'm here, Georg!" she called out above the crowd. Her voice rang out, sending a chill down his spine.

"Meet me in the middle of the road!"

The townspeople swallowed her up as folks pressed their way into the crowded restaurant. He lost sight of her. However, determined not to give up, he forged his way through, more determined than ever. As he did, a familiar voice spoke.

"You can do this, Georg. Just speak your heart." The firm voice stunned him. Georg looked behind him to see his father standing there. The older man placed a hand on Georg's shoulder. "I've been waiting for this day for years, son. Now find a place where the two of you can have some privacy and tell her how you feel."

"Yes, sir!" Georg worked his way through the crowd, stopping in the center of the street—the very spot where Peter and Sarah Jo had just tied the knot. He waved his arms and hollered, "Belinda!"

For a minute, he couldn't find her. And with the sound of voices ringing on every side—happy voices raised in joyful exclamation— he wondered if she could hear him at all.

Seconds later, she appeared, with flushed cheeks and hair slightly messy. "G–georg." She stopped in front of him, offering a girlish smile. "Did you want me to meet you here?"

"I did." Oh, how his heart raced! He begged it to be silent so he could hear himself think, but it would not! "There is something I need to tell you."

"O–oh?" She brushed away a loose hair, and he reached to take her hand, refusing to let it go. In fact, he promised himself in that moment that he would never let it go as long as he lived.

"Belinda, I..." At that moment, someone bumped into him from behind, knocking him forward. He ended up in Belinda's arms. Oh, happy day! He could not have planned this any better if he'd tried. Now in a comfortable embrace, he took his fingertip and brushed the loose hair out of her eyes. She gazed up at him, and for the first time he noticed her tears.

"No." Georg shook his head. "No tears today. This is a happy day."

"And these are happy tears," she whispered, gazing up into his eyes. "I promise you. Nothing but."

"Then cry all you like." He grinned and drew her even closer. Funny, with the crowd of people pressing in around them, no one paid much attention. Not that he cared. No, even surrounded on every side, he still felt very much alone with the woman he loved. Oh, but he could hardly wait to tell her! If only the words would come.

He garnered up the courage to speak. "I have something to say to you, Belinda Bauer. Should've said it ages ago, but I'm a foolish man. I let other things get in the way."

"O–oh?"

"Yes. And forgive me for not shouting it from the rooftops. That day will come. But I had to say it to you first. Had to let you know—"

Someone next to him let out a whoop and hollered, "Ain't it grand, folks! Love is in the air!"

Georg laughed. "Well, that's not exactly what I'd planned to say, but it's not a bad attempt. Love is in the air and I *do* feel grand. Mighty grand, in fact. Can't say as I've ever felt better, in fact." He gazed into her eyes. Taking his finger, he traced her cheekbone. Belinda's gaze shifted to the ground, but he gently lifted her chin so that they were eye-to-eye once again. "You've got to look at me when I say this, Belinda. I've waited too long, and I need to know you're hearing every word. It's too important."

She looked up, tears now flowing, and nodded. "Y–yes."

"Belinda, I told you once that I didn't need a wife. That I was happy as a single man. I was wrong. In fact, I've never been more wrong about anything in my life, and you deserve to know it."

"O–oh?" A smile turned up the corners of her lips.

"I was right about the part where I didn't need you to fetch me a bride from out of state," he continued. "In fact, I think I realized that almost from the beginning. In fact, I didn't need anyone to fetch a bride for me, because the Lord already had." He leaned in and pressed a tiny kiss on her cheek, and she flushed.

"Aunt Hilde once told me I couldn't see the forest for the trees," she whispered. "I think she was right."

"Me, too." The crowd finally cleared the street, moving into the restaurant in droves. "I have no idea what took me so long, but Belinda, I've got to tell you before I crumble into a thousand pieces...I'm in love with you. I've loved you ever since we were kids. I just didn't know how to voice it."

"R–really?"

"Really. Every morning when I get to the shop, the first thing I do is look across the street to catch a glimpse of you. For years, we've had this street between us. But no more. This is my Jordan, and I have surely crossed it, never to return." He kissed her wisps of golden hair on her brow, hair that both tormented and delighted him.

"Oh, Georg!" She flung her arms around his neck, her face wet with tears. "What took us so long?"

In that moment, it felt as if heaven and earth collided. Georg leaned down and, with the passion borne of years of waiting, kissed the woman he loved. She responded with the gentlest, sweetest kiss he ever could have imagined. Surely even a poem couldn't do it justice. Afterward they stood silent, wrapped in each other's arms.

"I've been as slow as molasses telling you all this. But no more. From this moment on, everything moves at lightning speed."

"O–oh?

He dropped to one knee, completely undeterred by the fact that folks from both sides of the street had now taken notice of him. What did it matter? They were alone in the center of the street. God had arranged the perfect time, the perfect place.

Off in the distance, Georg heard Hilde say something. Then his father. He sensed the eyes of townspeople on him, but he didn't mind. Not one little bit. No, the only thing that mattered right now was the woman in front of him, the one he planned to spend the rest of his life with.

* * *

Belinda's heart beat so fast, she wondered if she might faint. Could this really be happening? She looked at Georg, stunned. "Y–you're asking me to marry you?"

"I am."

By now, half the crowd inside Stanzas was back outside, gaping at the couple, including Greta and Sarah Jo. They looked on, clearly delighted with what they saw.

"Say yes, honey!" Sarah Jo hollered. "Say yes!"

Oh, she would say yes, all right. No doubt about it.

"Well, let me ask properly first," Georg called out to all who were watching. "Belinda deserves a decent proposal, and I mean to give it."

She brushed away her tears and focused on the man who knelt before her, the one the Lord had surely sent—not from another state, but from her own backyard. One who had loved her all along. One whose life rhymed with hers.

He looked into her eyes and, with a tremor in his voice, managed to speak. "Belinda Bauer, I love you with my whole heart, and I plan to go on loving you until I'm old and gray. I don't have much to offer, but what I do have, I give freely. I would be the happiest man in Poetry if you would agree to be my wife."

Belinda gazed down into Georg's tear-filled eyes and whispered, "You are the finest man I have ever known, and I would be honored to be your wife. I would love to marry you, Georg Kaufman."

He jumped to his feet and gave her a solid kiss, and the crowd roared with delight.

Once folks settled down, he whispered into her ear. "That sapphire ring has been waiting in my shop for weeks. Months. Belinda, it was meant for you all along. Would you—would you be happy with it?"

"Would I!" She let out a squeal. "I can't wait!"

He took her by the hand and sprinted in the direction of the barbershop. Once there, she waited at the door while he raced inside to fetch the ring. She giggled as he opened the box and pressed it on her finger. Sure, it was a little tight, but she didn't mind. Not at all. There would be no pulling it off this time. No, this time she planned to wear it for the rest of her life.

Chapter Twenty-seven

On the first Sunday in November, a lovely fall day in the town of Poetry, Myles Lott took Adeline Rose Jewett as his bride. The congregation looked on, many with tears in their eyes. Belinda had never seen a more beautiful wedding. Sweet Catherine, who had settled in at school and become Sarah Jo's prodigy for theatricals, stood up for her sister, wearing a lovely dress that Cassie had made. The bride wore white, an exquisite gown also crafted by Cassie. Corabelle, of course, took care of the veil.

Yes, it was a fine day for a wedding in Poetry. In fact, it was so fine that they decided to do it twice. As soon as Myles and Adeline tied the knot, John and Greta walked the aisle as well. Belinda stood in support of her cousin, with tears streaming down her cheeks as the "I do's" were shared. She'd never seen Greta look prettier. In fact, her gown, which Hilde had worn on her wedding day years before, held special significance. Oh, if only Uncle Max could have been here to walk her down the aisle. Belinda's papa had done the deed in his stead, of course, and done it well.

After the ceremony, folks nibbled on cake from Katie Sue's new bakery, Couplets. Belinda stopped by to chat with Katie Sue, making final arrangements for her own wedding cake.

"Have you settled on a date yet, Belinda?" Katie Sue asked with a twinkle in her eye. "I do hope you're going to give me some breathing room between ceremonies."

"Yes, we plan to wed just before Christmas," Belinda said. "It's going to be the prettiest winter wedding you've ever seen."

"Here at the church, I imagine." Katie Sue nodded.

"We haven't decided yet." Belinda shrugged. "I have a couple of other ideas, but we'll let you know. At any rate, we will need the biggest cake you can make. We expect nearly everyone in town to attend."

"No doubt they will come out to support you," Katie Sue said with a smile. "You and Georg are both well-loved in Poetry." Her eyes grew misty. "I know that I have come to love you as a sister, Belinda. And I'm not sure I can ever thank you enough for bringing me here. I've never been so happy in all my life."

"Oh, I love you, too!" Belinda reached over to give her a warm hug. "And I'm tickled that we're all becoming sisters. I had no idea it would turn out like this, but I'm thrilled that it has."

"Since we're sisters and all..." Katie Sue leaned in and whispered, "I guess it's safe to tell you my secret." Her eyes twinkled with mischief. "Bucky and I are going to have a baby."

"No!"

"Yes." Katie Sue nodded and blushed. "I've only known for a few days, but I couldn't wait to share the news with you. Oh, I'm the happiest girl on earth. And happier still, my parents have decided to move to Poetry. They are going to build a home near ours so that they can be close when the baby arrives."

"Oh, Katie Sue, all the news is good." Belinda gave her another hug. "Just be careful who you tell. You know how fast news spreads in this town."

"News?" Sarah Jo drew near. "Someone has news?" She took one look at Katie Sue and squealed. "I knew it! You're in the family way! When is the little one due?"

Katie Sue shook her head and laughed. Looking at Belinda, she whispered, "Why fight it?" then engaged Sarah Jo in a conversation, telling her everything.

Belinda left them to their own devices, looking for Georg. She found him sitting with her parents. As she came upon them, Belinda's heart flip-flopped as always. Something about seeing the man she loved just sent her heart racing.

He looked up, a smile creasing his mouth. "Well, there you are. I thought you'd gone missing."

"No, just chatting with friends." She smiled and he rose to sweep her into his arms.

"Well, how about a chat with me?" he whispered. "Want to go for a walk?"

"Do I ever." She smiled at her mother, who offered up a wink.

Belinda and Georg headed down to the creek, hand in hand. For a while, neither spoke a word. After they sat at the water's edge, however, Georg broke the ice.

"Belinda, do you remember that day you came running into town and knocked me down?"

"Yes." She smiled. "I was so embarrassed. But what brought that up?" She gave a little shiver, and he slipped his arm over her shoulder.

"Well, you said something that day that intrigued me. I've often wondered about it since but never thought to ask till now."

"Oh?" She shrugged, the whole thing just a foggy memory now. "I can't remember. What did I say?"

He grinned. "You said that one day I would thank you for running me down in the street. I've often wondered what you meant by that."

"Oh." She chuckled. "Well, actually, I was on my way to the post office to mail the letter to Corabelle, asking her to come to Poetry to take your hand in marriage."

"Ah." He laughed. "You mean the Corabelle who is happily married to James, of course."

"Of course."

"I always knew you would thank me if I ever found the right woman," Belinda said. "And I suppose that's what drove me all along... wanting your praise. Your approval."

He kissed the tip of her nose. "You certainly have it now. Though the road that brought us to this place was not without its pitfalls."

"True." She leaned against him and sighed.

"Remember that day in the mercantile when you told me I was lonely?"

"Yes." She sighed. "I'm sorry, Georg. I didn't mean to hurt your feelings that day."

"No, it's not that. I don't think I was honest in my response, that's all. I told you that I wasn't lonely. That my work at the barbershop was enough. But I was wrong. Until I won your heart, I *was* the loneliest man in the world. I just didn't realize it."

"And I always argued against marriage, saying the Lord had other plans for me," Belinda said. "Now I know His plans. No doubt in my mind."

"No doubt in mine, either." Georg gazed into her eyes with such tenderness that she thought her heart might burst. "I can honestly say I have never been more content."

"Me either."

They sat in silence for a period of time, listening to the sound of the water running over the rocks. "Tell me about the wedding plans," Georg said finally.

"Well, after waiting such a long time, it needs to be a celebration no one will soon forget, don't you think?" Belinda looked at him with a coy smile.

"I do."

"Memorize those words," she said, with a hint of laughter in her voice. "You'll be needing them again."

Georg chuckled.

"You know, I've had a revelation of sorts, Georg," Belinda said, growing quite serious. "All this time, I wanted to make Poetry a place of great beauty. Wanted it to rival the big towns. In the end, it *has* become more beautiful, but you know what I think?"

"What?"

"I think the Lord's real work wasn't in the town." She grinned just thinking about it. "It was inside of me. In my heart."

"And in mine, as well." Georg took her by the hand. "Not that I'm unhappy with the way the town is turning out. Things are buzzing along in Poetry, and it's all for the good."

"And all the better when the opera house is finished next month." Belinda nodded, anxious to see it finished. Suddenly an idea came to her. "Oh, Georg! That's it!"

"What's it?"

"The opera house!"

"What about it?"

"Why, it's the perfect place for a wedding. We can fit the whole town inside. And our wedding will be the first performance on the big stage. What do you say?"

He appeared to ponder the idea. A smile played at the corners of his lips. "I think we've had a fairly theatrical run thus far, so it makes sense. And you know Sarah Jo will love it. She will want to arrange the whole thing."

"And we will let her." Belinda paused then laughed. "To a point."

"Yes, please. Only to a point." Georg grinned. "She tends to run a bit on the eccentric side, wouldn't you say?"

"She does, but you have to love her."

"Yes, I do. The Bible says so." He gave Belinda a playful kiss. "So tell me more about this theatrical wedding of ours."

With joy filling her heart, she turned to him and did just that.

* * *

Georg leaned back in the grass, listening to Belinda's ideas. Every one felt right. Perfect for the two of them. They needed something special, something out of the norm. And no one could deny that getting married on the stage of the opera house would be memorable. If anyone deserved a special wedding day, it was the one woman who'd worked so hard to bring others together...in her own mismatch-making sort of way.

On and on she talked about their beautiful Christmas ceremony. Georg listened thoughtfully, chiming in when the opportunity arose. Most of all, though, he just loved listening to the sound of her voice. It rivaled the water running over the rocks in the creek below. And the excitement in her voice. Nothing could stir his heart quite as much.

Oh, Lord, my heart is so full. So full.

He closed his eyes, suddenly overcome. As he did, a memory overtook him. That day in Peter's office...he'd poured out his heart about Belinda. Told Peter every intimate detail. The things that took his breath away. The things that tormented him. The things that brought him joy.

Why had he shared these things again? So that Peter could compose a love poem. A love poem that, to this day, still remained unwritten.

In that moment, Georg decided to put together a verse for Belinda on his own. Why, with such love pouring from his heart, it would surely come as naturally as the water traveling across the rocks below. Indeed, it sprang from the very depths of his being.

Suddenly, Georg could hardly wait to look for pen and paper.

Chapter Twenty-eight

On the crisp, cold morning of December 14 Belinda prepared herself for her wedding, paying particular attention to her long, blond hair. The house was a flurry of activity, for she was not the only one dressing for this event. No, the many young women who would stand up with her had all come to help, each decked out in blue dresses crafted by Cassie. The town of Poetry had never seen so many matrons of honor.

Belinda smiled as Greta showed off her gown. Then she turned her attention to Corabelle, who, in spite of her expanding mid-section, had agreed to be in the wedding as well. Prissy was next, followed by Adeline, Cassie, and Katie Sue.

Marta and Sarah Jo fussed over the bridesmaids and offered their help to Belinda's mother, who seemed a bit frazzled. Finally, when all of the girls were ready, Belinda put on the white gown Cassie had made especially for today.

"Oh, Belinda!" Sarah Jo drew near with tears in her eyes. "You are the prettiest bride I've ever seen."

"Better guard your flattery," Belinda whispered with a chuckle. "You're saying that in front of a room full of recent brides, you know."

"Oh, posh." Sarah Jo waved a hand then dabbed at her eyes. "I told the others the same thing on their wedding days. No one cares."

Mama entered the room and gasped as she clamped eyes on Belinda. Her tears started almost immediately. They stood together, facing the long mirror. Belinda stared at her reflection, hardly believing the transformation. Surely her tomboyish ways were behind her now. The woman staring back at her was sophisticated. Refined. Very ladylike, indeed. Hopefully Georg would agree.

Georg.

The moment his name flitted through her mind, Belinda's heart came alive. She could hardly wait to get to the opera house, to walk the aisle and land in his arms.

Minutes later, Papa called for the girls to come to the wagon. They climbed underneath a half dozen quilts and made the journey to the south end of town, becoming the center of attention as the decorated wagon made its way down the street. Folks cheered all the way, many falling in line behind the wagon and walking the short distance to the opera house. All in all, it was quite a production, though the real show would take place inside. There, amidst a beautiful scenic backdrop of Christmas trees and twinkling candles, Belinda and Georg would exchange their vows. Then the whole town of Poetry would celebrate together with cake and punch. Katie Sue assured her the cake was the best she'd ever made.

When they arrived, Belinda and the other women made their way to a room on the side of the theater. Once there, she gathered her friends together and waited for their cue to enter the opera house. She closed her eyes and tried to picture the activity going on in the auditorium. Surely by now most everyone was seated. Sarah Jo would take her place at the piano, and the girls would walk up the aisle. Then, that magical moment she had waited for would take place at last. She would take Georg's hand...and his heart...as her own.

* * *

Georg stood backstage at the opera house with his groomsmen. He'd never seen the menfolk of Poetry so done up outside of a Sunday morning service. Georg took a final look at himself in the mirror, checking his hair for the hundredth time.

"She's going to marry you even if every hair isn't in place," his father said, slapping him on the back. "But just so you know, you look dashing."

"Thank you." Georg embraced his father. "I can't believe this day is finally here. I'm so excited."

"Have you seen the inside of the opera house?" his father said. "The ladies did a wonderful job of decorating it this morning. Looks like Christmas all over the place in there. Candles, trees, you name it. And that setup on the stage is pretty incredible. There's a hand-painted backdrop. Looks like something from a big city Christmas production."

"We have Sarah Jo to thank for that." Georg's heart swelled as he thought about the outpouring of love and support that he and Belinda had received from the community, particularly from those most recently wed.

Peter stuck his head in the door. "Georg, you almost ready? Sarah Jo is sitting at the piano. Listen for 'Joy to the World.' That's your cue."

"I wouldn't miss this for the world," Georg said with a smile.

Peter took a step into the room and drew near Georg, brushing off the back of the groom's jacket. "You know, I've been thinking about that day in my office when we talked about poetry."

"That's funny." Georg gave him an inquisitive look. "So have I."

"Well, I shared some of my thoughts with you that day," Peter said. "But I left out the most important thing. Perhaps it will be of some benefit to you today."

"What's that?"

"I have heard it said, and have often said myself, that the best poetry is not always written with words."

"What do you mean?" Georg asked.

"I mean, our lives are the greatest stories we will ever write. And if we write them well, others will read those stories and learn from the things we've done. How we've lived. How we've treated others. It's all in there."

"Ah."

Peter nodded. "Georg, I want you to know, your life is an amazing poem. You and the Lord have written it well. Your story isn't ending today. It's just beginning a new stanza, a fresh verse. And I have a feeling the lines left to be written are going to be even better than the ones you've already experienced."

"There's a scripture that says the same thing," Reverend Billingsley said, entering the room. "It's found in Haggai chapter two, verse nine, to be precise. 'The glory of this latter house shall be greater than of the former, saith the Lord of hosts: and in this place will I give peace, saith the Lord of hosts.' "

Georg gave him a curious look, not quite understanding his full meaning.

"The latter things are greater than the former things," the reverend explained. "The best is yet to come, my friend."

"Well, amen to that," Georg said. "The past has been really good, so I can only imagine how wonderful the future will be."

In that moment, the familiar melody of "Joy to the World" rang out. Georg gathered his groomsmen and began to make his way onto the stage. From there, he would have the best view in the house when Belinda, his beautiful bride-to-be, made her way down the aisle.

He slipped a hand into his pocket, checking to make sure the poem was still there. Breathing a sigh of relief, he entered the stage and gasped as he took in the magnificence of the room. *Oh, Lord, who has a wedding in such a place? This is breathtaking.* He stood center stage with the reverend and Mayor Mueller, who had agreed to share the honor of performing the ceremony. His groomsmen took their places to his left.

The back door of the theater opened, and the first matron of honor entered. Cassie made her way up the aisle and onto the stage. She was followed in steady succession by most of the town's most recent brides, one after the other. Georg did his best to stifle the laughter that threatened to creep up. He'd never seen so many brides converge upon a place in all his born days.

Oh, but the best was yet to come!

As Belinda appeared at the back of the room on her father's arm, his breath caught in his throat. Nothing could compare to the sight of her in that white dress. Georg whispered a prayer of thanks to the Lord and then waited with anticipation for his bride, the one he loved more than life itself.

* * *

Belinda walked the aisle on her father's arm, her heart beating so fast she felt as if she might faint. She hardly had time to take in her surroundings, though she knew the opera house was glorious. She had seen it in all its beauty earlier today. No, the only thing she focused on now was her husband-to-be, her perfect match. The one the Lord had given her from the start.

As they drew near the front, Belinda resisted the urge to hike up her skirt and race up the steps onto the stage. Instead, with her father's arm to lean on, she gingerly ascended, in front of the crowd, to Georg's waiting arm.

Once on the stage, Papa kissed her on the cheek and placed her hand in Georg's. Belinda found herself humming "Joy to the World" all over again as her heart swelled within her.

She and Georg took a few steps toward the reverend and Mayor Mueller.

The reverend opened in prayer and began the service. He started by gesturing to the married couples lining both sides of the stage. "All of these couples had a rather poetic beginning," the reverend said. "But none more poetic than today's bride and groom. For what can surpass the story of two people who've cared about each other all of their lives, finally realizing they are in love? No, they did not cross the miles to find each other. In fact, they only had to cross Main Street. But the miracle of their story is as grand as if they'd come together from opposite sides of the globe."

At this point, the mayor took over, offering the exchange of rings and the vows.

Afterward, Georg pulled a piece of paper out of his pocket. Belinda looked at him with some degree of curiosity, intrigued. He read in a voice that trembled with an odd mixture of stage fright and emotion, but Belinda could hardly believe the beauty of his words.

From Jordan's shore, I catch a glimpse
Of golden hair upon the wind;
A field of wheat, it beckons me
To come and lie, to simply be.
Her tender voice, it sounds the cry
A church bell peals across the sky,
Angelic choirs, sweet cherubim,
They woo me now to enter in.
Her heart, I find, an open book,
I chance to take a second look,
And reading there, am blessed to see,
A glimpse of our eternity.
My heart now beats in steady time
My life composed in perfect rhyme
For now we two are truly one
All praise to Father, Spirit, Son.

When he finished, the room was eerily silent. Then, despite her best attempts to the contrary, Belinda began to cry. Not just cry, really. *Wail* might be a better word for it. Before long, all the women on her side of the stage were a blubbering mess. The mayor leaned forward and patted Georg on the shoulder.

"You've got a real gift there, Georg," he whispered loud enough for only those onstage to hear. "Never knew you to be a poet."

"Well," Georg whispered in response, "writing the story of your heart is easy when you know the subject as well as I do."

Belinda's heart swelled with joy as Georg took her by the hand.

As the reverend pronounced them man and wife, she melted into her husband's embrace, enjoying his sweet kiss.

The audience came alive with applause, and Belinda felt her cheeks turn warm with embarrassment. Not that she planned to stop kissing Georg anytime soon. Oh, no. Standing here, center stage, with the lights beaming down on them, how could she help but play the scene for all it was worth?

Chapter Twenty-nine
....

After the service, Belinda and Georg made their way through the crowd, greeting everyone. Just when she thought they'd said hello to each and every guest, the mayor came bolting toward her.

"Belinda, I have to speak with you at once. I'm sorry to bother you on such a special day, but it cannot wait. The strangest thing has happened."

"O–oh?" She looked at him, her heart rising to her throat. "Pray tell, what is that?"

"A woman named Lena has just arrived in town, claiming to be my future wife. What do you have to say about that?" The mayor paled and looked as if he might faint dead away. Of course, if he did, Sarah Jo would sweep in with her smelling salts and construct a scene worthy of such an event.

"Well, Mayor, did you or did you not say you wanted a wife?" Belinda crossed her arms at her chest and stared him down.

"Well, yes, but..."

"And did you or did you not look through those newspaper advertisements with me some time ago?"

"Certainly. But you told me that you would pray before sending out a letter. I had it in my mind that you would also inform me, should you choose to do so."

"Well, I did pray, Mayor," she said with a nod. "But I was counting on the Lord to tell you the rest. I can say as a firsthand witness that hearing it from Him is better than hearing it from anyone else. You must trust me on this."

"But, Belinda, I haven't had time to think this through, and now she's here. Peter told me she checked into the hotel and told everyone she saw that she was here to marry the mayor. I—I'm the mayor."

"Well, at least she's got the right man." Belinda grinned. "Could be worse."

She gave him a knowing look, and he slapped himself in the head. "Well, if I have an incoming bride, perhaps you'd better tell me about her."

"It was all in the advertisement. Don't you remember? Her name is Rena Gebhardt, and she's from Maine," Belinda said, her heart quite full. "She sent several references. Rena is a widow, happy to remarry and settle in a small town."

"Not that our fair town is small these days," the mayor said, sounding a bit nervous. "Hope that part doesn't bother her."

"I'm sure it won't." Belinda smiled, finally able to relax, now that the mayor seemed to be adjusting to the idea. "Best of all, I understand she wants an authoritative man, one who has no trouble speaking his mind."

He grinned. "I am that sort of man."

"You are. And on top of that, she is looking for a man who loves the Lord and loves his community."

Mayor Mueller puffed his shoulders back. "Well, now. Is that so? There's not a soul in Kaufman County who loves his community more, and my love for the Lord is the primary focus of my life."

"No debating that fact." Belinda patted him on the arm. "Oh, and by the way, I should tell you that I met Rena face-to-face when Georg and I fetched her from the train station yesterday afternoon. We found her to be lovely, both inside and out. I'm sure you will agree. If you will just turn around, that is."

"W–what?"

Belinda took him by the shoulders and pointed him in the direction of the woman in question. The mayor gasped as he clamped eyes on the beautiful brunette with the winning smile and curvaceous physique headed their way.

"Oh my." Now the man looked genuinely ill.

"Indeed." Belinda nodded. "I couldn't have put it any better myself." She leaned in and whispered, "Now, go and fetch her before someone else does, Mayor. I have it on good authority that Jake Farris is looking for a bride. You don't want him to steal her out from under you."

"Jake Farris! That scoundrel! Over my dead body!"

Belinda laughed as the mayor sprinted in Rena's direction. Just then, Georg drew near and looked at the town's newest couple with a crooked grin. "So how did that go? Is everyone happy in paradise today?"

She looked at the mayor and Rena then offered her husband a smile. "I daresay, everyone is quite happy." She turned to face him, slipping her arms around his neck. "Oh, but Georg, I am the happiest of all."

"I could dispute that, but I won't." He smiled. "Let's just say we're both delighted and leave it at that."

He pulled her into his arms, planting a half dozen kisses along her hairline. "I am the most blessed groom in Poetry," he whispered.

"And I am the most blessed bride," she responded.

"Speaking of brides and grooms, I do hope things slow down soon," Georg said. "I'm getting a little tired of wedding cake."

Belinda grinned. "I know. I've put on five pounds in the last four months alone." She glanced at the mayor and Rena, who seemed to be getting along well. "On the other hand, what would it hurt to see more folks happily matched? Do we not wish them the same joy that we ourselves share?"

Georg laughed. "Of course. If only we can avoid some of the mismatches along the way."

"I cannot promise that," Belinda said with a smile. "I can only promise to pray ahead of time, as always. The rest, of course, is up to the Lord. Only He knows the next line to each person's poem. He, alone, sees the whole picture."

"You are right, as always."

As Georg leaned in to kiss her once again, Belinda was suddenly reminded of the beautiful verse he had recited during their ceremony. She longed to ask him about it. Had he actually penned those remarkable words himself? If so, then she had married a poet, one that could rival Peter Conrad any day.

In that moment, the perfect idea hit. If Georg could be compelled to write such a beautiful verse for his bride, perhaps he could be persuaded to write a few lines to include in letters to the town's incoming brides, as well. It was the least he could do. Right?

Caught up in the most glorious kiss she'd ever experienced, Belinda decided that question could most certainly wait for another day.

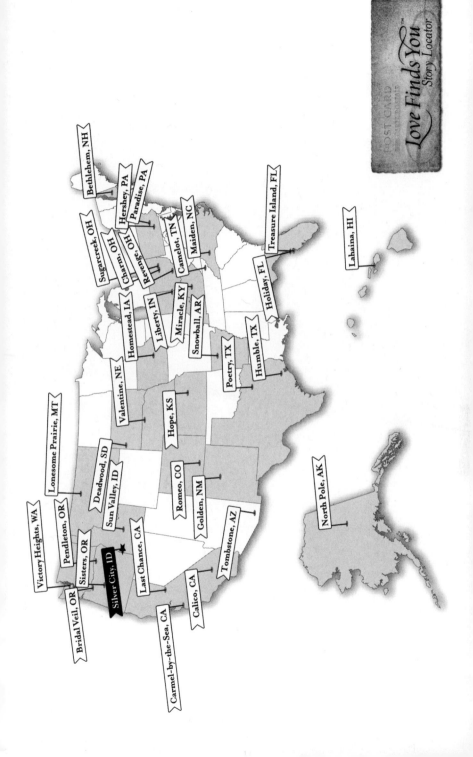